Dragon Prow Shadow

I0670681

Paul Hodson

For my wife:

The most amazing person I ever did meet.

Min lufian, min heafonfyr, min hleahtor.

With grateful thanks to Phil Keep who helped me edit
this book and gave me the Djinn joke
And thanks to Nathaniel Keep who read it

Art by Sylvain Lallouet
www.sya-artworks.com

ISBN – 978-1-9999046-0-9

https://dragonprowshadow.wordpress.com

Chapter 1

Dragon Prow Shadow

Robert spent most of his days with one eye on the clock, trying to work out how long it was until bedtime. Unspeakable fears and monsters lurked under the bed. And he had his suspicions about the wardrobe. At night, deep in the middle of the night when it's darkest he could hear them whispering about how they were going to eat him. This only ever seemed to happen when he was in that half asleep state. Then he jumped straight into full awake, yelling for them to go away. His parents had been assured by the family doctor that it was just a stage he would grow out of.

He'd seen a movie where the back of the wardrobe was some sort of doorway to lands that could transform him into a hero. He'd checked his wardrobe but there was no secret door. He mentioned this to his Mother, in the serious way that Robert had. And Robert could be very serious, his brown eyes glaring from under furrowed brow. His Mother was somewhat perplexed as to how best answer this statement. Not wishing to undermine him or berate his obvious and burgeoning imagination, the best she could come up with was that perhaps it was the wrong sort of wardrobe; then kind of shrugged her shoulders.

Not long after on a shopping trip to Ikea he went missing, he was missing for nearly twenty minutes. His Mum and Dad were frantic, tannoy messages were being played, security staff had been dispatched and the manager and assistant manager were looking very stressed indeed.

Someone had come to the customer service desk and asked if it was possible that the lost small boy mentioned in the tannoy message was the same small boy who appeared to be playing hide and seek "unsupervised" in the wardrobes?

When his Mum and Dad and Security Staff and Manager and Assistant Manager went to where he was last seen, they simply followed the loud banging noise to ascertain which wardrobe he was in. When his Mum asked between sobs what he was doing, Robert replied, 'Looking for a door', as if it was the most obvious thing to be doing. He then fixed the Manager who was a tall thin man with a nervous Adam's apple, with a serious stare and stated that he wanted to go and frighten the monsters whilst they slept in the daytime, the same way that they frightened him in the night. The Manager choked up with relief and wrenched his tie open a little, undoing his top button on his shirt, allowing his Adam's apple full freedom of expression. In his head he stopped writing letters of resignation and letters to lawyers and editors of the local press and tried to focus on the fact that all was well.

Robert enjoyed the free meatballs in the café.

Robert's Dad took to reading him bedtime stories where the hero always won and the monsters were vanquished, in the hope that it would take his mind off his fears and onto matters more positive. They'd even bought him a new night-light, a cd player and cd of soothing noises which they'd put on low volume and repeat through the night; bird songs, nightingales, rain, a mountain stream bubbling over heath land and ocean waves.

Not long into this new routine (which was having limited success), Robert's Dad, having checked under the bed with a torch, happened upon a story regarding a band of Vikings, sailing off in their longboat to distant lands, fighting sea monsters and dragons.

Robert had decided that whilst his Dad read this story, playing the sounds of the ocean lapping against the shore (or the side of a boat) would be a really good idea. It seemed a good idea to his Dad as well, as Robert was asleep before the end of the first page and remained asleep and undisturbed for the whole night.

The next night, whilst snuggling down, Robert noticed a shadow cast on the wall of his bedroom from the new bedside lamp and commented on how much it looked like a Dragon; his Dad, realising that here was the potential for another monster, established surprisingly quickly, that it looked more like the Dragon shaped prow of a Viking longboat, and that these dragons were the protectors and guardians of the Vikings, looking after them on their hazardous voyages. The shadow therefore was Robert's guardian dragon, who looked over him whilst he slept. His Dad was quite chuffed with how this had panned out given he'd made it all up on the spot. Robert seemed to like this idea; a contented nod was all his Dad got in response. So with the stories of Vikings in his ears, the sound of the sea gently slapping the side of his boat and the dragon prow shadow floating above his bed, it came to pass that Robert sailed out into the night sky to adventures new.

Chapter 2

'Boy!'

Robert blinked, steadied himself; then stumbled forward again as a half-eaten chicken drumstick ricocheted off the back of his head. He pushed himself up and turned around, his feet unsteady beneath him.

A tremendous smell assaulted Robert; uncleaned toilets and wood resin. Robert was nearly sick on the spot but managed to clamp his mouth shut; he spun around trying to take in his surroundings.

Before him sat a man so huge that Robert had never seen his like. Wrapped in animal skins, the apparition bellowed again, this time seemingly in rage, the man's face not a dissimilar colour to his huge red beard.

Robert turned around to look behind him in the vain hope that it wasn't him they were focussing on.

It was.

Slowly and with much drama, the man before him pulled his sword from his side, its blade hissing on scabbard; time slowed enough for Robert to really notice the sharp edge of the blade glittering in the sunshine, flashing the golden rays across Robert's face. Robert turned slightly and took a step back, the men around him quickly leaving a space. He looked at their faces; rough-hewn, grubby, unkempt, most had missing teeth and scars. These were faces that had been thoroughly lived in and beaten by the weather.

The huge man again bellowed, this time, 'Ragnar!'

The ship bobbed slightly, the floor fell away, Robert stumbled and sat bolt upright in his bed.

He gripped the side of his mattress as if to hold on as the room spun gently around him. When it stopped he listened with all his might, body physically straining at the intensity of his listening. There wasn't a noise, except for the sea lapping gently from his new cd. He lay back down, his heavy breathing subsided and sleep reclaimed him; the rest of his night remained dream free.

The next day there was a vague notion that he had dreamed; he seemed to remember the stench as much as anything. At breakfast his Mum had asked how he'd slept. Robert said he'd had a really vivid dream about people, not monsters. His Dad opened his mouth to say something but then seemed to just force a smile and continued reading some paperwork he'd got in front of him.

'It was all weird and jumbled, there was a man with a sword and he threw a chicken leg at me,' said Robert through a mouthful of breakfast cereal.

'That's lovely dear,' said his Mum, 'but let's not speak with our mouthful shall we? Nobody wants to see what you're eating.'

Robert half nodded, and decided it was generally easier to keep these things to himself, it's not like she was listening anyway, and he'd no doubt get into trouble about something he done or hadn't done.

'Don't forget Brian, I'll be later home than normal, I've got to pick up Robert from Stan's,' said his Mum.

'Ok,' replied Robert's Dad, still focused on the paperwork, he looked up as he folded it all up into his work bag, 'So you've got the whole summer off school now, what you and Grandad going to get up to kiddo?'

'Probably gardening,' sighed Robert.

'It's good for you, it's character building.'

'You say that about everything I don't like.'

Brian was somewhat taken aback by this response, so he just shrugged, scooped his bag and ruffled Robert's hair, 'Be nice, all the fresh air and plants and stuff. See you tonight. See you tonight love.'

Louise nodded from the sink and wiped her hands on

a towel, 'You got all your stuff together? We need to leave now'

Robert nodded and headed for the hall to wait, whilst his Mum found her car keys.

Chapter 3

That night Robert lay listening to the sea, not once taking his eyes off the dragon prow shadow on the wall, the words of the story from his Dad wrapping around him and floating into his ears. Robert's eyes flickered open, the shadow of the dragon prow was still there, but somehow seemed different, the light was darker, bluer, there was a gentle motion and about him the sound of men snoring.

Robert sat up and scratched his head, pulled something wriggling out of his hair that had lots of kicking little legs. He flicked it out into the night. Robert wrinkled his nose at the stench, felt the wood under him move, flexing and sighing, as if it was a slumbering beast. He eyed the dragon prow; the dragon prow looked back without emotion. Someone prodded him in the ribs, 'Fetch me some water boy.' Robert turned to looked at the face, still wrinkled from sleep, a mass of unkempt hair and a scar running right across his face, red and angry looking.

'Boy?' Said another figure sitting up abruptly, 'The boy child is back!'

Robert was aware of faces looming out of the darkness, peering at him, then whispering, the faces receding as people scrabbled to move away, the one who had prodded him just sat and stared at his own finger as if it might drop off.

Robert said 'Erm.'

Another figure appeared in front of him, old and knobbly. The old man looked like he'd spent his whole life sleeping in a hedge, but his eyes pierced Robert, almost nailing him to the floor. He was a whirl of grey hair, tied up with leather bits, beads in his beard, and a slightly funny smell about him.

'What are you boy?' the figure demanded, waving something in Robert's face.

Robert again said 'Erm.'

Robert had never been really frightened before, he'd had frights that had been and gone in an instant, but this was different, this was a lasting experience. He felt outside of himself, watching himself see the fine details of everything around him, not just the smells, but the texture of the light; a paleness to the sky off to one side and the light seemed to be seeping up into it, above him a falling star, a pin prick of light speared towards the horizon and was gone. Robert's breath hitched in his throat.

Never had he seen the sky look like this, the deep blackness of the night dusted with millions of stars, all glittering like those in the stories his Dad read to him. The man in front of him followed Robert's gaze up to the sky then looked back at Robert, 'You look in awe boy, like you've never seen the sky before?'

Robert shook his head slightly unable to take his eyes off the stars, 'The colours, you can see the colours,' he whispered.

The man in front of him, relaxed back onto his haunches, still unsure of what to make of the creature in front of him but feeling the threat of impending doom slowly fade.

With that the boat rocked gently, as if someone had knocked against it, there was a slosh of water from a sea that was otherwise as calm as a mill pond. Figures perked up in the gloom, arms reaching for swords and axes. Men scrabbled to peer over the side of the boat.

'What was that?' one whispered hoarsely.

'Did we run aground?' another asked.

'No, we're in deep water here and there was no grinding, it's was as if....' He paused, someone else finished the sentence. '... Something hit us!'

Robert felt the tension on the boat rise again, with the hairs standing up on the back of his neck, he scrambled backward to a corner and watched men leap to take look out positions, staring down over the side of the boat into the inky water beneath.

Torches flared into life casting mad, dancing shadows

in the pre-dawn gloom. Some of them glared over their shoulders at where he was hiding. The old man was still on his haunches staring at him. Nothing happened.

The sky got a little paler. Robert realised he was cold and shivering. Some of the men gave up the search with shrugs and furtive looks at one another. Grumbling and muttering letting sword arms and axes droop, then sheathing them, or tucking them in belts. A tense quiet descended over the boat. The boat lurched hard sideways, a great slosh of water surging over the side and splashing across the wooden decks. Robert screamed at the sudden cold drenching, opening his eyes and clawing the water away from his face, coughing and spluttering he peered out from between his fingers to find his Mum peering quizzically back at him.

'You ok honey?' she squinted at him, still not quite awake, her blue grey eyes bleary in her face. Robert sat and looked at her, mouth open, eyes wide and astonished, looking around his room like he'd never seen it before, then staring back at his Mum.

She pressed her hand against his forehead.

'Bad dream? She asked. Robert nodded, unsure of anything at the moment. 'Come on lie down, let me tuck you in.'

Robert lay down whilst his Mum straightened his bedclothes and tucked them in, pinning him to the mattress. For someone so fragile looking, there was a steeliness to her, not least her eyes. She kissed him on the cheek and left his room, whispering, 'Now go to sleep.'

Robert scowled, 'I was!' and turned his head and stared at the shadow on his wall. The shadow seemed unmoved by his plight. Robert was confused, he couldn't make out where he was, his Mother had expertly tucked him in and at the same time, he was trapped under some shattered benches, bits of broken boat clattered around him. A hand reached out of the darkness, and pulled at his shirt, about him men screamed, waving swords and spears, hurling axes.

The boat was listing badly, taking on water, which sloshed around in the commotion. Everything slowed down; Robert watched open mouthed as blood intermingled with the sea water, the foaming bubbles on the waves inside the boat, the stitching on the leather shirt of the man who was trying to save him from drowning, pulling so hard that the veins and sinews stood out on his arms. And then Robert noticed the huge horse-like head looming over them, one mangy, putrid tentacle clamped over the edge of the boat pulling it over.

A crab scurried from a hole on the beast's head and splashed into the sea. The beast's great yellow eyes glared down at the puny men beneath it. The thing stank of rotten fish and decaying seaweed. Tendrils of seaweed swayed around its blue grey body, which looked like it was covered in slime. Robert pointed and opened his mouth to scream but no noise came out. The man who was trying to pull him free, turned to see what Robert was pointing at, just in time to see a tentacle sweeping towards him, he lashed out with his sword and buried the blade deep into the flesh, the tentacle recoiled, snatching the sword from the man's grip. He turned, grabbing Robert by both shoulders and heaving him out and throwing him bodily up the boat to where a cluster of men were trying to stand their ground.

Robert was on his back, trying to clamber out of the way, sea water foaming around him, looking up, he saw the sword that had been embedded in the tentacle shudder free from the beast's flesh and tumble end over end in slow motion towards him, it plunged into the deck, point first, vibrating between his legs with a thwang. Men screamed and yelled threats and insults, shouting names and words he'd never heard before.

He looked at the sword, then at the monster, which had now clambered onto the side of the boat, men shouted and raged and jabbed at it ineffectually as it swatted at them. Robert reached out for the sword handle and gripped and pulled but he could not free it from the deck. Using both hands and pushing with his feet, he strained, his face lifted in a grimace, he looked at the monster and the monster looked back. It lurched forward, a dripping tentacle lashed out at the same instant the sword pulled free and Robert tumbled backwards, the sword blade swooping upwards through the air, slicing the tip off the tentacle, as he fell he crashed into a brace which held a flaming torch, which fell next to him, coughing and spluttering. Robert picked up the flaming torch automatically, so that it didn't burn him, blowing the flames away. And the creature recoiled. Robert jumped to his feet, waving the flaming torch in one hand, the sword in the other. As the men of the ship saw, others leapt for the nearest burning object and threw it at the creature. Quickly and with a huge slosh the monster, lunged off the side of the boat back into the sea, bits of burning detritus hissed in the foam thrown at where it had been. The boat wobbled and splashed as it righted itself, men and weapons and bits of boat tumbled into jumbled piles. Robert was on his knees breathing heavily, arms aching from holding his weapons, waiting for the boat to stop rocking: Then he realised that all the men were looking at him.

The Chief, the big man who had thrown a chicken leg at him, stepped forward, scowled at the boy, took the torch off him and peered down under the guttering flames, 'Where did you get the knife, little man?'

The man who had pulled him free from the wreckage spoke up, 'It is mine, the beast swiped it from my hand,' adding, 'The boy picked it up.'

Robert looked down at the knife, it was huge, he'd thought it was a sword.

The old man pushed his way forward, using knobbly elbows to great effect, 'The boy saved us, he frightened the Loki spawn off with the fire and sword!' his eyes gleamed under tremendously bushy eyebrows.

'But the spawn did not appear till the boy did?!' breathed the big man.

'No,' replied the old man who tugged on his long knotted beard, 'The boy came just in time to save us.'

He reached out then poked the boy hard in the chest.

'Ow!', yelped Robert.

'Well boy?' he added, 'What are you and where you are from?'

'And what does he want?' the Chief chipped in.

'Yes, yes, alright, that as well. Well?'

Robert said 'Erm,' and really didn't know what else to say, he was in the middle of a circle of very large, heavily armed men who were not overly thrilled at his appearance.

'Did you bring the sea beast upon us?'

'No!' said Robert, a little more petulantly than he wanted to. 'I, er, I don't know how I got here. I'm err....'

Robert for all the world looked like a terrified small child. This relaxed the old man a little as small frightened children were much easier to deal with than spirits, ghosts and Huldufólk.

The old man turned and looked over his shoulder, 'I say we get out of here before the sea beast returns, count our blessings that the child seemed to best the creature and worry about the other stuff later.'

The big man nodded and turned and started shouting at people and waving his arms around. The people he was shouting at did not seem to be inclined to do as they were told. So he got louder. The men of the ship returned to their posts but none of them were really taking their eyes off Robert.

'You're holding that knife like it's going to catch fire boy,' said the Chief turning back.

Robert looked at it and looked at it like he'd never seen it before, not like someone who had just fended off a giant octopus with it.

'Villi would you have your knife back?"

Villi appeared to be the man who had saved him from drowning and whose knife he now held.

The man shrugged and grinned, pushing back his mop of blonde hair from his smiling face, 'Who am I to argue with one so small yet fights off beasts the size of our ship!'

There was much muttering from the men within earshot, and lots of others asking 'What did he say?'

The Chief who had a knowing for how superstitious sailors could be broke into a smile, 'The boy did save us, you bring us luck boy, you fought well,' he turned to the original owner of the knife and in a loud voice proclaimed, 'I say he keeps it, he earned it, you can find yourself a new one, this is a sign from the gods, would you cross it?'

Villi just nodded, he seemed to be a man of few words. Some of the men broke into a half-hearted cheer. And some of the others said, 'Why are they cheering down there?'

The Chief stroked his chin, staring at Robert and then turned away to go look for his chair. Robert stood still, still dazed, blade pointing skyward as the men busied themselves around the boat, as if fighting off sea monsters was an everyday occurrence. It would seem whatever was happening had happened and that was that.

'Here boy,' said the man whose sword he now held, and he handed him a leather scabbard and belt from around is waist, 'Keep it in this. And don't cut yourself! We don't want our new lucky charm coming to a sticky end so soon.'

Robert placed the blade on the floor and took the leather and tried to tie it around his waist, his hands shaking so much it immediately undid and fell to the floor. Villi cocked his head one side, hesitated then knelt down. Robert marvelled at the scale, he was vast, his fingers were nearly the size of Robert's thighs. Villi took the belt, and tied it tightly in a knot around boy, who grunted and eyes popped. Robert thought he was going to be cut in two.

'A beast fighter you may be, boy, but a sailor you are not, eh?' rumbled Villi, grinning. He then picked the knife and slid it into the soft leather scabbard. The weight of it still caused it to hang low, but Robert hitched it up with his pants and said, 'Thank you.'

Villi stood up, winked one of his sky blue eyes and turned away.

Ragnar had watched this exchange unfold, his eyes squinting in thought, as he stroked his beard. Robert had that sensation of being watched and turned, meeting the stare of Ragnar who then hobbled towards him.

Robert was aware that he was now trembling and still frightened and no matter how real this all sounded and felt, he knew that it must be some kind of weird dream.

The old man appeared at his side, 'Come boy, we would talk,' gripping him by the elbow and manoeuvring him through bits of broken boat to a dark, quiet area.

Chapter 4

'Tell me, who was your Father boy, you would have heroes blood in your veins? Where are you from?'

Robert scowled at the old man, 'What do you mean 'was' my Father?'

The old man's head bobbed to one side, his shoulders sagged slightly, 'Where are you from?'

'England.'

'Ah, an Angle, and how did you get here?'

'I don't know,' Robert felt his eyes stinging, his throat tightened, he tried forcing himself not to cry, he tried to speak but all that came out was a burbling noise, so he clamped his mouth shut.

From behind them someone bellowed, 'Ragnar!'

The old man raised one very bushy eyebrow, 'That would be me, you rest here boy, stay from underfoot whilst we make her ship shaped again, we'll talk more later.'

The old man hobbled off, walking as if he had a stone stuck in his hip. Robert looked around; he was under some steps that seemed to lead to a slightly elevated area of the boat. It was dark and he pushed himself further back into the shadows, no one could see him, no one was looking for him. He watched the hurly burly and bustle of the entire crew at work, found himself sat on top of a barrel, back resting against part of the hull. Sleep slipped her arms around his head, comforted his furrowed brow and drew him into her dark embrace.

Someone was shaking him, he awoke with a start, sat bolt upright and a gasp in his mouth, 'Come on sleepy head, I've been shouting you for 5 minutes, get up!' exclaimed his Mum, who seemed more exasperated at him than usual.

Robert shook the sleep from his head, had the feeling he should be cold and wet, fearfully he checked that he'd not had an 'accident' in the bed. He hadn't, the bed was dry. He was dry. The curious sensation of dampness followed him throughout his whole day.

Robert pressed play on the CD player, adjusted the volume slightly and set it back onto the bedside table. Clambering into bed, his Mum tucked him in, kissed him on the cheek and said, 'Your Dad will be in a mo', being as though you did so much coughing and sputtering last night, I think a drop of this wouldn't go amiss.' A strange, old looking dark bottle appeared in her hand.

'What is it?' asked Robert.

'It's called Olbas oil; my Mum used it with me. It helps clear your tubes and breathe, here.'

She cracked open the bottle and let Robert sniff. Warily he acknowledged that it smelt quite nice even if it made your eyes water a little. She dabbed a few drops on his pillow and then on a clean hanky, which she tucked up the sleeve of his pyjamas, 'good night, sweet dreams,' she whispered as she kissed him on the forehead.

His parents passed at the door and his Dad plonked himself down on the edge of the mattress, Robert sloped sideways.

'What story you want kiddo?'
'The one about the Vikings.'
'Again?'
'Yes.'
'Are you sure, there's lots of others...,'
'No, I like the Viking one.'

Robert's Dad shrugged, to be fair this story seemed to do the trick, as although he had done some thrashing about in his dreams, he had only woken up once and there had been no screaming about monsters. Things definitely seemed to be improving, and whereas once upon a time, well a few days ago actually, it had been quite a challenge getting him to bed, he seemed quite eager tonight.

Robert felt a warm glow cast over him, saw the brightness surge through his eyelids, as his Dad slipped out of his bedroom door onto the landing.

Ragnar waved a flaming torch under the stairs where he had left the boy, he appeared to have disappeared and despite searching the ship, could not be found.

'Maybe he fell overboard?' suggested Villi.

Ragnar scowled at him, waved the flaming torch around some more and peered into the mist that the boat seemed to have settled in. The men were on edge, this was Dragon's Breath, or some said it was Odin's Breath, either way it wasn't good and now they had lost their lucky charm. Sailors have ever been a suspicious lot. Villi's face dropped, he said 'Um' and half heartedly pointed behind Ragnor, in the manner that suggested he didn't want to point in case the thing he was pointing at took offence. Ragnar spun round, the torch guttered and coughed as Robert stepped out of the shadows behind him, Ragnar said 'Oh.'

Robert looked around sheepishly, there seemed to be a lot of worried faces looking at him. There then followed much muttering and whispering and touching of lucky charms and a slight backing away from where the men had previously been stood, without seeming to move at all. Ragnar raised the torch, look passed Robert, over his shoulder into the dark recess, and then at Robert.

'I see' said Ragnar but he didn't. He leered around at men, 'Go on, be off with you, I would talk with ....' Ragnar spat on the floor.

The men half-heartedly wandered off, some straying not too far in case something interesting happened, like a battle of magic spells or some such.

Ragnar placed the torch in a bracket beside them, then pulled out a stick from up his sleeve, Robert could see some lines carved into it.

'Do you know what this is?' Demanded Ragnar.

'It's a stick,' replied Robert helpfully.

Ragnar looked at him blankly, then said, 'I can't make my mind up if you are as you appear or you are some Elf or Wight or such like, casting a glamour.'

Robert didn't reply, he just stood there a bit lost for words.

Ragnar continued, with some flourishing of the stick, 'This STICK, was cut from the Great Tree itself, it has been passed down through the generations, passed from Rune Master to Rune Master since Odin himself first sacrificed himself on the Great Tree.'

Robert's eyes focused on the end of the stick as Ragnar waved it around, there seemed to be a lot emphasis on the word 'himself' in that last sentence, but Robert wasn't sure why.

'You don't seem overly impressed by that boy.'

'Um, sorry,' said Robert, shrugging his shoulders, then he pulled his belt up a bit so that his knife point didn't trail on the floor. Robert realised that he was in strange clothes and shoes and not his pyjamas. His brow furrowed but then his attention was taken by Ragnar stuffing the stick back up his sleeve, then with great theatrics raised his hands above his head and bellowed, 'I am Ragnar, son of Ragnar, Rune Master, Mage and Wizard!'

Robert took a step back into the shadows but couldn't really see an escape route.

Ragnar sniffed, 'Look there is a form to this, a kind of traditional way of doing things.'

Robert bit his lip then said, ''I am Robert son of Brian?'

Ragnar pounced, like a cat on a mouse, 'Ha, Robert son of Brian, Brian is a Celt's name, you said you were an Angle?'

Robert shrugged his shoulders, 'My Dad's still called Brian.'

Robert recognised the Chief's voice, 'Ragnar, enough

with the boy, you'll wear his luck out or frighten him away permanently, come do your work, get us out of this mist! Talk is for wimmin folk.'

'Talk is for people who want to learn things' sneered Ragnar.

'You learn things by cutting bits off until they tell you what you want to know. Now get rid of the mist or get us moving! Or I'll start cutting bits off!'

Ragnar muttered under his breath, then grabbed Robert by the elbow, 'Come Robert, Angle son of a Celt, come hither, we don't want you disappearing into the shadows again, do we?'

The men parted as Ragnar walked up the centre of the boat, Robert stumbled and almost fell, but Ragnar's fingers were like iron pincers. Robert noticed that none of the men would not look at him directly, even Villi whose knife was now around his waist seemed a bit wary.

'Sit there, don't move and don't disappear' commanded Ragnar, adding in a whisper, 'the men are jumpy enough as it is.'

Robert sat down cross legged on the decking, it took him a few goes as his sword seemed to get tangled around his legs.

'You finished sitting down now?' enquired Ragnar politely, overly laced with sarcasm.

'Um, yes. Thank you.'

Ragnar shook his head, convinced this boy was too clumsy and unsure of himself to be anything eldritch or dangerous, then reached into a pouch at his belt.

Chapter 5

A circle of white splashed onto the dark wood decking, Robert thought it looked like liquid light and let out an involuntary gasp in delight. This seemed to please Ragnar immensely. Then a splash of some liquid in the middle, dark and sticky; Ragnar carved strange shapes in the air with his fingers, he spat and then he blew gently. A blue flame leaped into existence flickered and then died, burning away the liquid with a pungent wisp. Robert reeled back slightly. Then Ragnar threw some shiny pebbles onto the deck, each with a strange pattern etched into them.

'Oops!' he said, grabbed the stones and then dragged Robert to one side, in something of a hurry, throwing him to the floor.

Out over the ocean somewhere a great roar echoed.

Men stopped looking at Ragnar and grabbed weapons instinctively.

A huge dark sharp hurtled through the mist, illuminated briefly with a fiery glow

'Ragnar!' screamed the Chief 'I asked you to get us out of here!'

Robert looked up in complete awe as a black dragon the length of the ship flew across them, a massive fire ball fizzed and sizzled in the damp air then hissed into the sea nearby.

'You asked me to get us out of here or get rid of the mist, is the mist going!?'

'I didn't ask you to bring a great bloody dragon to burn the mist off.'

'Is the mist gone? Yes. Did you stipulate how you wanted the mist getting rid of? No!'

'By Odin's teeth Ragnar you push me to the limits and beyond!' The Chief had gone a strange crimson colour and was physically vibrating with rage.

'Then you should be careful what you ask for shouldn't you?'

Arrows skittered skywards and bounced off the scaly dragon skin as it flew again low over the ship, its tail whipped and snapped the very top of the mast off which plummeted deck ward; luckily it stopped half way down caught by the sail and rigging it was attached to.

Villi grabbed Robert by the arm, hoisted him to his feet and yelling, 'Get your sword out boy, start weaving us some luck with it eh!'

Robert managed to pull the blade from the scabbard without seriously cutting himself, then waved it above his head; more in the manner that was he was expected to do rather than with any enthusiasm. Robert was quite sure that none of this was real, therefore it didn't matter, and the dragon really was quite spectacular to watch. Great plates of skin like armour rippled over each other, the thing should most definitely not be able to fly, it was immense; yet there it was, flying. Robert let out an involuntary wow noise.

Ragnar watched the boy from behind a barrel, slightly perplexed by the whole thing, in all his learned years he'd never come across anything like this. A waft of cold air brought Ragnar back to the present; the great beast was hovering, in defiance of nature, great ponderous beats of its wings seemed to keep it stationary: The downdraught from the beating wings, blasting cold air and sea water skyward into huge vortices so that the beast was partially obscured by the swirling spray.

Robert's arm was getting heavy; the sword drooped slowly to the deck. He stuck it point first into the wood, taking great care to avoid his own foot. With his other hand he reached up the sleeve of his sword arm, pulled out the handkerchief to wipe the seawater off his face. Catching a whiff of the Olbas oil he sneezed loudly and dropped his sword which made a loud clanging noise. He sneezed again.

'Come on boy, thrice is the charm,' muttered Ragnar. A third sneeze echoed out. The dragon was suddenly awfully interesting in the small squeaky thing at the front of the big tree thing floating on the water. And not remotely interested in all the bigger squeaky things that were waving bits of shiny things. It moved in for a closer inspection, the beat of its wings eased, the spray no longer broiled in the air.

Robert wiped the tears and sea water from his bleary eyes and realised he was looking down the nostrils of a large dragon. The dragon's nose was twitching, like a dog that can smell sausages, Robert held out the handkerchief for it to smell, the dragon went cross eyed slightly, its mouth snapped open and it took a great intake of breath. Behind Robert was the noise of an entire ship's crew throwing themselves behind the least flammable object they could find: On a wooden boat, this didn't leave many options and led to some brief but quite vicious altercations.

Then it sneezed with all the ferocity of a tornado made of fire. Luckily most of it went straight over Robert's head but it hit the hanging sail full on, Robert was thrown to the decking as the ship hurtled away, the stern driving down deep into the water, a great bow wave of water pushing away from the boat. The dragon meanwhile hurtled backwards like a jet engine. Robert looked over the rail as the dragon sneezed again, with a kind of high pitched roar, again the beast rocketed backwards on a tongue of fire, its wings flapping up by its ears; by now it was quite some distance from the ship, both moving further and further away from each other.

Robert turned and looked down the length of the ship, there wasn't much left above head height (well his head height, which wasn't that high all things considered); there was a lot of smoking charcoal, wisps of crisped rigging, and the vague outline of a sail.

The crew began to emerge, unsure whether to cheer the banishing of the dragon or scream for bloody vengeance at the state of their ship.

The Chief stepped forward, the fur rim to his hat was gone along with his eyebrows and his moustache really wasn't what it used to be. He took off his hat and looked at it, wiping some of the soot off it with a sleeve. Tucking a singed lock of hair behind one ear, he spoke, very politely and through tightly clenched teeth, 'Ragnar, a word if I may,'

Ragnar popped up from behind a barrel, and looked around, at bright sunshine and calm seas, 'On the bright side at least the mist has gone,' he said.

It took three of the crew to hold the chief down, it was considered very bad luck to kill a Rune Master (a truism much marketed by the Rune Master Guild), and they really didn't want things getting any worse than they already were. The Chief screamed, the muscles, veins and sinews in his neck bulging.

Ragnar tiptoed around the seething pile of people, making sure to stay out of reach of the Chief's teeth, fingernails and feet which flashed and slashed at him, he thought it ill judged to suggest that he calm down lest he give himself an injury and better to put a little breathing space between them.

Villi stepped up to Robert, picked his knife up and helped him put it in the scabbard, 'Um,' was about all he could say.

'Sorry,' said Robert, 'It's only Olbas oil; my Mum gave it to me.' He held it up for Villi to sniff. He pulled his head away, then leant in, very warily giving the smallest of sniffs, 'Hmm, smells quite nice actually,' then sneezed.

It was one of those quiet, restrained, internal sneezes that comes out as a Gngngngnnngch! And nearly blows your eardrums out. He pushed his hat back off the bridge of his nose. 'You better find somewhere quiet to sit young Robert, cause it looks like we're rowing home.'

Chapter 6

What's Odin Dad?' asked Robert the next morning whilst he was sat eating his breakfast. His Dad who was trying to cram a slice of toast and some tea into his mouth at the same time and put his tie on paused and looked at his Mum, who was at the sink and she turned and looked at Robert. 'Why, where did you hear that?' she asked. 'Oh, I dunno, just heard it somewhere.'

'There's a T in don't know,' she replied curtly, emphasising each syllable as she went. Then his Dad who by now was staring down the garden, added, 'I think he was chief of the Viking Gods, I think Wednesday was named after him. And Thursday was Thor. I dunno who the others were.' His Mum glared at his Dad due to the lack of a ''t' in his 'dunno know.'

'How do you get Wednesday from Odin?'

'Erm, perhaps some people put a W in front, Wodin, Wodin's Day, not that far away from what we call it really.' His Dad shrugged, 'Not sure really.'

Robert nodded sagely, 'If I ask Grandad would he know about Vikings?'

'Why would your Grandad know... oh.. you mean because he's from the olden days?'

'Yes,'

'Ha, he's going to love that, yes ask away, I'm sure he'll be a goldmine of information.'

'What's the sudden fascination with Vikings?' his Mum asked his Dad, as if Robert wasn't still there.

'Dunno, he seems to like that book I read him at bed time, who cares at least he's interested in something other than monsters from under the bed and in the wardrobe. See you tonight.'

He kissed Robert's Mum on the cheek, then roughed Robert's hair, 'See you tonight kiddo,' and darted from the kitchen.

'Bye Dad,' said Robert through a mouthful of cereal.

'Come on you, hurry up, I need to get you to your Grandad's, traffic was awful yesterday,'

Robert hurtled up the garden path and charged the front door which was on the latch,

'Grandad!'

'Morning, Boy Wonder, what you been up to?'

'Grandad, Dad says you've got a golden mind and it's full of stuff about Vikings?'

His Grandad looked a little perplexed and then caught Robert's Mum's eye down the hall

'He's got a sudden fascination for Vikings and Brian has told him you being from the olden days, know all about Vikings.'

'Sure, you mean I've not told you about the time I saved Ethelred the Unready from certain doom.'

'No way!' gasped Robert wide eyed, looking up.

His Mum rolled her eyes, and turned away, 'See you tonight you two, thanks Stan,' and let herself out.

As she left heard Stan ask, 'And I never told you about the time that Eric the Red asked me to look after his magic sword? Come on to the interwebs dear boy, you can show me how it works and I'll find some pics of me as a lad in a daft hat with horns on.'

Robert's Dad was late home that night, something had happened at work, Robert was already in his pyjamas when he heard the key in the door.

'Hey Dad, did you know that Vikings didn't really have hats with horns on but only in old movies. And Grandad once looked after a magic sword for Eric the Red. And they had this big tree and they all lived in it.'

'Hello to you too kiddo,' said his Dad who was taking his coat off.

Robert's Mum, brought his Dad a mug of tea, 'Grandad has spent an almost productive day with Robert on the internet,' with a heavy layer of sarcasm on the word almost.

Robert interrupted excitedly, 'I have to show Grandad how to use the ''puter you got him, but we found an old picture of him, on a big poster made of sewing of a battle that had a comet over it. And he said that he told Harold not to look up, and that Norman should stop waving sharp sticks about cause he'd have someone's eye out with it.'

His Dad laughed, picked Robert up with one arm, carried him to the living room and threw him on the sofa, plonking himself down, Robert climbed onto his knee.

'Come on then, what else did you and Grandad find?'

Fact, fiction, myths, names, places and dates were all garbled up into one long sentence of events that may or may not have happened to his Grandad about the time when his Grandad was 'a bit of a lad'.

'And they did this thing called a blood eagle where they'd cut your ribs open and spread them out and all your squishy insides!' Robert was almost bursting with enthusiasm at this.

'Eww I'm not sure your Dad should be showing him stuff like that,' frowned Robert's Mum to his Dad.

'History is gruesome, when was the last time you saw him this excited about something? Maybe we could get you some of those horrible history books?'

'Do they have ones about Vikings?' asked Robert.

'I don't know, but I'm sure we can find out, anyway kiddo, it's about your bed time me thinks,'

'Aww Dad, but, but.'

'No buts,' replied his Mum,

'Dare I ask which story you'd like read?' asked his Dad. Robert just scowled at him for asking a daft question.

'Go on, clean your teeth, put the CD on and in bed, your Dad will be up in a minute.'

Robert leapt off his Dad and bounded up the stairs.

His Mum and Dad now stared at each other across a suddenly tranquil living room,

'Well, that was weird; I've never seen him get up the stairs to bed so quickly?'

'No.' Robert's Mum couldn't think of anything else to say.

'Still as long as he doesn't start trying to pull out people's ribs or whatever it was, we should be ok,' said his Dad.

'Hmmm' was the only reply he got as she stood up and went to make sure Robert was actually doing what he was supposed to be. She half expected him to be in investigating his ribs in the bathroom mirror, but as it was, he was in bed, duvet up to his nose, the sound of waves gently splashing.

Chapter 7

Robert didn't dream of Vikings that night. When he got up the next morning, he seemed a little peeved.

'What's the matter?' asked his Mum?

'I didn't see any Vikings last night,' bemoaned Robert, 'I think I might have to apologise after the dragon singed most of their boat,' he looked up but his Mum seemed to be reading the ingredients on the breakfast cereal box instead.

When Robert's Dad got home that evening, there was a strange smell, which wafted over him as he opened the front door. Robert was sat on the bottom of the stairs waiting for him.

'What's up kiddo?'

'Something went wrong with the slow cooker Dad. Mum says that we won't be having stew tonight. I'm staying here till she stops banging things around.'

'Oh. Probably for the best, what you get up to with Grandad today?' he asked as he took his jacket off and slung it over the bannister on the stairs.

'We found some more Viking stuff on the interwebs, apparently they used to own Dublin and York and most of England and people had to pay them to make them go away. And they used to rob churches a lot.

But we found these amazing pictures of belt buckles and stuff made out of gold, with trees and dragons all in complicated patterns. And then we made chocolate biscuits.'

Brian raised an eyebrow, 'Your Grandad is not supposed to have chocolate.'

'Oh he didn't, but I let him lick the bowl out,' replied Robert helpfully.

His Dad snorted a laugh, 'Come on let's venture into the kitchen and see what your Mum's up to,' he held Robert's hand and they tiptoed down towards the kitchen.

'Evening dear!' Said Robert's Dad in his best cheery voice.

'Yes. Well I'm not sure what we're going to have to for tea, as you can probably smell. Could well be beans on toast.'

There was a strange mist in the kitchen and Robert's Mum had opened all the windows to try and let the smell out.

'On the plus side, the house didn't burn down.' She added.

'I'm sure beans on toast will be just lovely. We can add some Worcester sauce in the beans, what do you say Robert?'

Robert who had seated himself at the small table nodded vigorously.

'Robert tells me that he's be making chocolate biscuits today.'

'Well, yes, more melting of chocolate and then dipping biscuits into the melted chocolate,' she snapped back.

'Dad did you know that Normans' king was not called Norman but William and they're called Normans cause it's short for Norse Men, that's Vikings Dad who moved to France and took over a bit of it?'

Brian broke into a smile, 'You know Robert, I knew the bit about William, but I did not know that Normans was short for Norseman. That's excellent Robert, well done.'

His Dad beamed, even his Mum seemed impressed.

'Can I change my name to Norman?'

'No,' said his Mum

'What about Eric?'

'No!' more emphatically this time.

'Ragnar?'

'You are not changing your name to anything,'

His Dad leant across, 'How about Ethelred?'

'He was a Saxon Dad, not a Viking.'

'Oh.' said his Dad looking a little dejected.

'And you're not helping either, come on do something useful, butter the toast,' requested his Mum. 'And Robert wash your hands. And you too, Brian.'

His Dad lifted Robert up so he could reach the water coming out of the tap,

'Vikings invented washing, they had a bath every Saturday,'

'Hmph, I never knew that either, is there anything Vikings didn't do?'

Robert went quiet for a moment, as he sat down at the table again clearly thinking hard, 'I shouldn't think so.'

'Enough about Vikings now, let's eat our tea eh,' said his Mum as she placed the plates down on the table.

Chapter 8

Robert could smell the burnt slow cooker when he went to bed. And he could still smell it when he woke up. But the smell had a different texture and there was a low droning noise.

'Ah the boy returns!', it was Ragnar who had been sat cross legged by the barrels under the steps on the Viking ship. His face was creased like he'd been fast asleep, but as Robert stepped out of the shadows, he unfolded himself with remarkable grace considering he walked like he had one leg shorter than the other.

'I was beginning to wonder if you were coming back, we missed you.'

Robert blinked in the bright sunshine, noticed that the crew had stopped mending the boat and were looking over at him, most touched lucky charms and muttered things, a few whispered to each other, all perplexed by his appearance, only Villi stepped forward,

'Ah our lucky charm, I hope you've been taking care of that knife boy,' he nodded to the scabbard slung at Robert's hip.

Robert looked down, not realising it was there, 'Erm yes, yes, I've looked after it. Um, where are we?'

'Home boy', said the chief pushing passed Villi, 'where have you been?'

Robert looked down perplexed, he knew this must be some kind of dream, he went to bed in pyjamas but here he had itchy leather clothes, little leather shoes and blooming big knife that was nearly as long as his leg. He remember that the Chief had said something, 'Erm.. Home..' he replied.

The Chief nodded, 'Seems fair enough. You keep turning up when we're about to be attacked, so what have The Sisters got in store for us today do you think?'

Robert looked around the faces of them all studying him with great seriousness and had no idea what to say. He looked at Ragnar pleadingly.

'I think the boy Robert has no more of an idea of what the Sisters weave than we do, Thunor.'

It was the first time, he'd heard the Chief's name, Robert remembered his Dad telling him about Thursday being named after Thor's day and wondered if the Chief was named after Thor as well. Come to think of it he didn't know what his own name, Robert meant, or even if it had a meaning.

Ragnar reached out and prodded Robert in the chest with a long, thin, boney finger.

'Ow!'

'Just making sure you're really there, come on boy, let's go see the village,'

'Villi go with them, make sure the boy doesn't stumble across any ice giants or dragons or such like,' rumbled Thunor.

Robert followed Ragnar off the boat, along a plank to a small wooden pier, with Villi behind.

A small throng of people had gathered to welcome the crew home; there was good natured shouting and kids clambering on the boat, hugging fathers, presents being sought. Villi had stepped off to one side to see his wife and Robert presumed his daughter, he could only see her from the back but she had the most amazing red hair.

The people parted almost subconsciously for Ragnar, nobody really taking that much notice of Robert, and soon Villi had fallen in step behind them.

Up above the shore, wooden houses clustered around each other. They all seemed to have very sharp pointed roofs made of thatch and on some of them the roof seemed to come down to the ground, with the grass growing right over the house as if they were all still part of the land. Behind them, thick forest stretched up and up towards jagged mountains in the distance. There was no wind, and smoke hung around the village in strange curled shapes. Robert realised that the smell was as bad as on the boat, but it was masked a little by the wood smoke, there seemed to be a ring of burning torches around the village. And he realised that the low, droning noise was some sort of singing.

'What's with the torches and the singing?' He asked.

'One of the elders died whilst we were at sea, the torches and singing keep unwanted attention away till it is time,' replied Ragnar, in a loud whisper from the corner of his mouth. Robert was unsure whether to ask some more but that was more taken by the fact that some of the people they were walking by were now stopping and staring and they were being followed by a small group of children; at a safe distance all whispering to each other.

Robert felt very hot and uncomfortable; he walked awkwardly, the knife banging on his leg putting him off his stride.

As they got to the centre of the village, the singing seemed to be coming from one house. Set apart slightly from the others, it had white smoke coming from its chimney. Robert thought they were heading for that, but Ragnar led them to the largest house that was pretty much in the middle; inside was dark and dingy and smelled of sweat and wood smoke. In the gloom Robert could make out straw on the floor, sprinkled with what looked like dried herbs and flowers with bench tables running the length of the building.

People who were milling around, stood staring or peeked from around pillars, Robert sat at the table with the others (who all managed to sit without stumbling over their knives, swords and axes) and they were brought them some wooden bowls of what looked like stew by grubby looking children. Cups carved from thick branches with beautiful patterns carved in the wood were plunked down unceremoniously.

'What is it?' asked Robert, prodding the contents of the bowl with a wooden spoon but looking at the carvings on the on his cup.

'No idea, but it will taste alright,'

Robert tried a small taste, it had the consistency and texture of porridge but didn't taste like it, Robert couldn't quite put finger on what it did taste like, but it wasn't bad. He noticed some flakes of what looked like meat but they had a fishy quality. He tried the drink, it was water, with a kind of bland, sweet honey after taste, he wasn't sure if he liked that, but thought it would be considered rude if he didn't drink it.

As his eye became accustomed to the gloom, Robert could make out strange carvings on the beams and pillars that ran around the room, creatures, vines, branches, spiral patterns all seemed to twist and writhe such that it was difficult to tell where one started from another. And they all seemed to focus towards a large chair at the far end. He assumed that to be some sort of throne, it wasn't hugely bigger than anything else in the room, nor was it overly decorated, but it was definitely a throne. Behind it a tree, an oak tree, that reached up and grew through the roof, as if the roof had been moulded around its branches.

Ragnar and Villi watched Robert study the room,

'That's a tree,' said Robert.

Both men looked at the ancient oak, then back at Robert, as if he had stated something blindingly obvious.

'It is, yes.' Ragnar eventually replied, wondering where the conversation was going.

Robert kept looking at the tree, as he spooned his stew, 'Is that the tree that you all live in.'

Villi was lost, his brow furrowed, he looked at Ragnar who had that look on his face, that twinkle in his eyes and thought he was best out of this one.

Ragnar's face broke into a crooked smile, 'It is, and it isn't,' he replied enigmatically.

Robert nodded. He thought he understood but wasn't quite sure.

Ragnar seemed overly pleased by this exchange.

A flurry of activity announced Thunor and the rest of the men, who all seated themselves on the benches around the hall. People brought out more stew and drinks. As Robert suspected Thunor took his place on the throne under the tree. There was much chatter and banter and back slapping; the energy of the room had gone from quiet contemplation to bawdy in an instant.

Whilst Thunor seemed quick to anger, he was also quick to laugh, loud and boisterously. In fact they all were. Despite the armour, chainmail, huge knives and axes, all embellished with ferocious beasts, they were almost permanently gleeful and found humour in almost everything.

A woman came over, she wore a strange apron dress that had lots of keys dangling from her apron, she whispered something in Ragnar's ear, he nodded and stood up, 'Robert I have things to attend too, you'd best stay with Villi.'

As Ragnar left there was a loud rapping, Robert turned to look, Thunor was banging what a looked like a large walking stick on the floor. He rapped it three times, and the room fell silent.

'We've brought a stray home with us.'

The room turned to look at Robert and he felt himself go crimson.

'This is the Boy Robert. He walks his own path, but twice now he has saved us all from certain death at the hands of Loki's children.'

A great roar erupted from the hall, Robert wanted to crawl under the table.

'Some would say there is no valour in being saved by a boy, I would say there is no honour in denying his courage!'

Another huge roar from the men, all banging the table with whatever was at hand.

'He carries a knife, he earned it. Let us hope that thrice is the charm when, if, we have to call upon him again.'

The room looked at Robert. Robert looked back.

Villi lent over, trying to squash his considerable bulk towards Robert's ear, 'It is your turn to speak now.'

Robert opened his mouth more in fear than anything else as nothing came out, his mind was blank all he could feel was the adrenaline screaming around his body, he stared wide eyed at the room full of people.

Villi nudged him and whispered, 'Stand up boy when you speak here, thank your host eh.'

Robert stood up, not that you would notice, so Villi grabbed him by the scruff of his neck and hoisted him up so that he was stood on the bench, the room broke out into laughter, which eased Robert's terror. He'd never stood on a table before, his Mum would go mental if she found out.

'Erm thank you Chief Thunor, erm, thank you for the food and the drink,' Robert stammered and squeaked.

'Tell me boy is your Father's Hall as grand as this one!' the Chief thundered, looking around, one arm raised wide.

Robert looked up, his bottom lip pouted a little, he thought about his house, it was a nice home, but it definitely was not like this.

'It is not Chief Thunor, I can honestly say I have never seen anything like this in all my life.'

The honesty and awe in his voice chimed through, it brought more cheers from the men.

Thunor beamed, 'Come here Boy Robert, I would gift you, a knife is not enough for saving the lives of my men. Wife, bring your keys and bring the chest.'

Robert walked up through the lines of men who slapped him on back and shoulder, tousled his hair, nearly knocking him flat several times.

As he approached the throne, Robert noticed two huge men, straining to move a heavy wooden chest towards Thunor, their veins and sinews bulged, the chest thudded to the floor and Thunor motioned for his wife to open it. When the lid flipped back a golden glow erupted from it, bathing Robert's face.

Robert said only one, long word, 'Wowwww!'

Thunor ran his fingers through immense red beard, eyes glinting in the golden light, the chest was full to nearly overflowing with gold. Gold cups, goblets, rings, arm bands, belt buckles, dragons, coins, little statues of wild animals; that all seemed alive and flowing and writhing and shimmering in the torch light.

Robert had never seen such treasure and just stood there opened mouthed.

'I bet you've never seen the like eh boy? The wealth of the tribe,' Thunor stood and stooped down, picked out a large ring, large enough to go around a man's bicep muscle and held it out, 'I suspect it might be a bit big yet,' he winked. 'Villi, take him to see Smvor, get him to turn this into something that fits.'

Villi stood up and nodded, he seemed to have found a cooked chicken from somewhere and had one drumstick in his mouth, the other he waved in the air.

Robert turned, holding the ring out in front of him like it was truly fragile, he couldn't take his eyes from it, then remembering his manners he looked over his shoulder straight at Thunor, 'Thank you,'

Thunor nodded, looked like he was going to say something then turned and sat back, taking a goblet with one hand and stroking one of his hounds between the ears with the other he watched the small boy walk up his hall, arms outstretched mesmerised by the golden ring.

Chapter 9

'Smvor!' bellowed Villi, there was no answer except the clanging of metal on metal. Robert wrinkled his nose at the smell of soot, heat and burning metal, then was taken aback when a man so huge Robert thought it impossible, threw open the large black doors. A wave of heat and fumes blasted out making Robert's eyes water. The man looked at Villi then looked at Robert, 'This is the Boy Robert, Thunor would have you make something for him.'

Smvor was vast, he was a head taller than Villi, and his chest and upper arms were an impossible size. A singed leather apron covered most of his front. Robert wondered at the size of the beast it had come from and stood open mouthed.

Villi nudged him and Robert stopped staring and held out the arm ring, it looked tiny in Smvor's hands, yet it was probably big enough to go over Robert's head.

'Something that fits,' added Villi with a smile.

'Isn't that your knife,' grunted Smvor nodding at the blade at Robert's side.

Villi, snorted a laugh, 'Not anymore.'

Smvor raised an eyebrow and nodded once, 'Hold out your arm,' he said to Robert.

Robert complied, and Smvor rummaged in his leather apron, found some twine and measured Robert's bicep. He rumbled a laugh, 'I've made bigger wedding rings than this, and that's for the bride.'

Villi laughed.

'Come back in a couple of days, I'll have knocked something up for you.' And he pulled the door shut, leaving them looking at the wooden slats.

'He's not one for talking our Smvor and he gets grumpy if the forge cools down too much, but you'll struggle to find a better metal-smith.'

With the door shut Robert noticed how chilly it had got and twilight was upon them, the sun seemingly long since slipped behind the distant horizon.

'Come,' said Villi, 'We go find somewhere warm to sit until later,'

Robert turned and scurried after him, 'What happens later?' he craned to look up at Villi's face.

Villi just grunted, his normally gleeful face strained into something altogether more serious, then said, 'Ragnar will explain these things to you.'

And with that they walked in silence towards the great hall again. Inside flickered with shadows and fire. Burning torches lined the beams, a fire was being tended by a small boy in the middle of the hall, the wood cracked and spat with a loud snapping noise, all around in the shadows Robert could see people lurking. And they all appeared to be in full battle armour – a fearsome sight. There was an atmosphere in the room, a sort of trepidation but not. The hairs on the back of his neck stood up and not for the first time on these journeys he felt frightened and stopped dead in his tracks.

Some of the men had stepped aside to let Villi and Robert through, Villi turned to motion Robert to sit down and realised he was still stood by the door, 'Come Robert,' he nodded, a smile on his lips, 'there's nothing to be afraid of here. Whatever is out there should be afraid of us, eh?' and he nodded towards the coming night.

Some of the men bashed the armour on their arms against the chest plates and grunted in agreement. Villi beckoned him again with a nod, 'Come sit here for a while, till it is time.'

Robert slipped in between the huge men, suddenly realising he was gripping his knife handle and did not know why, his knuckles were white. A young girl with beautiful red hair appeared, older than him, but not by much, she gripped the bicep of his sword arm, and motioned for him to take the goblet she held in her other hand, pulling his hand away from the sword,

'There's nothing to fear but fear itself, here drink this, make you feel better. All is woven.'

Robert took the goblet, he didn't understand really what she was talking about, but he didn't care because she was quite the most beautiful girl he had ever seen. She winked and disappeared into the dark; Robert stood staring at where she had been, cup still in hand, then realised everyone was looking at him again; he went bright red and the men around him started laughing loudly.

'Villi,' said one, 'You'd best watch for your daughter as well as your knife.' Everyone seemed to think this was hilarious, even Villi smiled. Robert just blushed even more if that was possible, plonked himself down on the bench and took a big gulp of whatever was in the goblet. It smelled of honey, it tasted of honey and it warmed him inside. The girl was right, at least about the feeling better bit.

The fire crackled, shadows danced, low voices murmured in the darkness, occasional ripples of low laughter splashed up against the walls of the hall. Robert sat in silence, a warm glow in his tummy, watching and listening. He felt warm, content, possibly even more so than when he was at home. In the firelight and dancing shadows he could well imagine strange and wonderful stories unfolding.

Out in the night a long drum began to beat, a slow rhythm, everyone in the room stiffened, stood up, one man had appeared by the door with a flaming torch and as the men and women of the village walked out into the darkness many of them lit their own torches from his. Villi tapped Robert on the shoulder, 'Stay close to me Robert, do not stray, that is very important, we stand together, yes?'

Robert nodded solemnly, his head felt a bit fuzzy and when he stood up it was like his feet were suddenly too big, he followed Villi out into the night. It was quite cold, but it felt nice, fresh, cleansing and the first stars were blazing high up in the sky.

The people had formed two parallel lines up to the far house where Robert had noticed the white smoke coming from earlier, the torches coughed and guttered in the cold air. Villi gripped Robert's shoulder and motioned for him to stand still.

Once the lines were fully formed, Ragnar appeared out of the house, followed by 4 men who were bearing what looked like a stretcher. They walked down, in between the lines of people, as they passed the people fell in behind them, passing the great hall down towards the boats at the little quay.

Robert saw that there was an old man on the stretcher, he looked to be asleep, he was wrapped in furs, a great golden pin holding them in place, and a huge ornate sword lay down the length of his body, one cold hand on the handle.

No one spoke the only noise was the gentle lapping of the sea and the burning torches roaring. The village had gathered on grass just above the shoreline. At the end of the short wooden pier was a boat. Dragon's head carved into its prow, Robert noted it looked like the shadow on his bedroom wall, then realised he'd not been overly concerned by these trips or where his parents were. He was interrupted by Ragnar's voice ringing out clearly on the night air.

'This is Ealric, son of Eolric son of....' the list of names seemed to go on forever, but everyone else was listening with the utmost concentration. The man lay there, the waves lapped gently at the shore, the torches guttered, wheezed and crackled. Robert could smell the sea, smell the night, smell the frost in the air. A list of Ealric's deeds were read out, which monsters he had fought, which battles he had won, land taken, gold taken. Of how the gods had seen fit not to take him in battle, but to leave him here so that he may pass on his battle skills to his son Thunor.

Robert realised the dead man was Thunor's Father. Thunor stood immobile one hand on sword, the other holding a flaming torch near the front. The only other man bigger than him was Smvor the Smith; he searched the crowds and could just make out Smvor's vast figure looming in the gloom. Looking about the crowd of people he caught the eye of the girl who'd given him the drink, Villi's daughter, she flashed a small smile and he blushed looking down at the floor, then up at Villi who was still focused on proceedings. He glanced at the girl but eyes were now looking out to sea.

A wind had picked up coming off the sea, it swirled about them, snatching Ragnar's words and whirling them away into the night. Robert could feel the wind tugging at his hands, legs, hair, he could only make out odd words; that Ealric had died gripping... trusty battle blade, singer of death, would take this blade to the lands of his Fathers....' Robert looked up at Villi's face for reassurance and maybe some guidance as to what was happening but his face was impassive.

The stretcher was lifted and carried onto the boat at the end of the pier, the four men then retreating into the crowd so that Thunor could step forward. He hurled his burning torch onto the boat, it dimmed as it hit, then caught something flammable with a gentle woof noise.

Ragnar stepped forward out of the crowd, turned to face the sea and put his arms in the air, Robert could see his lips moving, but could not make out the words: The drum beat that he'd forgotten about had increased to now twice what it was before. The wind swirled and fidgeted about them, now seemed to be coming off the land. Ragnar turned and moved towards three tree trunks sticking out of the ground, half as tall as him again, Robert realised they were crudely carved into heads and faces, each one slightly different. Ragnar lay before them, stood up again,

Robert couldn't see what was happening there were too many people in the way, the drums were getting ever so slightly faster and faster, Robert's heart beat was now keeping time with them. Above his head he heard a great sizzling, he looked up, ducking slightly before noticing a smile curl on Villi's lips. He could see great ribbons of coloured lights flexing and snaking across the night sky. Head as far back as he could go, he could not take his eyes off the ribbons of light dancing across the darkness, blues, greens, pinks, white – nobody else seemed to be taking much notice of them. He tugged on Villi's sleeve and pointed at the sky, Villi just smiled knowingly, nodded and returned his attention to the proceedings down on earth, as if it was perfectly normal for shimmering lights to be dancing in great ribbons across the sky.

So mesmerised was he that he barely noticed the flaming torches arcing into the boat. Had he been watching he would have seen Ragnar lightly touch the rope that held the boat to the pier and see the knot tumble undone. He would have seen Ragnar blow towards the boat, the simple sail billow and the boat sail out, sail out on the wind, flaming and burning under a ribbon of lights in the sky that Robert could not take his eyes off, it was almost as if the sky itself were aflame. He could feel himself falling backwards, but it didn't matter, nothing mattered, nothing except the lights in the night sky. His head bounced off something soft. And he lay back into it, realising it was his pillow, in his bed, he was home again. He sat bolt upright in bed. Looked around the room, checked the floor, the ceiling and then sleep claimed him again.

Chapter 10

Robert ate his breakfast in silence, still pondering last night's events. His Dad was trying to put on his jacket, check his phone, eat toast and drink tea all at the same time, and his Mum was loading the dishwasher. He thought about saying something, but then decided against it; maybe he would ask his Grandad later.

Robert pushed open the front door and walked down his Grandad's hallway; Stan was in the kitchen, the clanking of tea spoon on mug stopped and his head popped around the door; Robert, flickered a smile and went into the back room where the computer was. He heard his Mum talking to his Grandad in a low voice; 'Don't know, he's been very quiet and sullen this morning, I didn't hear him in the night though, so ...' then they'd moved down towards the front door and Robert couldn't quite hear them anymore.

His Grandad ambled in with a mug of tea, 'You want some juice or something?' he asked, Robert shook his head, intent on firing up the internet.

Stan plonked himself down next to Robert on another dining room chair, 'So.... where we off to this morning?'

Robert looked at his Grandad, he was quite short, square looking, pale, grey hair and slightly watery blue eyes. Nothing like his Dad who was slim, tall and all warm browns. But they had the same sense of humour, when they got together they would laugh for hours, just like the Vikings.

'I want to see where the Vikings lived.'

'We can do that. Click on images and then type in ''S c a n d i n a v i a',

'What's that?' asked Robert.

'Scandinavia is what we call all those countries that are in Northern Europe, sometimes they're called Nordic countries as well I think. See.'

His Grandad pointed to the images, all of which seemed to be maps, then with a big square finger, pointed out some of the countries, 'See we is down here, that's Norway, Sweden, Finland, over here is Iceland.'

Robert squirmed in his seat slightly, which Stan knew was code for 'Robert getting impatient but he didn't like to say', 'But I'm guessing that you don't want to look at maps?'

'No, I want to see pictures of where they lived, what does the land look like, is it all mountains and forests?'

'Oh, well type in landscape after Scandinavia, there you go.'

Pictures of mountains, and lakes and forests flittered up the screen.

Then Robert jumped up and pointed to the screen, 'What's that!?' he shouted.

Stan jolted and slopped tea over his leg, 'Ow, that's hot.'

Robert ignored him, 'Look Grandad, what's that there, make it bigger, look the green fire in the sky.'

Stan wiped a hand over his leg, put the mug down and peered at the screen, he clicked on the thumbnail and dark landscape flipped up, above it green bands of ethereal light flexed across the sky.

'That's the Northern Lights, here type 'n o r t h e r n space l i g h t s ,''

Robert was ahead of him, clicked on search and then sat there mouth hung open, eyes as wide as could be, he finally made a noise, it sounded something like that ''Woowwwwwww', before adding, 'What, how?'

'It's a natural phenomenon, it's caused by solar particles from the sun, being attracted to the North Pole and they sort of charge up and glow. Your old

Grandad knows a thing or two you know.'

Robert couldn't take his eyes off the pictures, but turned his head slightly, 'What's a solar particle Grandad?'

Stan choked a single laugh, his shoulders dropped slightly, and he clicked on the short cut to Wikipedia.

Robert spent the rest of the day reading much but understanding little. And accumulating a vast folder full of pictures he'd downloaded.

When the doorbell rang Robert ran to the door, grabbed his Mum by the hand and dragged her into the back room, 'Look, look at these!' He showed her dozens and dozens of pictures of the Northern Lights, and some close up pictures of the sun and sun spots they'd found.

'Very nice,' said his Mum, not showing nearly as much enthusiasm as she should, thought Robert.

'Come on, let's get home and get tea on the go before Dad gets in, thanks Stan.'

'No problem, see you Robert.'

Robert ran over and gave his Grandad a hug then scampered for the car.

Robert's Dad appeared from around the living room

door, 'What you up to then?'

Peering over the laptop that nearly entirely covered him, Robert broke into a smile, 'Hey Dad, come look at these.'

His Dad dropped down onto the sofa, causing Robert to list seriously sideways and the laptop nearly rolled off his knee, 'Careful Dad,' squirmed Robert, pushing the laptop back, 'Mum said I could use this only if I was careful with it. Look.'

Robert pointed at the pictures,

'The Northern Lights' said his dad.

'Yes.' Robert seemed surprised that his Dad knew that.

'Your old Dad knows a thing or two you know.' He added.

Robert scowled as if he'd just uncovered some kind of conspiracy, 'Yes that's what Grandad says,' he replied with a hint of suspicion.

'They're caused by particles from the sun converging on the north pole, they follow the magnetic lines.'

His Dad's hands mimed the solar particle, converging on the top of a globe.

Robert nodded sagely.

'Come on it's on the table,' shouted his Mum from the kitchen. Robert closed the lid of the laptop, slid it off his knee and followed his Dad out into the kitchen.

'So is it like lightning then but in space?' asked Robert through a mouthful of food.

'I think the effect is the same, but I think the causes are different, I don't know to be honest, and I don't think science knows for sure, you getting into some pretty weighty stuff son.'

'So if Vikings saw the Northern Lights, they must have been really amazed by them, thought it was the Gods or something?'

'Yeah you're probably right,'

'Maybe it was the Gods, back then or still is, they just kind of start it, and stuff.'

'Maybe,' agreed his Dad.

'So do people in Scandinavia still believe in the Viking gods?'

'I think some still do. Not many though.'

'So if our names of our days are named after them

and Vikings used to own big parts of this country, they must have been pretty important here once?'

Robert's Dad broke into a wide grin, 'That is very fine bit of thinking and logic; Yes, you're right?'

'Logic?'

'Coming to an understanding of something, that the Viking gods would have been important, from knowing something else, the names of the days are named after them. That's very good Robert. Well done.'

Robert felt very big, 'So what happened, why don't we have those Gods now?'

'Gosh whole books have been written about that, I guess it boils down to personal choice of people.'

'Which God do you believe in then?'

Robert's Dad looked up towards the ceiling for a moment, 'I don't know, not even sure there is one, and all this squabbling that my God is better than yours is pretty childish. Each to their own I say.'

Robert frowned, not completely satisfied with the answer, but he caught the look from his Mum to his Dad, pretended he hadn't and concentrated on the food.

The rest of the meal continued in silence. Robert thought about mentioning the dreams, but his Mum didn't seem that interested and seemed to be grumpy about him asking questions about this stuff. He might ask his Dad later.

'Can I go back on the laptop Dad?' Knowing that asking his Dad was a better option than asking his Mum.

'Sure I'll come through in a mo, I'll just tidy the dishes up,'

Robert darted from the kitchen. Behind him his Mum was stonily silent. After a couple of minutes of this his Dad interjected, 'Look, a few weeks ago we lost him in Ikea, looking for monsters in wardrobes, now he's suddenly interested in history and asking science questions that I don't know the answer to. And I like to think I know stuff.'

His Dad didn't wait for reply but instead took his mug of tea into the living room and sat on the edge of the sofa next to Robert. The rest of the evening was spent looting the internet for information on Vikings and Northern Lights and anything they could find that might be interesting... Robert was chuffed that his Dad was sharing his interests, so happy that some forty five minutes after his bedtime he volunteered to go to bed, just to show he was grown up.

'I think I'll got to bed now Dad, thanks for looking at

stuff with me,' His Dad scooped Robert up from under the laptop and gave him a hug, 'No problem son, I enjoyed it too. You want me to come up and read the Viking story?'

Robert shook his head, 'No it's ok, am quite tired, it's late I'll just go straight to sleep. But can I have the waves on?'

'Sure you can.'

Robert squirmed from his Dad's arms, and padded over to kiss his Mum, 'Clean your teeth,' she whispered, 'Sweet dreams.'

He nodded and slipped from the room.

'No bedtime story; Gosh, our little boy just not so little anymore.'

Robert did dream that night; a confusing maelstrom of images and sounds that he couldn't make head nor tail of. He saw bright lights of coloured fire in the sky, burning ribbons, flexing and writhing and upon them whispers of dark shadows and black misty cloud in the shape of a horde of horsemen charging across the sky as if the ribbon lights were somehow a road. He saw the shore where the funeral had taken place, the burning boat, the villagers. The three wooden totem poles seemed to come to life but remain where they were at the same time. Giant figures reached up to the sky and waded through the sea beside the burning boat. Three women stood out on the water, as if guiding the burning boat towards them. Everywhere he looked he could see shapes of figures, faces, eyes, wings like some fantastical surreal drawing somehow embedded in the landscape. And then the lights faded, the boat slipped below the water, the figures, faces and creatures had all disappeared. There was just Robert, hanging on the wind, high above the calm sea, looking towards the houses. He could just make out the sound of people laughing and singing, occasional snatches of a voice. A falling star caught Roberts eye as it darted across the sky, Robert looked at the hundreds and thousands of stars, which dusted the black, and felt strangely comforted. The quiet sound of the waves, the gentle pulling roar of the wind guided him back home.

Chapter 11

'Ragnar?' whispered Robert, nervously reaching out to touch the old man; Ragnar's eyes snapped open, and focused on Robert's face.

'Ah, you woke up.'

'What happened?'

'You seem to have passed out, the great hall was a tad noisy, so we brought you to the cow shed, it's warm, and there's plenty of fresh milk,' Ragnar winked.

Robert seemed to notice where he was for the first time, the sweet, sickly, slightly malodorous smell, the gentle sound of cows chewing and digesting. And he noticed all the cows seemed to be looking at him. He couldn't decide if it was a judgemental look or not.

He turned back to Ragnar, 'Ragnar I dreamed I was walking on the lights in the sky, and there were horsemen on it and I looked down and could see you and figures and faces in the landscape.'

Ragnar's eyes twinkled, he nodded spoke softly, 'Come boy, tell me what else you saw.'

Robert curled up in the straw, it was itchy and scratchy but he ignored it, 'I saw three women out to sea, and the wooden poles with faces grew into men, and they reached right up to the sky and they walked out with the boat.'

'Thunor will be pleased at this news, he was worried that his Father had not died a hero's death, but had died a straw death in his bed. And these faces you saw, where were they?'

'Everywhere, it was like your eyes deceived you, where you look at something and then realise that there is something else there after all.

'Elves.'

'Elves!?'

'Yes Elves, don't you have Elves?'

'No' gasped Robert, 'They are the stuff of stories? I've never seen an Elf.'

Ragnar raised an eyebrow, 'Well with a bit of luck, you'll see one tomorrow. It's a strange world you come from Robert, with no Elves.'

'Tomorrow?'

Ragnar, giggled and rocked slightly, 'Tomorrow we go on a trading mission to find some Elves, I think it would be wise if you came with us?'

'Where do they live, what do they look like?'

'They live in the hollow hill and secret places, in old trees and by babbling brooks in ancient woods. As for what they look like, well you'll see later. They are not called the Shining Ones for no reason, boy; they are glorious and beautiful and will put a glamour on you just as quick as blink. But they keep their words, you make an oath with an Elf, you know it will not be broken, but they're canny about it all right. And if you cross an Elf, not a power in earth or sky can save you. Anyway, close your eyes, it's a while before dawn yet, and tomorrow will be long.'

A door banging open followed by a cold draught woke Robert from his sleep. His eyes blinked open, he could make out the huge silhouette of Thunor, 'He's back with us then?'

'Aye,' replied Ragnar and elbowed Robert in the ribs, offering a wooden bowl full of slightly warm milk. Robert slurped on it, wiping the white moustache from his face with his sleeve.

'Tell Thunor what you told me, go on, leave nothing out.'

Robert felt incredibly shy under Thunor's gaze even though all he could see was his dark shape, the pre-dawn light pale behind.

'Erm,.... I dreamed I was walking on the lights in the

sky, and there was this horde of horsemen charging over them, and I saw three ladies standing on the sea waiting for the boat. And three men who were the faces in the poles stood up and reached up to the sky and everywhere I looked I could see faces in the hills, trees and rocks.'

Robert was aware he'd been gabbling his words. Ragnar reached out, put one hand on Robert's forearm, 'See Thunor, the warrior hosts themselves, the great hunt, came to escort your Father. The Three Ladies and the Gods of our Tribe watched over his journey. And the Shining Ones themselves came to pay their respects, eh? How's that for a send-off?' Ragnar chuckled.

Thunor didn't move, then he turned for the door, he half turned over his shoulder,

'Thank you Robert. He comes today?'

Ragnar replied, 'He comes today.'

'Well get a move on, the day is nearly done.' And with that he walked out.

'The day nearly done?' enquired Robert, puzzled looking out the door as he stood up and pulled bits of straw off himself.

Ragnar snorted slightly, 'Sun's not up yet, it's all part of his charm. Come on.'

At the quayside men were loading supplies into a long boat. Villi appeared behind them, he had a short axe and a long-handled axe tucked in his belt, two long daggers, one on each side and he carried a spear.

Ragnar bundled Robert into a dark corner of the boat, under the steps, 'No disappearing now eh?' Robert watched as men busied themselves loading stores and weapons under the benches and in nooks and crannies. By the time the sun had burnt the early morning mist off the surrounding forests they were out on the whale road, the sea slapping at the sides of the boat, ropes singing and thrumming taught. With the smell of salt and fresh air assaulting his senses, the slash of the boat through the waves filled Robert's ears he found himself beaming with excitement.

Ragnar appeared next to him, for man with such a hobble he could move remarkably quietly and quickly Robert thought to himself.

'Now then young Robert, let me tell you of the Elves and how it will be. Do not believe your eyes, or your ears; eat and drink nothing that is proffered; do not speak without first consulting me. And most of all Robert, do not wander off. Do not leave my side. Do you understand?'

Robert nodded solemnly.

'These are very dangerous folk Robert, never underestimate that.'

'Where are they, where do they live?'

Ragnar paused, clearly thinking, 'Well, we head north, they live in the wild places, away from man, every year we have to travel further and further. I suspect this is because every year we encroach more and more, chopping down forest and such like. They are clearly pained by our visits, because of the iron we carry, our swords and mail and such like...' Ragnar just shrugged.

Robert didn't know what to say. Ragnar looked up to the clouds scudding over blue skies, then continued, 'In the time of my grandfather, they were everywhere, a common site. And now I meet you Robert who has never seen one. The world is changing. The Wyrd grows more complex.'

'Wyrd?' queried Robert.

'Yes you know, the weave of life, the weft, the pattern..'

'Oh.'

Robert opened his mouth to ask more, but saw that

Ragnar had once again drifted off, deep in thought, he could see the reflections of the clouds passing over Ragnar's eyes.

Robert sat back, watching the men on the boat go about their business, shouting and laughing; they were always laughing he thought, no matter what happened laughter was not far behind. A cry went up, Robert stirred and rolled, found he'd fallen asleep and had pins and needles in his left leg and left arm... rubbing them awake, Ragnar peered in from the bright sunshine, 'Come, we make landfall.'

Robert clambered out from his hiding hole, the sun making him squint and blink and cover his eyes. The boat felt unsteady under his feet, not the gently undulating of the wide ocean, but the ragged rise and drop of waves rushing to shore. Thunor glanced at Ragnar who gave an almost imperceptible nod, Thunor turned and flicked his head, three men clambered towards the prow and began manhandling the dragon prow, twisting and turning, such that it no longer faced forward but cast its benevolent glare along the length of the boat, looking back over the crew. Robert noticed some of them bend or make a gesture...

Robert pulled on Ragnar's sleeve, 'What's happening?'

'Hmm?'

Ragnar was concentrating, looking at the sky and the slash of land on the near horizon.

'Why do they turn the boat head around?" asked Robert.

'Ahh, we don't want anyone there to think that we come for reasons of war, we have no fight with the people who live here.' And then added 'Nor do we want one, eh?' and chuckled. 'We, erm, our Dragon's Head, she's our guardian and also our guide and, it's difficult to explain, really. We don't want to upset folks with her scary face, eh?'

Chapter 12

A shale beach, with rocky outcrops to the left and right beckoned them; behind the shore, thick, dark green forest, with wisps of mist clinging to the upper branches of trees so huge they really seemed to scrape the sky.

Ragnar noticed Robert's look, 'This is ancient forest Robert, ancient beyond the memory of my Fathers. There is powerful magic here, and powerful folk.' Ragnar squeezed Robert's shoulder.

The boat slammed into the beach, all spray and noise. The boat juddered and rocked, Robert stumbled and by the time he'd got to his feet half the crew had already splashed down into the surf and were spreading out in a half moon shape up the beach. They stopped at a line of seaweed and watched.

'Come Robert, we learn nothing here,' Ragnar leapt for the water, Robert was less sure of this course of action, but Villi appeared behind and gave him some encouragement via a gentle shove.

The water was freezing, the water was beyond freezing it was colder than anything he had ever experienced. Pain snapped him in half, paralysed his brain, ripped his breath away. On most people the water was waist high, Robert had noticed that on Thunor it had barely come above his thigh. On Robert it was almost neck deep and with the fall, it went right over his head. All his sensations shut down, he should have been overwhelmed by the salt, the sea, the swirling sand and seaweed. Instead he was overpowered by the sheer freezing quality of the water.

He felt himself being lifted by the back of the neck, suddenly he was gasping lungs full of cold air, and being carried then dropped splashing around in the surf where the beach and sea met. Villi laughed, 'Come on little fish, you'll find it more comfortable on the dry bit,'

Robert lay there, shaking, spluttering, eyes streaming, cold water surged up his legs, he crawled up the beach some more to escape its clutches and eventually forced himself to his feet.

Cold, bitterly cold, damp, squelching, covered in wet sand and bits of seaweed he shivered uncontrollably. He looked around, other than Thunor and his men, the beach, the edge of the forest was deserted, but he felt like he was being watched. And of course, he was.

Camp was struck, a fire was lit, guards were set. No one else seemed remotely bothered by the bitterness of the temperature and being wet.

Villi called to Robert, 'Go find some driftwood for the fire, the quicker we get it going, the warmer and dryer you'll be eh? Bring back all you can carry, but don't go beyond the line of men, understand?' He jabbed a finger at Robert.

There was no mistaking Villi's point.

The beach was all stone, sorted by the tide into different sizes, and varying degrees of smoothness; here and there a strand of seaweed or crab shell lay pale in the late afternoon sunshine. Thunor and his men were strung out in a half moon shape, watching the tree line, hands on axe and sword handle, some 100 paces from the boat. Robert started to collect broken bits of wood and soon had an armful, wandering back towards the boat, he kept looking over at the trees, certain he was being watched. By his third trip he'd pretty much reached the limit he was allowed to go. Just beyond was a large pale log. Once a limb on a huge tree now wind blasted, sun bleached and salt soaked.

Robert eyed the large branch speculatively, he doubted in all seriousness that he could drag it on his own, it was as long as he was. The man nearest to him, Robert didn't know his name, turned to see what he was doing. Robert pointed at the tree, 'for the fire,' he said.

The man looked around, up and down the beach, to the tree line, back to Robert, he simply nodded and slowly stepped toward the bit of tree, never taking his eyes off the forest. Right hand still on his sword, he bent towards the tree, scooped it up with one hand and hurled it towards Robert. The lump of wood flew over Robert's head and clattered into the stone beach, sending stone flying. Some of the men looked round to see what the noise was then returned to their vigil.

By the time Robert looked up again, the man who had moved the wood was already fully focused on the forest. Robert walked over to the lump of the tree and pulled on one end. The tree didn't move. He tried again. And it didn't move again. He tried rocking it and managed to roll it a little, once it was moving, he managed to start to drag it towards the boat but the log kept ploughing into the stones, and catching his feet, making him stumble slightly. After dragging for what seemed like an age, for so long his arms ached, and his chest hurt from the breathing so heavily he had to stop. When he looked round he realised he's hardly dragged it any distance at all. Again, he tried rocking it from side to side and then dragging and in a flurry of activity stumbled backwards the log followed, nearly running him over.

Robert sat on the floor panting, and a shadow loomed over him, 'Good effort little Robert, you nearly got it to the boat, this will make nice fire,' rumbled Villi.

He picked the log up, spun it onto his shoulder and walked off down the beach; Robert turned and watched him go, shaking his head at the fact that he could barely move the thing and Villi carried it like it was a twig. He clambered to his feet and trotted after Villi, wet clothes slapping, chafing.

Robert plonked himself down by the new fire, it was already warm and steam was rising from him.

There was a quite a pile of wood now, others had brought wood from the other side of the beach, but with some pride, Robert noticed none of the bits were as big as the bit he'd brought. Villi laid into it with his long axe, a few thwacks later, and he'd split it into three large pieces. It occurred to Robert that every time anything was done, it was often done by three.

Looking over his shoulder, back towards the boat, he watched the sun slip below the horizon and into the black water, the sky changing through every hue imaginable and it seemed, some that weren't. Robert was still freezing, the part nearest the fire was singed and burning, indeed one arm and leg was so hot it felt like his flesh was singing. The rest of him was bitterly cold, this was going to be a long, cold, miserable night. For the first time since he had first come to these shores, Robert wished he was at home, in his own bed.

'Here,' Robert recognised Villi's voice and turned, a rough tunic landed on his head, 'Take your wet clothes off, put that on, you will feel better. We'll get some broth on the go soon, you'll feel better again, then you'll look back on the cold water and laugh!'

Robert raised a smile, even snorted a small, sarcastic laugh. They found humour in everything.

Robert peeled off his wet clothes; normally he would have been mortified to have to do such a thing, in an open place, surrounded by strangers, but sometimes the uncomfortableness of a situation is worse than that required to change things. And anyway, everyone was busy doing whatever it was they were doing, not remotely interested in what he was up to. The tunic was rough on his skin but at least it was dry and it had some thickness to it. He laid his wet clothes out, they made a slapping noise on the stones. Villi was right, he did feel better already. He sat down and pulled off his boots, it took more effort than he would have thought possible and at one point he over-balanced, tumbling backwards. Robert looked round to see who was looking, he caught the eye of one of the men, who winked at him and smiled at his acrobatics. Robert blushed and returned his attention to his feet, which were freezing, he rubbed them, and then tucked them under his what he now realised appeared to be a long dress. He thought about this for a moment he was wearing a dress. He then realised he didn't care, it was much more comfortable than the immediate alternative.

Wood crackled and popped on the fire, embers gushed up into the twilight, Robert watched them, watch them rise and spiral, and twirl, dancing on some unfelt breeze as they rose towards the first stars, as if hurtling off to join their kin. Then the night grew thicker and blacker, the half-moon of men around the camp withdrew nearer the fire. Robert could not get comfy, he snuggled a hollow with his bum in the small stones of the beach, but how comfortable were you ever going to get on a stony beach? The side of him nearest the fire baked, anything away from the fire was freezing. A wooden bowl appeared in front of him, it contained a hot stew for which he was grateful, it was thick, smelt of fish but tasted of meat. When he had finished a hand loomed out of the fire light and swapped it for some sweet water, Robert held onto the drink, sipped it carefully and slowly, eyes mesmerised by the flames and dancing sparks which twirled and leapt for the night sky.

'Come on then, someone start a story?' said a voice from the darkness.

'You give us one, must be your turn,' a few people laughed at this.

'Ok, then, did I ever tell you the time that my Grandfather...'

'Yes!' a chorus of voices interrupted, 'We've heard everything your Grandfather did?'

'And a few things he didn't.'

Everyone laughed at this.

'Aye well, a stories not worth telling if you can't add a few bits here and there, so I'll begin...'

And with that, the deep, rich voice wove a story of deeds almost lost to memory, of Gods and Goddesses who intervened in the life of mortals, of heroes and wild beasts, of heroic deeds and tales of renown. The man brought to life the vague flickering images Robert saw in the fire. He must have nodded off at some point because when he next opened his eyes the story had finished, there was no noise, apart from some raspy snoring, and the crackle and hiss of the fire.

There was a shuffle and murmuring and some of the men got up, buckling on sword belts and helmets, stumbling out up the beach towards their comrades who kept guard. And stayed with them for quite a while, until it seemed to be mutually agreed that they return and places were made for them by the fire with stew and drink. Ragnar appeared next to Robert, folded himself down into the ground, Robert leaned over but didn't really look at Ragnar and whispered, 'The ones that have gone to take over, why don't the other's come back why do they both wait?'

Ragnar pulled his mouth down, then said, 'The ones at watch never face the fire, it blinds them. The ones that go cannot face the dark, for they see nothing, the brightness of the flame has overwhelmed their eyes. So they stand until their eyes have become accustomed to the dark. Who would have blind men stand watch?'

Robert nodded and let a quiet 'Ah'.

Ragnar continued, 'You seem to know many things Robert, yet other times you seem to know nothing. A quandary you are?'

'What's a quandary?' Robert asked with a cheeky grin.

Ragnar opened his mouth to reply then realised Robert was teasing him, 'I think you know full well, young Robert,' and laughed

'Hehe, it's a word my Grandad uses.'

'Tell me of your Grandfather?'

Robert grinned, stared deep into the fire, its flames dancing in his eyes and spoke. He spoke of how his Grandfather had won battles, saved magic swords for Kings, saved entire kingdoms; was mighty in battle and kind in peace. Most of what Ragnar heard was a jumble of names and places that were incomprehensible to him. Of Arthur and Merlin and their sword Excalibur, King Harold, how it was Stan who burnt the cakes and not King Alfred like everyone thought. Of Robin and Hoods and his Maid Marion.

He smiled at Robert's enthusiasm, smiled at the tales a Grandfather tells his Grandson, but held his tongue, who was he to dissuade Robert or malign his Grandfather? After all, this child had banished a dragon and seen the Gods, perhaps his was a mighty bloodline indeed.

Ragnar leant forward, eyes glinting, lapping up the words and the stories, Robert's enthusiasm infectious. Perhaps there was hope yet.

Robert yawned and blinked in the fire, his face was ablaze, he seemed to have run out of words, and found himself on empty.

'Come Robert, lie down, sleep, tomorrow we must be up before dawn. It will be a long day. Again. And we don't want to use up all that rich word hoard do we.'

Robert frowned at Ragnar's words but he was already asleep before it mattered.

Chapter 13

Dawn seemed to arrive unreasonably early, Robert felt like he had barely slept but instead spent the night tossing and turning. He was bitterly cold and could not stop trembling even after someone had thrown some more wood on the fire, giving the embers a severe poking. Robert looked up at the sky, it looked like it had been painted by God; or Gods, depending on your point of view. Away to the west, night still claimed the horizon, stars dusted and dazzled, embedded in deep purples and blues. But to the east, a pale band of light crept ever higher, bleaching the dark with lavender, gold and burnished orange. Breakfast was dry bread and dried meat, which took a great deal of effort to chew and in truth, wasn't really worth all of the effort. The watch was swapped and the men who had been stood out on the perimeter huddled by the fire and gnawed on their rations with a quietness about them.

Villi loomed over Robert, 'You should change again, put your clothes back on from yesterday, they should be dry enough. We have a long walk today.'

Robert grimaced at the phrase 'dry enough'. He reached over and on the whole they were surprisingly dry. And surprisingly stiff, it was as if they had become made of cardboard overnight, though the sound they made when he peeled them from the beach was distinctly unappealing. He brushed the sand and stones off them, and fought his arms and legs down the respective holes. Standing there, feeling all stiff and scratchy, he folded up the smock he had been wearing and looked around for someone to give it to. It was nice to have his feet inside something resembling a shoe, he squidged his toes, feeling the life and a little warmth coming back into them. But he couldn't for the life of him figure out where that smell was coming from. Then he realised it was him; gingerly he sniffed his top, and pulled his nose.

'You smell like a dead fish little one,' laughed Villi has he took the smock from Robert's hands and stuffed into a leather bag. 'If that water had been any deeper you might well be a dead fish!'

Villi seemed to find this more amusing than Robert thought it actually was, and sniffed his top again; dead sea weed, dead crab, dead fish came to mind.

There was the hustle and bustle of men preparing for a long walk, rations shared, bags packed, weapons checked. A couple of men trotted off towards the tree line, a couple of men stayed behind on the boats, one standing on the prow behind the reversed dragon. When Thunor was happy everyone was about ready, they set off, crunching up the beach, past the line of seaweed and dead crabs, up past the fine sand to where they long grass tufted and whined in the early morning breeze. Before them the forest loomed, dark and twisted.

'Mind your feet young Robert, it's said the tree roots here can snap a man's ankle if they don't like him,' whispered Ragnar.

Robert peered into the gloom, he'd never heard of tree roots attacking people before, but then there were many things he'd experienced in this place that he'd always considered to be fairy stories.

It was slow going, but the group of men, of large, heavily armed men, moved with surprising quiet through the forest. In fact Robert, the smallest and lightest of them made more noise than all of them put together, no matter where he put his foot dead leaves rustled or twigs snapped. He also realised that the smell of the sea salt had been replaced by the smell of trees, leaves, rotting vegetation and living forest. A vibrant green smell.

About them birds sang in the branches, unseen wings flapped, things scurried off in the undergrowth, everything smelled alive and lustrous which was a strange thing, Robert felt like he could feel the forest through all of his senses, like the whole forest was one huge living creature.

Robert whispered to Ragnar, 'It's alive!'

'What is?'

'The forest. The whole forest and everything in it, it's

like it's one big thing and I can feel it and taste it!'

Ragnar grinned, then stopped, gripped Robert by the shoulder and halted him. Robert looked up and around, all the men had stopped, no one moved, or breathed, Robert noticed Villi, a few paces ahead, his hand ever so slowly drifted down towards the handle of one of his short axes that hung from his belt.

Then there was some unseen signal the tension eased and the party moved on, but Robert still noticed that men's hands were never far from weapons. And they all looked about them, left and right and above like predators. Or maybe prey.

He could make no sense of the forest, where he was or where he had come from, he was unsure whether they had found a path or were forging a new one; on either side of him was a twist of trees, saplings, leaves, bushes, gnarled branches all broken up amidst pools of shadow and quiet sunlight. Then they were in a clearing about 30 paces wide. In the middle was a standing stone, it was just a simple, roughly hewn stone, about the size of his Dad. The men didn't seem to want to get to near to the stone, nor did they want to get to near to the tree line which circled the clearing, so they kind of hovered in a mid-line orbit. Thunor flicked his head at Ragnar who scuttled towards the stone, pushing Robert before him.

On closer inspection the stone had spiral grooves etched into it, but they looked ancient and weather-beaten and there was moss and lichen growing all over it. He reached out to touch it, but before his fingers had reached the stone, he heard Thunor say ''Gnnnnnnn!' and noted the eyes wide look of distress on his face, Ragnar's hand shot out, grasped Robert's wrist and gently pulled his hand away from the stone.

'That would be considered very bad luck and very bad manners by some folk in these parts, young Robert and we may not be able to explain it away by just saying you're not from around these parts, mmm.' Ragnar's eye brows rose a considerable height up his forehead.

'Sorry, my Mum's always telling me to look with my eyes and not with hands.'

'A very wise bit of advice. Now I would like you, to erm, just stand there, don't say anything and don't touch anything, these could be delicate negotiations and our erm 'friends' can be a tad fickle sometimes.'

A voice hissed out from the trees, it boomed and seeped and roared and whispered all at the same time from every direction.

'Fickle! You old fool Ragnar, you insult us, after we have traded secrets across the winters and summers!'

Everyman of the group gripped their weapons but did not draw them or raise them. Ragnar stiffened and looked around, opened his mouth to speak, eyes wide and head spinning like an owl, not sure which direction to address.

'A bad choice of words to illustrate to the boy, he has never seen your kind before.'

'I suggest that your men withdraw to the south, and abide by our rules' said the voice.

Ragnar nodded, flicking his head behind them, the men withdrew to the far side of the circle, leaving Robert, Ragnar and Thunor by the stone; Robert was quietly impressed that everyone knew which direction was south. On days out with his Mum and Dad, there was usually a row at some point about which way to hold the map, where they were and what direction they should be travelling in.

Thunor waited, stared at the tree line, bristling at being told what to do, Robert could see the indignation on his face. Ragnar grunted and motioned with his head, and Thunor walked backwards staring intently into the dark shadows of the forest.

'Have you any iron on you boy or steel?

Robert thought about it, 'other than the knife, no, and the end of the belt maybe?'

'Give them to me'.

As he undid the belt, Robert looked back to the men, across the grass that was clipped short for a wild place, everyone was deliberately not making any sudden hand moves and all communication was being made by head nods and eyebrow twitches. But the colour had left many faces; eyes were wide, muscles tensed. In fact if you looked carefully you could see the veins standing out on Thunor's neck.

'Stay here,' and stepped towards the men. Robert felt very alone, his head spun round, trying to take everything in. He looked to the tree line, feeling very vulnerable and afraid, the pit of his stomach dropped away. He turned back, Ragnar seemed to magic a short knife from up a sleeve, a really long knife that looked more like a short thin sword from within the folds of his smock, his belt, a ring and some sort of pendant and place them all in a pile by his sword. They clinked together in the green grass, Robert aware of the prickly sensation all over his skin, the pounding of his heart in his ears. Ragnar slipped back to his side, put a reassuring hand on his shoulder, 'Calm yourself boy, take slow deep breaths.'

'Non should be calm in our presence, do you not know us?' boomed the voice.

Ragnar's eyebrows wriggled a like a furry caterpillar roaming across his forehead.

'Shall we continue, lest we endure,' said Ragnar, his eyes narrowed.

There was silence, Robert had the sudden feeling that he was the cheese on the mousetrap; Ragnar squeezed his shoulder, and then stiffened. Robert looked to where Ragnar's eyes were pinned but couldn't see anything, he looked back, Ragnar was concentrating furiously but Robert could not see what he was looking at. Then where there had been twisted branch and root, and shadow, and patch of sunlight, seemed to form into figures, it's as if they had been there all along, you just needed to know how to look, like one of those trick pictures his Grandad had shown him, with the face in the wine glass or grain of wood, but this wasn't a trick, it was real.

The figures stepped out of the tree line, and as slow and imperceptible as the dawn, colour bled into them, bright vibrant, living colours. Robert squinted, they seemed to be far away but quite near at the same time, a wave of nausea broke over him, the distance and perspective was all wrong. Half closing one eye, he managed to get the figures to be in some sort of equilibrium view. And they were magnificent, and beautiful and terrible and Robert could have spent the rest of his life quite contentedly just looking at them so glorious where they. Tall and splendid, perfect skin, high cat like eyes with no hint of emotion, thin lips and nose sneered out at the world. Their clothes were bright and colourful and theatrical and tiny bright lights danced about them. Long fine swords and knives hung about their belts, even from here Robert could see the workmanship of dragons and beasts wrought in the metal and the creatures seemed to dance and move all of their own. The Elves moved with a gentle, lithe grace. They were taller than he expected. They were utterly terrifying.

They moved towards the stone, a leader and three on either side of him, a pace behind, looking languid, lazy and bored. One of them stared at Robert, he couldn't look the creature in the face, could not hold its gaze but was instead mesmerised by the large war axe hefted on its shoulder. It glinted and gleamed in the sunshine and the metal work figures squirmed about its haft and blade. The blade was so sharp it seemed to never end; Robert imagined what it would feel like to have that blade slice through him, it would be a pleasure to experience the workmanship of that blade so directly. He leant forward to take a step, eyes unblinking fixed on the cutting edge, Ragnar jolted him back by pulling on his shoulder and scowled.

'My companion plays that is all; do not take offence so easily' a voice whispered petulantly.

The voices thought Robert, they're like soft tentacles that could crush you in an instant, but you want to listen to them, but you'd never leave their side in case you missed something, they were there to be adored.

Ragnar dug his nails into Robert's shoulder and he snapped out of his reverie. The nails, reminded Robert of being scratched once by his Aunties' cat, and then he realised that these Elves were like cats, not just their eyes but their whole demeanour, they were perfectly adapted to killing, and beautiful to look at and utterly evil to anything they considered to be of a lesser species than them (which apparently, was everything). And cats like to be adored.

Robert bowed deeply, swung his arm out and around like he'd seen them do on that play his Mum had watched about Shakespeare.

The voice seemed to be amused, 'See that's your problem Ragnar, you and your kin, you don't know your place in life. Who is this boy you bring from far?'

Robert could feel Ragnar go all brittle next to him, then through clenched teeth, Ragnar hissed back,

'We don't bow before our Gods, we stand and look them in the eye and we stand straight and tall, I bend my knees to no thing or no one.'

'Yes so I see.'

'Let's not forget *Lord*, you need us as much as we need you. You few might be able to best us in a fight here and now, but others of us will come back, with their iron and their ploughs and their axes and we all know what will happen then, cause what we also is, is very, very, very stubborn. And overall there's a lot more of us than there is of you. The boy comes from a place where your kind don't even exist anymore!'

The Elf wrinkled his nose as if he'd smelt something unpleasant, his head nodded back ever so slightly and then he held out his hand. One of the other Elves, handed him a leather bag in a very relaxed, almost couldn't be bothered manner. The lead Elf then tossed it to Ragnar who caught it. Robert noticed him squeeze the bag slightly, making sure there was something in it.

'Don't you trust me Ragnar?'

'If you was trustworthy you wouldn't need all the charms, and enchantments and beguiling and glamour that goes about you?'

The Elf's lip twitched, 'just some pretty things in another wise drab world. And you still haven't told me why he is here?'

Ragnar turned, looked Robert in the eye, seemed to think for a moment, bit the inside of his bottom lip then turned back to the Elves, 'As a reminder, that we keep our word, our oath remains, our pact is sealed. And to show you what could be.'

Robert was aware of adults talking over his head but he wasn't sure what was going on.

'I think we are done here.' sneered the Elf.

'Yes.' Ragnar gripped Robert's shirt and pulled him gently away towards the rest of the men, after a few steps he spun Robert around and pushed him towards Thunor and the others. Ragnar kept walking backwards never taking his eyes off the Elves. Villi stepped forward, helped Robert put his knife and belt on, held Ragnar's stuff for him whilst he tucked away the sword and knives and the like.

'Trust to iron now boy, move quickly. Do not stop until we get to the boat and then don't stop, just get in.'

Chapter 14

Robert was bundled forward towards the tree line by Villi, he managed a quick look behind him, but already the Elves had gone, faded, there was something there, in the shapes of the trees, the way the light fell, but he couldn't be sure. Then then they were in the dark of the forest, now was nothing but green and shadow.

Villi gripped Robert by the scruff of the neck and launched him upwards, Robert managed to grapple himself over the edge of the boat, half tumbling, half skipping out of the way as the men clambered up and over and around him. Robert's legs got tangled in his long blade and he stumbled to the floor as the men started undoing ropes, tying ropes, some jumped down into the rowing stations and began heaving on oars, and suddenly the boat was ploughing through the waves at a pace.

Thunor was shouting orders at people, but everyone seemed to know what to do without him.

'What was that!?' demanded Ragnar and prodded Robert in the chest, glowering in his face and looking really angry.

Robert was frightened, he'd clearly done something wrong but he didn't know what, he looked around the boat but no one was looking back at him.

'Erm what?' he stammered.

'The bowing and scraping?'

'I was erm, just trying to be polite...'

'Polite! You can't be polite with them, they'd rip your head off and use it for decoration as soon as look at you.'

'I thought they were a bit cat like, and my Aunty has cat, you stroke it, it purrs,' Robert spluttered.

Ragnar fixed him with a beady stare, and chewed the inside of his lip, 'make the cat purr you say?' and then roared laughing. ' Boy, you make life interesting that's for sure. You might have something there though, however I am not bowing to anything, let alone an Elf.'

'But surely, I mean what if they had attacked us?'

'Then I'd be supping mead with my forefathers in Odin's Hall, with fine woman and fine men for company, swapping stories in front of a roaring fire. Not a bad place to be eh?'

'But you'd be dead?'

'I'm going to die anyway, we're all going to die boy, all

that matters is how you lived and how you died. And bowing is not happening.'

They both looked at each other like the other one was insane.

Robert looked at the floor, unsure what to make of all this, in fact he was very confused. Ragnar seemed to have calmed down now.

'What was in the bag?' asked Robert looking to change the subject.

Ragnar stooped down and whispered, 'a secret, a sunstone, if you know the magic, and I do, they tell you where the sun is even when you can't see it?'

'How?'

'Hmph, some things are not meant to be shared.'

'So what did we give them? You said you'd given them something, and it was very formal, very erm I don't know the words.'

'You ask a lot of questions boy.'

'My Grandad says it's how you learn, you should always ask questions of everything.' Robert looked up at Ragnar defiantly.

Ragnar nodded, a glimmer of a smile, 'Hmmm

indeed, I think I would like to meet your Grandfather.'

Robert wasn't sure if he was being sarcastic.

'We have an oath with them, that we will not encroach on their lands, the forests to the north are theirs. That's why we push east and west. Iron poisons them, we left the iron to one side, though even that close it pains them, hence the face like he was sniffing a dead rat. If we were to pick a fight, we would most likely win, eventually and at a heavy cost. The world is big enough for everyone. Especially where they are not. Besides, with it hanging in the balance as it is, they kind of pay us to stay away. It's good for trade,' Ragnar winked.

'Danegeld?' exclaimed Robert.

Ragnar glared at him, his eyebrows scurried to and fro, Robert could tell he was thinking.

'We have iron and steel everywhere at home,' he offered.

Robert knew that Ragnar knew that Robert was changing the subject (again). But Ragnar seemed to content to play the game for now: 'And that young Robert is why you've never seen one before, it poisons the land and them, but they are the land. It's...complicated.'

'So, we head for home now?'

'No, now we head south, to see a friend, this we just acquired us for us to trade,' he stood up and looked over the side of the boat to the rolling waves and white horses rushing towards the horizon, 'my friend knows someone who will like this and will venture much to gain one. Enough with the questions now, I have tasks to attend to.'

And Ragnar walked off. Robert felt a bit confused, almost tearful, like he'd let everyone down, but most of all himself. He stepped back into the shadows, clambered up onto the top the barrel and wiped a tear from his face. It's not like he'd met Elves before, and as for your going to die anyway thing. He felt edgy and unsettled as he closed his eyes.

Chapter 15

Robert swung his legs and padded down stairs. Everything felt strange; he couldn't tell what time it was, or even what day it was. In the living room his Dad was reading the paper. In the kitchen his Mum was busying herself.

'Mum?'

She turned, put the dishcloth down and scooped him up. This was not like his Mum, 'What's wrong?' he asked.

She kissed him on the cheek, 'Nothing, your Dad and I need to have a chat with you?' and headed for the living room.

He heard Dad's paper rustle as he folded it up.

'What day, is it, why aren't you in work?'

'Enough with the questions kiddo.'

Robert scowled and made a 'hmph' noise. He stood between them looking at them for what seemed like an age.

'Your Grandad has been poorly and he had to go to hospital, it's not serious so there's nothing to worry about, but he needs to take things a bit easier ok?'

This all seemed to get gabbled out as once, 'We need you to be grown up about it Robert. Especially whilst you're there during the holidays.'

'Ok' replied Robert matter of factly; then screwed his face up as a thought occurred to him, 'If there's nothing to worry about, why all this?' Robert waved his arms around hoping it conveyed the drama of the situation.

'Yes, right, well then, erm.'

'What's wrong with him?'

'Well it's something called diabetes, it affects the amount of sugar in your blood, which is controlled by what you eat.'

'What your Dad is failing to say is that one of the things which might happen is your Grandad might go a bit light headed. He might even faint and you need to be not frightened by that and know what to do. And you need to be able to help him make the right decisions, he's looked after you, now you need to look after him.'

Robert nodded.

'This is the difficult bit, and this is really, really important now; he's not to have sweets or chocolates or biscuits. But if you think he's gone a bit light headed or, um, weird then give him something sweet.

But it's really important that he doesn't have them just in the day, his medicine will control things. Do you understand?'

'Ok.'

'It's kind of like a seesaw, a balance, if it swings one way or the other too much, then he'll be poorly again.'

'So you understand, no sweets, biscuits or chocolates unless he starts going a bit funny. And if he faints, he'll crash to the floor, the first thing you do is phone us. Ok?

There was a slightly awkward silence.

'Is there anything else?' asked Robert.

His Mum and Dad looked at each other sideways then back to Robert.

'Nooo. What we will do is leave your Mum and mine's mobile phone number on Grandad's fridge and if for any reason you think there is something you phone one of us. Ok?

'Ok.'

His Mum and Dad briefly looked at each other again in that strange sideways manner again. His Mum frowned and rested her hand on her chin.

'You ok, you seem remarkably calm, you do understand, yes?.'

'Yes, you said it wasn't serious but if Grandad starts to feel a bit funny then phone you. And if he goes really funny, give him a chocolate biscuit as well.'

'Yessss.'

'Ok then. What do I do if there are no chocolate biscuits?'

'We'll make sure there is.'

'What happens when I go back to school, when the holidays are over?'

'We'll worry about that when the time comes.'

'Ok.'

'Ok.'

There was an awkward silence.

'So where is Grandad now?'

'He's still at the hospital, as soon as you're dressed......'

'And washed and cleaned your teeth,' interjected his

Mum.

'…..We'll go get him,' continued Dad.

Robert hurtled out of the room and thundered up the stairs, splashed water on his face, squirted some toothpaste in his mouth, smeared it around with his tongue then spat it out and was down stairs pulling his jumper and pants on and hunting for his shoes under the stairs before his Mum and Dad had even got off the sofa.

He stood in the doorway of the living room curious as to why they hadn't moved, 'Come on then!'

Grandad was sat in a high backed orange chair, there was an empty plastic cup on a plastic table next to him and he seemed to be staring out of the window. They were on a floor high in the tower block which offered fantastic views to distant hills, but Robert didn't really notice the expanse of sky, instead he wrinkled his nose at the funny smell which had been even more pungent in the lift on the way up.

'Grandad!' Robert ran towards him
'

There were hugs and smiles and a general morass of greetings. Then there seemed to be quite a bit of hanging around, as they had to wait for a doctor to come and talk to them. Robert was bored, fidgeting and peering over the window sill to see what he could see; people driving around the car park looking for a parking space. Two men seemed to be angry at each other, but Robert couldn't hear what was being said, just saw their arms waving around.

Finally, a brisk man turned up who seemed to be far too busy to have time to talk to anyone, went over what seemed to Robert to be an awful lot of boring stuff, then he wrote things down on a piece of paper and whirled off.

Robert's Mum did not seem to be impressed by any of this, she took the piece of paper off his Grandad and put it in her purse and then said ,'So that's that then, shall we go and get a cup of tea?'

Robert held his Grandad's hand in the lift. He looked up at his Grandad and wrinkled his nose. Grandad nodded with a tiny motion and wrinkled his nose back.

'What's in the bag Grandad?' Robert asked, looking at the blue and white plastic bag, with thin blue plastic rope handles.

'Oh just some overnight stuff, tooth brush and such like?'

'I could carry it?'

'Sure kiddo,'

And with that off they toddled off to find the car.

They seemed to spend a long time in the car, stuck in traffic, the lights always seemed to be red when they got to them. Robert sat in the back with his Mum, Dad and Grandad in the front. Robert was still fidgety, he felt part of him was still in bed, part of him was still on the Viking ship and this was a dream. And then he had this sudden surge of adrenalin about his Grandad and a whole load of 'what ifs' ploughed through his mind.

The car pulled up outside Grandad's house; inside was chilly compared to the mild summer's day outside and it was dark. His Mum went in the kitchen and started filling the kettle, his Dad went into the front then back room to open the curtains.

Chapter 16

'Grandad can I put the 'puter on?'

'Sure,'

Robert sat on the computer chair, legs swinging, waiting for it to get to the desktop.

His Dad and Grandad came in and pulled up chairs at the table behind him, his Mum was still clattering in the kitchen.

'What's this?'

Robert turned around.

His Dad was holding up the carrier bag, the rope handles were knotted in a complicated and perfect knot. His Grandad took the bag and looked at the knot,

'Robert this is a great knot, you thinking of joining the boy scouts?'

Robert just looked at them, shrugged then turned back to the computer, in the reflection of the screen he watched his Mum come in with some mugs of tea and Grandad gesticulate at the bag then Robert.

'Where did you learn to tie a knot like this Robert?'

She asked.

Robert shrugged his shoulders ''Dunno, off the internet I guess.'

'Don't know,' she replied emphasising each syllable, 'and what do you mean, you guess?'

'I don't know, I wasn't even concentrating, I just did it in the car!' Robert certainly felt he was being got at for doing something well.

His Grandad caught the look, 'It's a fine knot Robert, maybe you were a sailor in a former life, eh?'

Robert half nodded a scowl, and turned back and started looking up pictures of Viking ships.

He heard his Grandad kind of expel air as he stood up and came over, put a hand on his shoulder and squeezed, 'Look at the carving detail on that.'

And placed a stubby finger on the screen as a dragon's head peered at them from the end of the ship.

Robert 'ummed' in response, 'See this Grandad, there's no benches, they sit on chests with their stuff in, each man has his own place, the shields go over the side.'

Robert guided his Grandad over the painting of a

Viking ship they'd found, Robert's Dad pulled a chair up and sat next to him.

'This is brilliant Robert, you found this all out yourself.'

'Well, erm yes. Erm, Grandad helped sometimes.'

'Points make prizes that's what I say,' he chipped in and winked conspiratorially.

'You can't have any biscuits unless you go weird,'

His Grandad crossed his eyes and pulled out his tongue, Robert laughed, 'doesn't count.'

'Well done son,' his Dad squeezed his knee, 'and what's this?', pointing at something on the screen Robert was looking at.

The day ambled on, Mum bought in some ham sandwiches with mugs of thick soup. Robert left the crusts on his plate, and pretended he hadn't heard the comments about hairs on his chest or growing up big and strong. His Mum just tutted when she picked his plate, his Mum always seemed to be able to find something to tut about. He could hear her clattering the in the kitchen, his Dad and Grandad were sat behind him now, reminiscing about days long ago. But not as long ago as the days he was thinking of. Then he screwed his face, a sudden sense of confusion about the half listened to conversation.

'Grandad?' They stopped talking and looked at him.

'How old are you Grandad?'

'Seventy years and a bit'

'And they had horses and carts when you were my age?'

'They did, seeing a car was a real rarity.'

Then his Dad said, 'I remember the rag 'n' bone man coming up our street when I was young man with a horse and cart.'

'What's rag 'n' bone?' asked Robert, expecting something gross as an answer.

'Just a bloke who collected large bits of rubbish, mainly metal I think, but the big stuff that the bin men wouldn't take away. I used to give their horse a carrot when I was kid.'

'That wasn't the same horse they always had you know?' interjected his Grandad.

'Wasn't it?'

'Nooo. When old Jed passed on they decided to retire the horse, which was called Ned, Jed and Ned, ha. When Jed's son took over, who was called Jethro if I remember right, they got a new horse, but it had the same markings, but it didn't have the furry feet that Ned had. Can't remember what the new horse was called.'

'What happened to Jed?'

'Well, apparently he just had heart attack or something part way around his route. No one noticed, he just died on his cart and sat there, old Ned had been pulling Jed for years, knew the route and Jed was only noticed when he got back to their yard and never got down, poor old sod.'

His Dad nodded in agreement then turned back to Robert, 'Er, yes, when I was a young man, horses and carts were rare, most people had cars then, but in your Grandad's day, they were a real luxury.'

For a moment, Robert thought that at the mention of the world 'luxury' they were going to break into recounting something called Monty Python, he held his breath but they restrained themselves. But instead a smile and something unspoken passed between them.

Robert continued, 'your Dad's Dad' pointing at his Grandad, who nodded.

'So what did your Dad have Grandad?'

'Horses, but mainly walking, which we used to call

Shanks' Pony, no idea why, but only rich folk had horses and you rarely travelled beyond where you were born.'

'So why hadn't someone invented the car?'

'I guess it needed the technology and then someone to come up with the idea.'

Robert seemed a little unsatisfied with this answer, but then said, 'So there's you' pointing at this Dad, 'and then you,' pointing at his Grandad, ' Then your Dad, then his and his and his, how many of those are there till you reach the Vikings?'

The two men looked at each other and then his Dad said, 'I think we are going to need the internet and a calculator.' He pulled his chair closer to the computer, 'get up Google and type in 'how many years is a generation.'

Robert picked out the letters surprisingly quickly thought his Dad.

'Generation?'

'Yes each set of kids is a new generation, so starting with your Grandad, I'm his kid, so that's two generations, your mine, that's a third generation and it goes back.'

'For how long?'

'For ever, right back through the early men that looked a bit like apes, back to apes, back to fishes back to plankton, you remember that 'tree of life' we saw in the museum and it showed where everything was connected going back in time?'

Robert sat with his eyes wide and his mouth open for several seconds trying to process this, and then said, 'Wyrd.'

'I guess it is a bit weird when you first think about it, but there's a common sense, a logic and science behind it, people have studied this for many, many years. A man called Charles Darwin was the scientist who first came up with this tree of life thing.'

'No I mean *Wyrd*, that everything is connected.'

'Yes.'

Robert's Dad felt like he's missed something but wasn't sure what.

'So how many generations till I was a fish?'

'Well that's a bit of a guess really, even back to your Vikings they didn't write down much, the evidence they left behind rots in the ground, so we, well the archaeologists who dig these things up have to piece together what they can. But we can do how many generations to the Vikings. I think.'

There then followed several minutes of his Dad gradually taking over the control of the computer with much scrolling, clicking on links and 'hmming' noises. Eventually he said, 'Right well, the consensus would seem to be that a generation is 30 years, that takes into account when people have babies and the fact that in olden times when they had more wars and less medicine, people didn't live as long.'

He sat back looking quite pleased with himself, 'So what do we need to do now?'

Robert looked at him blankly, then at his Grandad and then at his Mum who was now stood in the doorway drying her hands on a kitchen towel. He shrugged.

'Ok well we know the Vikings period came to a close in 1066, is that right?'

Robert was taken by surprise that his Dad was asking him a question, and just nodded.

'That's a little under a thousand years ago, but if we say a thousand years ago that puts us dead in the time of the Viking and makes our maths easier. So we need a calculator,'

Robert slipped his arm to the mouse, 'There's one on the computer, here.'

'Ok, so typed in 1000 divided by 30 then press

equals.'

'33.3333333333 and lots more threes' Robert frowned, 'I don't understand.'

'So what we've done is we've said is if we have a thousand years, how many 30's are there in that thousand. Or put it another way, if you multiplied 30 years by 33.33333333 you'd get 1000.'

Robert was silent.

Then his Grandad stood up, his knees creaking, went to his sideboard and lifted out the tin cup which he kept his copper in.'

Then with the aid of lots of one pence pieces Robert was shown how three lots of 33 came to 99 and if you took one whole penny and could split it across the 3 piles of coins you'd end up with a third from each.

'How can you have a third of a generation though, I thought a generation was a person?'

'Excellent question, Robert and obviously you can't have a third of a person.'

'Unless you chopped them up' added his Grandad with some glee, Robert's eye lit up at this.

'No, no chopping up of people, thank you. The maths

we've done is just, can't think of a word to describe this, it's, um, an abstract.'

Robert gave him the, I've no idea what you're talking about look.

'Ok, it's something we use to give us a view but it's not the same as the actual thing. Kind of if you know what I mean?'

Robert gave a half-hearted shrug; there was a glimmer of understanding but a lot of fog as well.

'What we can do though, instead of getting hung up on the maths, is kind of forget about the .33333's as they are quite small and don't really mean much.'

Robert nodded vigorously at his.

'And concentrate on the 33. So we now know that in the last 1000 years there has been 33 generations. That means that if you wrote my name down, then you grandad's, then his dad, then his dad, then his dad and so on, you'd have a list of 33 people to write down to get back to the Vikings.'

'Let's do that, we can use the computer to type them out and then print them off!'

'Well, we don't know their names.'

Robert stopped stock still for a moment, 'Why not?'

'Well erm, we just don't, people move and not much was written down.'

Stan leant forward, 'Robert do you know who my Grandad was, that would be your great-great Grandad?'

'No.'

'Why not?'

'Well, I er, I've never met him and we never talk about him.'

'Exactly. And so they get forgotten, it's kind of sad but it's just the way of things.'

'But the Vikings remember, they sit around the fire at night in the great hall or when they're on adventures, telling stories about their kin folk.'

'But we don't,' replied his Grandad.

'Kin folk?' his Dad laughed.

'Yes it's important to them, Ragnar son of .... etc'

'Maybe it was more important to them than us? They didn't have cars and televisions and internets and games back then, they hadn't been invented, so they sat around telling stories.'

Robert sat back with a sigh, an unbelieving look on his face and looked at them both.

Stan leant forward and looked at Robert at eye level, 'As things get old, they degrade, they break and wear away. Look at me, I used to jump around like you, now I struggle to get out of a chair and one day, I'll die...'

'Stan!' interrupted Robert's Mum.

'No, Louise, this young man is growing up and he's asking questions which have to be answered, it's good that he knows. Knowledge is always good. Knowledge leads to wisdom.'

Robert was aware of a tension in the room, he'd never heard his Grandad say 'No' to his Mum before.

Stan continued, 'Even metal and stone wears away, till there's virtually nothing left, and they're a lot stronger than I am. I like to think that my soul, the bit that's me goes on, but this bit,' he pinched the flesh on his forearm, 'This is not everlasting, far from it.'

'But they might have done amazing things and we don't know about them?!'

'I'm sure they did,'

'And their blood runs in you, so it means you can too.'

Tears became to run down Robert's cheeks, he stared at the space between where his Dad and Grandad sat. Stan leant forward and held Robert's hand.

'Why you crying, there's nothing to cry about.'

'I don't understand,' sniffed Robert, 'if the stories are forgotten and everything rots, what's the point?'

'Aye, well I'm not sure I understand either, it's a lot to take in. But it's just the way of things, and so it can't be bad can it?'

Robert shook his head.

'Anyway, who'd want a bunch of old people hanging around the place, clogging the place up, getting in the way all the time?'

Robert sniffed back a laugh, the mood lifted slightly.

'And speaking of clogging up the place, we should go, let you have some peace Stan,' said Louise.

'Aye, well I could probably do with a power nap.'

They left Stan; on the way home they called in the Chinese takeaway as Mum didn't want to cook. And the rest of the evening was spent watching television, nobody talking. Robert curled up in a chair, eyes open but not watching, he'd no idea what had been on; his mind was elsewhere. At some point he got up and took himself to bed, and at some other point, he fell asleep.

Chapter 17

'It's so bright' mumbled Robert, which it was: The sun was a blazing, blistering presence in the sky.

Ragnar nodded as he reached into the dark and pulled Robert up onto the deck, 'Aye, not much more I can add to that.'

'Where are we?'

'In the south, heading towards Muspelheim, the Kingdom of Surtr, though if the Gods are with us, we won't stray that far.'

Ragnar looked pensively to the horizon, and half chewed his bottom lip, his grey straggly hair and beard blowing in the wind.

Robert opened his mouth to ask who, but Ragnar placed a finger over his lips to be quite.

'Don't say his name boy, it'll attract his attention.'

'But you just...'

'I know, but I have charms and protection, I can guide my words away from his ears. We call him the Swarthy One, he's all dark skinned, like the people of these lands, all fire and heat, he carries flames about him like we do furs, and a sword of fire so bright man cannot look upon it. It's said that at the end of days he will come north and unleash his fires upon us.'

'Worry not little one,' Villi slapped Robert on the shoulder, nearly pushing him over, 'we'll sell his folk some Freyja's Tears in exchange for some gems and maybe a kiss from one of his daughters!' Villi roared laughing at this. Ragnar just rolled his eyes.

Villi ambled off down the centre of the boat, coiling a rope from hand to elbow still chuckling to himself with a low husky rumble.

'Who is that?' Robert pointed at a boat, some distance from them, a sleek strip in the gleaming waves.

'Another trader, many come here from across the world to trade, we come to one of the great centres of the world young Robert. When we get there...'

'I know, don't touch anything, don't talk to anyone and don't wander off.'

Ragnar sniffed a laugh, 'Yes, I'm sure you get fed up hearing that, but you're something of a lucky charm for us. And anyway, we'd miss you should you be stolen from us.'

Robert gulped.

Ragnar ruffled Robert's hair and turned away leaving

Robert to stare at the view.

The sky was a kind of blue he'd never seen before, so intense it made your eyes hurt to look at it. And he'd heard people talk of the blue ocean, but he'd never actually seen it. When he'd been to see the sea it had always been a sludgy grey brown colour. This ocean was a dark, rich blue, covered in gentle waves all tipped in silver and twinkling.

And then on that infinite line between sky and sea a smudge appeared. A cry went up, and the boat was suddenly a frenzy of activity. Robert found his barrel to sit on and watched the smudge of a line grow thicker. Slowly colours faded into view, then a few sparse trees, and sand. They scudded along the coast, the swell greater here and more boats could be seen dotted about the ocean. And then a town, all mud bricks and white, protected by high walls; a thousand hawks whirled over it, tiny black drops which fell and soared. And then the smell; the smell was evil; Robert coughed.

Robert's eyes were still watering when Ragnar came up, he cackled, 'don't worry you get used to the smell, around the time we're set for leaving, heh. We land soon, stay here, there's things we have to do. I'll come and get you.'

Robert nodded and watched. He watched the Dragon Prow be turned to face down the length of the boat and away from the land. He watched the sail drop and the oars come out. He watched the men sweat as they rowed. After what seemed like an age, the boat bumped into a pier teaming with people and boxes and livestock.

Stretching away from them down the quay, more boats lined up all being loaded and unloaded. It was all so vibrant and chaotic. Everyone shouting at each other, and dressed in so many hues; he realised his Vikings looked quite drab, they did however tower over the lightly armed locals who gave them a wary respect.

Ropes were thrown and the boat was tied up. Thunor and Ragnar jumped from the boat and met a man he was bundled up in layers of white cloth, seemingly wrapped around him many times, they spoke and a small coin purse was exchanged. Thunor turned and nodded his head, Villi jumped down and was passed three large wooden stakes. He placed them on the floor, at the end of the pier, with his axe quickly hacked one end into a point, then hammered them into the dry earth. With a smaller axe and minimum effort he made crude faces in the wood then stepped back. Ragnar stepped up, poured what looked like mead at the base of the three pieces of wood, crouched down. Robert couldn't hear anything but was pretty certain words were being spoken.

There were people of every race and just about every style of garb you could think of. And some you hadn't; and they all watched, even those pretending not to.

Villi and Thunor's huge and threatening presence made sure they kept their distance.

Robert looked at them as if for the first time, there was no fear now, no apprehension, he could calmly just sit back and watch. It was as if the comparison of so many brightly clothed different ethnicities brought them into contrast. They almost all looked big, clumsy and lumbering, sweating profusely in their armour, the hair braids and twists slick with it. So much so that you might think their tattoos would just run off their skin. But then when you looked closer, you noticed the amazing and usually lethal metalwork dotted about their person, the intricate patterns in leather, metal and wood that told their stories, stories of the earth, of the colours they were dressed in. In this new land, people wore pristine white, crimson, sky blue, sea blue, silver, gold... Robert guesses these were the rich folk, because scattered around there were plenty of people wearing rags and sometimes barely even those.

Ragnar pointed at Robert, made eye contact and waved him to come down; clambering down off the boat he found his place by Villi's side, who laid a huge ham sized hand on his shoulder, but kept his eyes on the crowd and his other hand on the axe at his belt. About half the crew assembled on the quayside; Ragnar walked towards the prow of the boat and looked down its length; raising his hands and clasping them over his head. He kept them there, shaking them slightly, eyes closed, then flung them open and clapped. There was a peal of thunder from the blue, cloudless sky, many of the locals fell over themselves in an attempt to flee; boxes, baskets and chickens scattered all over the place; from dark corners and under boxes, terrified wide eyes stared out to see what would happen next. A soft, gentle wave of light pulsed from Ragnar's hands then splashed up against the boat, and ran down her length; the whole structure shivered slightly, sending ripples out on the water.

Ragnar then turned his attention to the crew assembled on the quayside, he winked at Robert, then raised his hands again, more locals ducked, eyes flickering skyward, but he just waved his hands and nothing much seemed to happen. He nodded to Thunor and a barrel of water appeared, crude wooden jugs were passed from man to man, slurped and splashed and poured over heads.

'Ragnar, what, I mean..?' Robert's mouth hung open.

'Hehe, just some lights and noise to let the locals know who they're dealing with.'

'Oh. But then you did it to us, I mean, nothing erm..'

'That's because I didn't do anything: Magic you can't see or hear is always much stronger than magic you can eh? They don't know what they're dealing with, so everyone will make something up.' Ragnar chuckled to himself. 'And that is the strongest magic of all, what people believe they saw.'

'Ah. And what about them?' Robert pointed to the carved stakes Villi had hammered into the ground.

'Them, well them's our Gods which we brought with us, Odin Tyr, Thor. But first we ask the local Gods, it being their land and all, if we can bring them and us ashore. It's always wise not to upset other people's Gods, you never know when they're going to get all shirty about these things.'

Robert pulled a face, which he hoped conveyed a great deal of understanding about what the heck was going on.

A sudden commotion somewhere in the crowd, people pushing and shouting, instantly hands reached for sword and axes, then a cry went up 'Ragnar! You old fraud!' the words had a strange accent to them.

Ragnar's eyes twinkled and he broke into a smile, he raised a hand slightly, the tension amongst the crew eased, even though hands never strayed far from weapons.

The crowd parted and a long white haired, white bearded, white robed old man pushed and clubbed his way forward, using his walking stick, elbows and knees to part the way. A blue spiral tattoo snaked around one side of his face and a large gold torque shimmered at his neck. His beard was so long it tucked into his belt.

'Haha, knew it was you, one of my minions saw the square sail and as soon as I heard the thunder, I thought, Ragnar's boys must be in town!'

'Elwynn!' the two old men hobble towards each other, and hugged.

'How are you, you don't look any different?'

'Meh, the climate's good, plenty of fruit and a long walk every day to think!'

'Excellent, this is Thunor,' Thunor stepped forward and offered his hand.

'Thunor?' queried Elwynn waved his hands around knee height, 'Yes, that's him,' replied Ragnar.

'Crivens, I remember you boy when you came here with your Father, you've sprouted a bit since then,' looking up at him and taking in the width of chest and shoulders, 'They been feeding you well eh?'

Thunor's brow furrowed, 'I, remember, I think, grey hair, was that you?'

'Aye, still an old man, just with white hair now. How is your Father?'

'He passed not long ago,' Thunor looked at the floor.

This news seemed not to phase the old man at all, it was all very matter of fact, 'Did he, well chin up Son, the wheel turns and the Sister's weave, he had a grand life, they still sing songs about him round these parts,' Elwynn winked conspiratorially, 'His seat in the Great Hall is assured, make no mistake.'

Thunor smiled; Ragnar spoke loudly, addressing the whole crew, 'This is Elwynn, an old friend of mine, he met the ships of you Father's when they landed in this land.'

'Aye and some of your Father's fathers' Elwynn chipped in.

Someone shouted if he knew who Jork's Father's was as nobody else did not even Jork, everyone found this uproariously funny, but Robert didn't understand the joke.

And then Elwynn turned his attention to Robert, pierced him with that same glare Ragnar did.

'And who is this fellow, he's...' Elwynn bent down prodded him in the chest, 'He's... there's something different about this fellow.' Elwynn's face was uncomfortably close, to the point that Robert could probably have counted the hairs in his beard.

'Indeed, he found us on one of our voyages, saw off a

Loki Spawn, then a Dragon, he's been on quite the adventure with us since then, seems to be our lucky charm, deals with all manner of danger without breaking into a sweat.'

'Does he now?. How interesting,' as if Robert wasn't there.

'He seems to come and go as he please,'

'A world walker!' Elwynn's eyes grew wide in amazement, 'One of the Sidhe, or Huldufolk?'

'Perhaps, but I don't know, we took him to see our lot, they were none the wiser. Am not sure the boy even knows, he seems as bemused as old Thor does sometimes. But I'll bide my time, you don't see a tapestry by pulling at the threads.'

'Very true, very true,' Elwynn continued staring at Robert for a moment longer, before standing up, slowly one hand on his back. 'Well come on, come to my house, I've some fine wine, and a few things to show you.'

'Thunor?'

Thunor, looked about, up and down the quay, then frowned, 'No, I'll stay here, help unload the ship, you go, take the boy.'

Chapter 18

Ragnar nodded, and off they went. Robert made sure he was never more than a few paces behind the two men, the last thing he wanted was to get lost. Elwynn talked animatedly, arms gesticulating. He was all white hair, white beard, white robe, where Ragnar was grey and silver and some other murky colours Robert couldn't quite put a name to. Elwynn had minimal adornments, a simple silver band on one wrist, a gold torque at his neck. This contrasted with Ragnar who's hair and beard had leather ties and beads in, his wrists were full of bits of metal and leather and around his neck numerous charms. They were very similar and at the same time as different as could be.

They climbed up stairs and steps and narrow alleyways between white buildings, the shade from the buildings was only marginally more tolerable than the full glare of the sun. They passed dark doorways and windows; occasionally he'd see a face in the gloom watching them pass, before it was lost to the darkness. The lives of sparrows could be heard unfolding on the flat roofs above them and the laughter of children added to the distant cacophony. As they rounded a corner the laughter stopped abruptly. Large dark eyes set in grubby faces stared at them. Robert looked back, realising that they were not much younger than him, he tried a smile but their faces remained impassive. As they rounded a corner, he heard the pounding of tiny feet, he glanced back, a bob of tousled black haircuts peered back at him from behind a low wall. And then they continued to follow them up the hill, always keeping a safe distance.

Near the top of the hill, their guide led them through a simple doorway that opened into a thankfully cool courtyard. A man wrapped in a white cloth was there to greet them; he bowed slightly without actually looking at them. Robert noticed the sound of running water. As they walked further in, they stepped through a stream that ran through the middle of the building, washing ice-cold water over their feet. Robert giggled and laughed.

'Nice to be out of the heat, eh boy?'

Robert barely murmured a response as he looked around; rooms ran off in various directions, other small courtyards and the shimmer of reflected water danced on surfaces; here and there a fruit tree either grew up through the ceiling inside the house or partially through the walls, hanging brightly coloured orbs within easy reach. And everywhere the sound of birds singing and chirping echoing through the hallways. It was like the outside was inside, the walls bringing only the loosest of definitions to the house.

They were led out onto a balcony that looked out over the city, a tasselled canopy sheltered them from the harsh sun, but a warm breeze still buffeted them.

Robert could make out their boat, right on the end of the quay. Beyond that a perfect blue sky over a blue sea that was flecked with white tips. The two old men, creaked down onto cushions on the floor, Robert followed, still trying to take everything in. In the room they had passed through he could see but one decoration, a small figuring of a lady. It looked like it was made from red clay, would probably fit in the large man's hand and was very definitely a lady. Robert blushed slightly at the huge chest and huge bum cheeks. And she didn't seem to be made up of much else. She sat in an alcove tucked away in the wall staring at the world without judgement.

The man who had greeted them entered the room carrying a silver tray, with silver cups and what looked like a kettle, and he poured out three drinks, a thick, dark fluid, then he backed away silently. A small boy followed bringing a bowl full of fruit. They were also placed on the table in front of them.

Ragnar reached forward and picked up a yellow, round fruit, the size of a small apple, 'What's this?'

Elwynn said something which Robert didn't understand, 'We call them lemons,' he added helpfully.

'Lemons' the two men overly pronounced slowly and at the same time, as if the word didn't fit their mouths.

'You have seen these before?' asked Elwynn

'Yes, lots of times. We erm use them for flavour. My Grandad makes a drink with it in, gin and tonic.'

The two men looked confused, 'a Djinn and tonic?'

Robert wasn't quite sure where the confusion was, 'yes gin and tonic,' he said slowly, 'and when he's ill, with hot honey and lemons.'

Elwynn and Ragnar looked at him, as if sizing him up. Elwynn pushed his lips together and forward, as if pondering something... then said, 'Show us.'

'Erm, Ok.'

Elwynn shouted something and the man in the white robe appeared, Elwynn then fixed Robert with a look and said, 'What do you need?'

'Erm.'

'We're right out of erms boy, come on what do you need?'

'Boiling water, some honey and a knife to cut the lemon' gabbled Robert quickly.

Elwynn clapped once and white robbed man disappeared.

Ragnar sniffed the lemon, wrinkled his nose, rolled it in his hands.

Elwynn leant forward, 'Cut the skin off and taste inside, but don't get any in your eyes, it stings like a scorpion.'

Ragnar who had pulled a small knife from about his person and already had it pressed against the skin, momentarily pulled back and more carefully than perhaps he was about to, cut into the lemon. Taking one half he rather messily tried to cut the fruit out.

'Pungent, a clear smell,' he said and popped a bit into his mouth. The effect was immediate, his face screwed up and pinched, his eyes barely open streamed and his head reflexed to one side. One leg came up and a hand to his jaw. He managed to swallow and then exclaimed, 'By the Gods! That's sharp.'

Elwynn roared laughing, slapping his knee, Robert was more amused by Elwynn's reaction than Ragnar eating the lemon.

Ragnar picked up the other half of the lemon, wiping the tears off his face, he held it out a bit, 'May I?'

'Of course, we've got trees full of them.'

Ragnar cut out the fruit from the half skin, and displayed a not dissimilar reaction to last time, 'It doesn't get much better even when you know what's coming,' and coughed loudly, wiping the tears from his cheeks.

The man in white appeared, another silver tray, more silver pots, one steaming.

'Ah, excellent,' Elwynn nodded at Robert who sat up and reached for the silver jug of steaming water.

 'We need to do this quickly because it needs to be drunk hot, 'said Robert.

The two old men nodded, Ragnar still wiping the tears from his eyes.

'Could you cut me a lemon in half please, Mum says I'm not allowed to play with knives.'

Elwynn, did as requested, 'Saw off Loki spawn you say?' looking at Ragnar from under an eyebrow.

Ragnar smiled, half nodded his head, 'Seen it with my own eyes.'

Elwynn shook his head and smiled in a kind of, wish I'd seen that, then went to hand half a lemon to Robert, 'Squeeze the juice into that empty cup please.'

Elwynn nodded with an amused look in his eyes (that also said, he wasn't used to being told what to do and found it momentarily refreshing) and did as he was requested.

'Now add the hot water and stir. And then add a really big spoonful of honey and stir.'

The silver on silver clattered between them, the 2 men concentrating on the cup, which Elwynn then picked up and offered to Robert.

Robert took it and took a sip, 'S'good' and handed the cup back to Elwynn, who sniffed, 'Smells good' and sipped, his eyes lit up and he broke into a smile, 'That, is very pleasant.'

Ragnar took the cup and murmured happy noises as he took a drink.

'Cures ailments eh?'

'Well, my Grandad makes it when he's got a cold or feeling a bit worn out. I think it more makes you feel better than makes you better. But lemons are good for you as well.'

'I've always said that people's ailments are often in the head, change what they're thinking and you change them.'

Ragnar nodded in agreement.

The honey and lemon was finished, the two men smacked their lips and picked up their other cups.

They sipped their drinks in silence for a moment, then Ragnar said something which Robert didn't quite catch but it didn't matter, because he was warm and comfortable, and the sea breeze twiddled with his hair, the sunlight glinted off wave tops as far out as the eye could see and the two old men spoke over Robert in a sing song manner that just seemed so comforting. They spoke of times gone and times to come, but the words washed over and around him.

Chapter 19

A gull or a hawk or something screamed and flashed past the balcony, closely followed by another, some noisy dispute over a tasty morsel. Robert's head snapped up and his eyes opened wide. It was like he'd been asleep but awake at the same time. And he was on his own. His eyes darted, scanning the piers, the ship was still there, but where was Ragnar? He tried calming himself, Ragnar wouldn't leave him, he called him their lucky charm, Robert then noticed the man wrapped in white sitting cross legged in the other room. He walked over, the man stood up and bowed slightly. Robert bowed back. The man didn't speak, but turned silently and padded out of the room. When Robert didn't follow he stopped and kind of half looked back around his shoulder, Robert followed, the man set off walking again.

The two old men, were in a garden terrace examining fruit trees, Robert smiled with relief, looked at the man in white and said 'Thank you' very quietly. The man bowed again. Robert got the impression there was much more going on with him than the silence.

A space had been cleared in the trees, there was a large stone in the middle which sparkled in the sunlight and lines had been drawn in the ground from this middle tall stone, to smaller round ones around the edge. Robert stepped towards and stopped at the edge, looking at it.

'What do you think it is, eh boy? asked Elwynn.

'Is it for measuring where the sun and the moon is?' replied Robert.

Ragnar broke into a wide smile and Elwynn snorted a single laugh of disbelief, recovering he said 'Do you have these where you come from?'

'Only old ones, we don't really use them anymore, everything has been measured and is written down in books.'

'Books?'

'Erm, yes what we know is written down, so everyone can read it.'

Both man raised their eyebrows.

'Everyone? Reads?'

'Most people, yes.'

The two old men seemed to be lost for words.

Robert got the impression that saying more was going to complicate things, so instead he stood awkwardly, and tried furiously to look like he was even more interested in the stones in front of him.

He saw them look at each other out of the corner of his eye. Ragnar indicated with a single nod of his head that Robert should follow them.

They moved between the trees, the ground was parched but the trees were lush and full of fruit. Birds and insects sang and buzzed and flapped and crawled about them. They came to what looked like a wooden lid over a well. Elwynn touched something around his neck, muttered something and waved a hand. A light oozed out from the grain of the wood, like stored sunlight. And then was gone. There was a clicking noise and then Elwynn kicked something with his foot; the lid lifted and a handrail seemed to unpin itself on what looked like the insides of a clock. Down the hole was a spiral staircase, which curved away into the dark.

At the bottom Elwynn reached for a torch which hung from the wall at head height, he pulled off a metal cap and the flames coughed into life, a thin black smoke swirled off it. Robert saw him look to see if they had seen this, he seemed particularly pleased with it.

They were in a large room, compact, red earth for floor ceiling and walls. All around hung things, shelves cluttered, benches and tables full to over flowing of stuff; bits of plants, animals, metal, it was the archetypal wizard's workshop. Robert realised that there was more light in the room than there should have been. The whole place was remarkably well lit, by a sort of diffused sunshine, but the only source of light was the torch by the entrance.

'Where does the light come from?' he asked.

'Good question boy,' and proceeded not to answer him.

Robert looked at Ragnar who tapped the side of his nose, like his Grandad did when he wouldn't tell him a secret, or what was for tea or something.

Robert just shrugged and accepted it.

Elwynn waved them in and found them some stools to sit on, and then reached for a rolled up parchment which he stretched out on the table; pushing all manner of monstrosities out of the way in the process. A tortoise shell, a lump of molten glass, a piece of crystal and a clam shell, which was full of a moss, which Robert realised was glowing where it had been used to hold the map flat. It was this moss that was throwing light out. There must have been shells of it all over the workshop.

Robert could see the coast, the town, and then nothing, lots of nothing and then some mountains. A bony finger pointed at a valley that wove in and out of the mountains.

'This is where we are headed', Elwynn said.

Chapter 20

They'd walked for two days, at dusk and dawn. They camped during the heat of the day and the pitch darkness. And sand was everywhere. Robert hated sand. He didn't mind making sand castles and spending a few hours on a beach looking for shells but this was relentless sand, like it had a purpose and its purpose was to irritate. There were no shells; in fact there was nothing but ripples and dunes, and in the haze that was the near horizon where some pale mountains scratched at the vivid blue sky. They'd passed bleached white bones late that afternoon; they looked like a horse or maybe a camel. No plants, no trees, no rocks, no markers of any kind, but Elwynn seemed to know exactly where they were going.

And he was so tired, the heat was everything, then there was perhaps an hour or more each day when it was tolerable. And then the freezing night, he was amazed anyone survived and sleep had eluded him, it was either too hot or too cold. He had no idea how his Viking friends coped having grown up in snow and ice, but they did and they did with good humour. Laughing, joking and banter remained the glue that held them together.

Around a timid fire made from bits of brushwood, as they always seemed to do, stories were told, raucous, rude and irreverent. Always three of the group were on guard, looking out into the dark, never turning round; they stood on the edge of the shadows, several hours at a time, until at some unspoken moment, others swapped their place.

Robert didn't remember falling asleep but he must have as someone was shaking him awake.

'Come on little man, time to rise.' A cup of tepid water and dry bread was thrust at him. The bread didn't taste too bad. What had been the camp, mere hollows in the sand for them to sleep in, was quickly left behind.

They stopped to allow the ferocious midday sun to pass, hiding in what shadow they could from the bits of poles and cloth one of the camels carried, the heat subdued any conversation, instead they dozed, eyes half open. Villi was drawing snake shapes in the sand with a huge finger.

Robert watched the shapes form and disappear in the sand, then asked quietly, 'Do you know what it is we are going for?'

Villi looked up and smiled, 'No, a trinket or something, it doesn't matter.'

Robert's face scrunched up into a questioning frown.

'It's an adventure boy, for the stories to tell and the

paths to tread, the why is not important. It's that we did it that makes it important. Maybe when I am old, I will tell my children's children of the time I went to the desert with Ragnar and Thunor and the World Walker. And they will say, what is a desert?'

He rumbled a laugh to himself, Robert returned his attention to the horizon, but out of the corner of his eye, he was saw some of the others nodding in a agreement.

As the sun reached the halfway point between straight up and the evening horizon, Elwynn stood up and went over to one of the camels they were (which stank incidentally and were grumpy and chunnered and burped constantly) and rummaged around in a leather bag.

He pulled out a handful of bits of strings with something attached and brought them back, throwing them in the sand.

'Everyone take one each; wear it around your neck. Do not under any circumstances take it off. Make sure it is outside your armour, it must be visible.'

There was an extremely stern manner to Elwynn's words, which made Robert nervous, he reached out along with other hands and picked one up. It was a necklace, a small silver box, with bells on. One side had intricately carved swirls and patterns wrapped around each other. On the other a blue eye, in a blue triangle stared out impassively.

'Which side is front or back?' asked someone.

'Eye goes against your chest, watching your back,' replied Elwynn.

'These bells, they'll hear us coming from miles away,' grumbled Villi.

'That's the point, you don't want to be looking like you're sneaking up where we are going. And don't try and pry the boxes open to see what's inside.' Elwynn glared pointedly at one of the group who had it raised to his ear and was shaking it experimentally.

Elwynn, frowned, 'Where we go, who we go to meet, is a creature of fire, of strange magic, who can appear and disappear at will: A magician of great skill. Do not trust it, underestimate it, or deviate from what I tell you.'

'It?' asked Villi.

'It is not human though it can take human form, it is a creature of Surtr, it is one of his kin. The locals call them Djinn. They are not really of this world, but some are trapped here, some are given a purpose and some are just plain mischievous.

'Sur...' Ragnar held a finger up at the speaker forcing him to silence with a glare.

Then realising the error of saying the name continued... 'Are you insane, why did you not mention this before?'

'It matters not. There are many terrible, ferocious things to be frightened off in this land, and you're one of them!' Elwynn prodded at each man in the group as he spat each word.

There was a tense silence amongst the group, all faces looking at the two shamans.

Some of the men nodded, a smile of pride on their faces, others chewed their lips and some just seemed to ignore the conversation at all. Villi, slowly, calmly and methodically sharpened one of his axes with a stone, examining the glimmer of the edge with great scrutiny.

One by one they tugged the necklaces about their heads and then set about gathering themselves to leave. There was some muttering but Robert could not make out what was being said.

The walked and as they walked the silver boxes tinkled, adding random, chaotic music to their steps. The mountains were larger now, looming above them; the scale of the desert had masked their true size. The men dragged themselves out of the desert and into the shade of a wide ravine, foot weary and broken by sweat. A wind gusted against them and some rocks rattled down the scree side caused a stir amongst the companions. The baked, sweat feeling was lifted for a minute by the cooling breeze and where there had been complete silence from the landscape, was now dry leaves and crickets rattled amidst a few thorny bushes; and then they stopped. And the wind stopped. And out of the haze, appearing right in front of them a high dry stone wall that ran across the ravine blocking their way. Robert looked up at the top, craning his neck, it must have been at least twice the size of a house. As Ragnar walked up to the wall, a door appeared out of the air, shimmering into view, made of beautiful, shiny wood simple in design. There were no real features except the arched top and a shape of a letter dancing in fire in the grain. There was a gasp of awe from some of the men. Elwynn, turned, 'Remember no matter what happens, do not take those talismans off....and do not lose them.'

Ragnar pressed his hand against the door. It swung open easily and silently. Robert was a bit disappointed; he wanted it to creak or groan, or some great work of magic to open it. However inside was stunning, a beautiful garden, filled with mature blossom trees, plants, flowers, butterflies, bees and dragonflies and open woodland glades with pools of sunshine glinting in every direction. The men moved quickly through the doorway and spread out in a line, hands on weapons, uneasiness amongst them.

Chapter 21

Villi gripped Robert by the shoulder and pulled him behind him, making sure he was protected. From somewhere to the left of them, came a blood curdling scream and two fireballs hurtled out of the trees. Elwynn jumped forward (rather spryly Robert thought) and held up the talisman shouting something. Chasing the fireballs and closing fast there was some kind of screaming man. He was sculpted of fire, tendrils of flame flickering from the edges of his form. Robert yelped, Villi pulled weapons from his belt and stepped forward.

The two fireballs dissipated into gentle, flickering, warm, washes of light with tendrils of black smoke, which buffeted the Vikings, causing them to stagger slightly and blink their eyes. The flaming man raced up to Elwynn's face, screaming and waving its arms above its head, but then finally stood silently and swirling and spiralling and swooping on the spot. He had no legs but moved on what looked like a tendril or tentacle of fire.

Elwynn seemed completely unmoved by the show. The creature danced up and down the line of men it peered closely into each man's face, as if it couldn't see them properly, finally returning to stand before Elwynn. The men almost relaxed, as if the initial threat was over, Villi breathed out very slowly and very completely.

Out of this man shaped column of fire, its visage began to form something that resembled Elwynn, then altered to look like Villi. The creature's face and shape kept morphing and alternating between all of them before finally settling on some weird combination of them all, occasionally shimmering into more like one than the other.

'You break into my house, you dare come here with those!?' - the man bellowed unnervingly close to Elwynn's face, glaring at the talisman about his neck then bobbing up to stare eye to eye. The sound of crackling fire, hissing and spitting emanated from the figure but curiously no heat.

'Without these we would not have got over the threshold. Would you not offer us hospitality, it's been a long trek across the desert, and you have guests,' replied Elwynn.

The Djinn made a 'Hmph' noise, like a fire suddenly igniting, and half turned its head, curling its top lip in disgust. Three women appeared out of the undergrowth, they moved slowly and methodically with an air of tranquillity, accompanied by delicate tinkling bells as they swayed. The women were carrying trays with cups, a head covering that looked to be made of silver chain-mail hid their whole face except for their eyes and ended around their necks with tiny bells, charms and glittering gems. They were swathed in silks and more silver chain mail that flickered like sunlight on water. Around their wrists and ankles more tiny, silver bells.

They walked down the line of men offering cups of water. All the men were taken by their eyes; they were smokey, blue, gray, the colour of dark blue ink swirling in water and were quite beautiful. Robert took a cup when it was offered, it tasted like nothing he'd had before; it was sweet and refreshing and sparkled in the mouth. Immediately his senses were refreshed, the smells and textures and light of this place popped and came alive for him. He looked at the empty cup as if not believing what had just happened. He noticed that the men seemed to have relaxed, Villi noticed the questioning expression on Robert's face, 'We will not be attacked now, we are guests.' He paused then added, 'Unless we provoke him,' and winked.

The woman then returned behind the Djinn and stood in line with the others.

'Are you rested travellers, have you drunk your fill?' the Djinn sneered, flames leaked out from around his hairline, ears, eyes, nose and mouth, like he was wearing a mask but his inner fire was trying to burst out.

'Thank you, your welcome has been most kind,' replied Elwynn sweetly.

'Now, what do you want?' the Djinn raged.

A tiny spark flashed from the Djinn's lips and landed on Elwynn's white toga, which he absent-mindedly patted out.

'We've come with a proposition....'

The Djinn's head flew back and he bellowed laughing...'Why would I want to associate with you, you, you, you..... filth, you dirt, you! Hahaha!' The Djinn spiralled and spun on the spot, as if dancing with glee, the flaming tentacle it moved on flashing and flickering, black smoke spiralling from its tip. 'I am made of fire and light and magic, what could you possibly have that I want?'

'Because,...' Elwynn continued unfazed.

The Djinn grew in stature, now half as big again as Villi, he appeared to be solid, but fire boiled within his form. Robert looked up to his bald head, his flaming eyes flared and glared, a thin plaited beard of fire swung as he moved his head. He folded his arms, looking for all the world like something out of an advert for a pantomime, but with the potential for outrageous terror.

Elwynn continued unperturbed, 'We bring something of great value, of great value that we would trade.'

Elwynn held out his hand, not taking his eyes of the Djinn and Ragnar placed the small leather pouch in his hand. Slowly and with considerable drama Elwynn took a milky coloured, oblong stone out of the bag and held it in his open palm. The Djinn nearly exploded, tongues of flames lashed around his form, he spiralled on the spot and then imploded down to regular size with a 'woomph' noise.

'What is that?... is that?.... is it?.... it is!' he demanded, clapping his hands with excitement and glee. Clouds of sparks and embers flashed from about him.

'This is as you have correctly seen, a Sunstone'

The Djinn roared, then flashed up and down the line of men, examining each one closely, then back to Elwynn looking closely at the stone without touching it.

'A Sunstone, a real Sunstone, from the Huldufolk?'

'Indeed it is.'

'I could take it!' The Djinn was now vast in size, as big as a house, some of the men recoiled, weapons half drawn. Ragnar put his hand up, 'No!' and looked up and down the men.

'You could' replied Elwynn, 'but you know, it would not be that easy.'

'Easy! Easy! I am of Them; I am of Fire and Light and

Love and Lust! You are nothing, mud! You are nothing compared to I.'

Elwynn remained silent, let the Djinn stare at the stone, then added quietly, 'But we are your guests we have sipped on your water, are we not in your house? Would you break the ancient rules?'

Great wings of fire, like giant bat wings flashed out and the Djinn growled like a rumbling log in the hearth.

'Think what you can do with this, think that you could become one of them, truly one of *them*?' added Elwynn

The Djinn was vast, but slowly it recoiled down to its original size, its face flickering once again through the facial forms of each of the Vikings.

Elwynn remained silent, the Djinn pulled a thoughtful face, tugging on a long fiery beard with a flaming hand 'What do you want for it, what would you have in trade?'

'The last of the Kemry, sits atop a hoard,'

'I will not lead you to him for you to slaughter! He is old, ancient and must remain that way.'

'No, we wish him no harm, there is something in the hoard we would have.'

'You wish him no harm?'

'None.'

'And the hoard?'

'Nothing, just this one item?'

'What is it?'

'A trinket, nothing of..'

The Djinn interrupted, 'Do you take me for a fool, you did not trade with the Huldufólk of the north, then wend your way here to trade a Sunstone, for the location of a trinket!'

Now it was Elwynn's turn to pull a thoughtful face, there was a long pause, 'There's a coin, an amulet, with an inscription on, which would be of use. It would be trivial, as naught compare to the magic you possess, but to us, to us it is of value.'

'Indeed,' one of the Djinn's fiery eyebrows raised, 'You give your word that the Kemry will not be harmed?'

'I do.'

'You give your word that the hoard will not be ravaged?'

'I do.'

'I will take your oath and your Sunstone.'

The Djinn whirled around on the spot, then rolled towards Robert. He looked at him very closely, reached out a long finger and gently bopped him on the forehead. Robert's head rocked back his eyes closed and there was a sensation of warm water washing over his body.

The Djinn moved back to Elwynn, 'I will not tell you how to get there, or where it is, gold makes fools of men and their tongues, follow the boy, he will lead you to the Kemry.'

The Djinn grabbed the Sun Stone and erupted into this whirlwind of fire that twisted away and disappeared into the orchard: Leaves and petals billowing after him.

Everyone looked at Robert, Elwynn looked at his now empty hand and swore loudly.

Robert looked up and down the line of them.

'What is that on his forehead?' asked Thunor.

'Let me see,' said Elwynn, 'There's nothing there, a soot mark,' and he tried to rub it off, which prompted an Ow from Robert.

'No it glows, see.' Thunor gripped the boys chin and moved his head. When he faced a particular direction the mark that had been left on his head glowed a bright fiery orange yellow, as he moved away it dimmed to almost nothing.

'Bloody Djinn's' grumbled Elwynn, 'That gentleman, is your way, point the boy in the right direction and keep going until you find what you are looking for. If you lose the boy, then that was that.'

'Considering the boy wanders off at his own will, that is not comforting.'

Robert frowned at being talked about, then raised a hand to his head, rubbing his fingers on his forehead, he couldn't feel anything.

'So what do we do now?' asked one of the men.

'Well the Kemry is not of these lands that much I know, back to the ship!'

Chapter 22

There were some groans and sighs, Robert noted the usual good humour seemed to have evaporated with all the excitement. It was a long walk back across the desert, and as yet there had been no reward.

Ragnar and Elwynn had already set off a couple of paces before they realised that the others hadn't really moved much.

Both men turned at the same time, Ragnar put his hands on his hips, 'Well?'

The Vikings shuffled about a bit in the sand, seemingly unsure which was worse, the glare of the sun, or the glare of Ragnar.

After some non-verbal, you ask, no you ask, raised eyebrows and such like at one another, one finally spoke up, tugging and twirling his long blonde beard as he spoke.

'The thing is...'

There was a long pause with more beard twiddling, followed by some egging on by the others.

Robert couldn't believe how hot it was, the sun was unbearable, and right now he didn't care much what the thing was, he just wanted to get out of the sun.

He looked over at Thunor who was stood exactly halfway between the group of Vikings and the two shamans.

The man continued, 'The thing is, we've done a lot of running around in this heat and it's really hot and we're more of a cold climate bunch and..'

'Get to the point,' said Ragnar calmly.

'Well, erm, why are we doing this? What's so special about this coin? I mean we're all for going off adventuring and seeing new things and maybe helping ourselves to some of it, and having grand stories to tell when we get back and all that, but this one has a been a long one Ragnar, and we don't know what we're chasing?'

There was a long silence.

Then Ragnar seemed to relax a little and nodded, and everyone else relaxed a lot.

'Well,' said Ragnar, 'the coin itself isn't really up to much, it's what's on the coin that's important. Some runes.'

At the mention of runes, some of the men perked up and looked a little less exhausted.

'That when written on steel, make that steel much stronger, and keep its edge sharp.'

There was more excitement at this.

'Now I'm thinking that our smith can copy these runes and put them on sword, axe, blade and spear...'

There was another long silence and a lot more speaking without talking, nodding and looks of well, yes that does sound like a good idea.

The man who had asked all the questions leaned forward and said, 'My wife's not going to be learning these runes is she, she's sharp enough as it is?' and he winked at Robert.

The laughter broke the mood and the two shamans turned and set off towards the horizon.

The next few days were a blur of blistering heat, aching cold and sand. The days were white hot and the nights were black cold. And then out of the shimmering haze the town appeared, all towering white buildings, red roof tiles, brick and stench.

As they entered the town, the crowds of traders, vendors and gawpers parted like water, Robert was surrounded by the band of Vikings, looking and feeling for all the world like he was invulnerable despite being exhausted and sweat drenched.

They must have looked incredibly intimidating; head and shoulders taller than anybody else, broader than anybody else, all leather armour, chainmail and sharp edges.

Kids chased up to them and then ran off squealing. People fell over boxes and stalls to get out of the way. A great cry and hubbub went up, by the time they reached the docks, the men they'd left behind were armed to the teeth and looking mightily relieved when the rest of the crew appeared from the throng.

Elwynn's voice cut through the noise of the traders, the watchers and that of a ship about to set sail, 'A word before you go, I knew your Fathers and some of your Father's Fathers, I am old beyond my time. I gave my oath, you heard it. If you break it, I would speak with your Fathers and those gone before them, my time here is nearly done and I will be with them soon in the Great Hall. And do not underestimate the power of the Djinn, his reach is far and terrible. The Kemry must not be harmed. The only thing to be taken is the thing for which we have traded. Nothing else!'

The Vikings looking a lot like naughty schoolboys being scolded, stood in a line nodding their heads. Robert stifled a giggle at this, more out of nervousness than anything. They looked like they could take on an entire army and win and here they stood looking all bashful and just a little bit goofy.

Elwynn looked at Ragnar and smiled; they hugged and slapped backs, 'Till next time.'

'Aye, wherever that is eh?'

Then Elwynn looked at Thunor and the two nodded a parting.

The ship bobbed and weaved, crashing through white and grey waves. Salt, spray and wind whipped at them as they raced towards deeper, calmer, more powerful swells; the noise moving from slashing and splashing to the constant thunder of the sea. The sweat and sand now gone, blown away. The sky was still bright blue and the sun glared down on them, but they were on the road home. A road they knew so well.

Robert sat on his barrel, Ragnar joined him, half pointed at him, as he leant against a wooden spar, 'What now?'

'Me?'

'Yes, you.'

'I don't know. I...er, I don't know anything about all this, I try not to think about it.'

'You're key to our success now,'

'I know, but I... I don't know what makes me be here, or home, I go to sleep and I wake up. What is it we search for, what's a kemry and this thing it has?'

'We must trust to the gods,' Ragnar, patted one of his knees, winked and hobbled off into the bright light, Robert was reminded of his Grandfather.

Robert rubbed his fingers over his forehead but could feel nothing.

Chapter 23

When he opened his eyes, it was his Mother's hands on his forehead, she was looking down at him with a worried expression on her face, she pressed her palm and then wiped his face with a nice smelling cloth.

'How do you feel?'

'Urgh' was about all he could manage. He felt hot, cold, shivering, sweaty, clammy and achy.

'You have a heck of a temperature, you're burning up, I'll get some honey and lemon.'

Robert was vaguely aware of shadowy shapes of people, different people, of hands on his forehead, of shivering heat and burning cold, unable to comprehend where he was, as if he was in two places at once.

And then he was awake, feeling vaguely empty but lying in his bed staring at the ceiling wondering what had just happened.

Padding out of bed into the bathroom, he stood on tiptoes still couldn't see his forehead. His mum appeared behind him, 'What are you doing?'

'Oh erm, nothing.'

'You feeling better?'

'Yeah, kind of I guess. Have I got anything on my forehead?'

'On your forehead?'

Robert leant forward for her to look, she ran a thumb over his head, her face screwed up in bemusement, 'No, like what?'

'Nothing, just feels... itchy.'

'You want some soup and cheese sandwich?'

'Yes please,'

'A splash of water and cleaning your teeth might help to make you feel better.'

Robert screwed his face up in suspicion, she'd said that before, he considered it just a ruse to get him to have wash and clean his teeth unnecessarily. But he gave it a go.

Downstairs he saw the time 'It's one o clock!'

'Yes, you were asleep most of yesterday and last night, I nearly called the doctor this morning, but your fever seemed to be breaking.'

'What day is it?'

'Monday, I took the day off.'

'Oh.' Robert was stunned this had never happened before. 'What's Grandad going to do today then?'

'I'm sure he'll be fine.'

A bowl of soup and some cheese sandwiches appeared before him.

'Thanks Mum,' in between the first and second mouthful. He was starving.

Dropping the bowl into the washing up water he turned around and padded into the living room, where his Mum was dusting, 'Can I go on the laptop Mum?'

She half nodded.

Robert wasn't sure why going on the laptop was such a big deal, but sat down and opened the lid; thus began his afternoon's research into Djinn.

When his Dad came home Robert was flagging, he pushed his tea around his plate, not eating much, not saying much.

'You ok kiddo?' his Dad asked.

'Yeah, tired, and hot and my head itches,' Robert sighed.

'Do you think perhaps going back to bed might be a good idea?'

Robert nodded in agreement, got up hugged his Dad and then his Mum then padded out of the kitchen. I'll bring you a drink up in a minute.

'How's he been?' asked his Dad.

'Quiet, seems better, but he did fall asleep on the sofa this afternoon when he was on the laptop, I don't think he realised.'

'Do you think he should go to the Doctor?'

'I'll see how he is tomorrow morning, his fever's broke, I think he just needs rest and fluids now.'

After they'd done the dishes, his Mum took Robert a drink up, he was fast asleep.

When she came down Brian had opened the laptop which had numerous browser tabs open, Djinn, Genies, Spirits of the Desert and lots of pictures of desert caves, mountains and wilderness.

'I'm not sure what's fired his imagination at the moment, but I have to say I'm pretty impressed.'

Louise nodded in agreement then pressed the remote for the tv.

Next morning Robert awoke a bit concerned to find himself in his own bed, he knew his Viking friends needed him more than ever now.

He went into this Mum and Dad's bedroom, part of him marvelling at how tidy and un-lived in it looked and went to the full length mirror to check his forehead, he could still feel it itching.

'What are you doing?' asked his Mum, she'd been cleaning the bathroom.

'My head still itches.'

She followed him in.

'Maybe if you left it alone.. There's nothing there, it's a bit red from where you've been scratching it.' She gripped his chin, and moved his head around then placed the palm of her other hand on his forehead, 'Still a bit warm though, how do you feel?'

'Ok. Hungry though.'

His Mum nodded and nearly smiled, 'Well that's a good sign, come on let's get some breakfast.'

'You're off work again?'

'Yes.'

'Sorry.'

'Well you can't help being ill, but I'll probably have to go into tomorrow.'

'Ok, I can go to Grandad's.'

Chapter 24

And the next day he did. And the day after that. By Friday the world had returned pretty much back to normal. He didn't even feel like he'd been ill.

Robert had lost track of the number of days till his friend's made landfall. He'd asked his Grandad if there was anything he could do to make him dream at night, he'd said cheese, but his Mum had told him no, it would give him indigestion.

Robert had never had indigestion, but the way his Mum carried on about it, it would seem to be something to very definitely avoid.

And his head still itched or at least he was certain it still itched.

Robert had discovered that when he moved the itching seemed worse when facing one direction He'd asked his Grandad what direction that was, and he'd told him it was West, the direction of the setting sun.. what lay to the West? Wales, Ireland, the Atlantic Ocean, Canada... then... back home..through China, Russia, Mongolia, The Steppes, Urals and Northern Europe. ..Robert spent ages looking at maps, drawing lines.

His Grandad left him to it, it gave him to time to do a spot of gardening but after two days of this, he suggested they go for a walk into town. Go to the café by the market for some lunch, then maybe the library?

Robert and his Grandad had got a bus into town, which as bus rides went was fairly uneventful. Robert wasn't a fan of bus rides, too often there were people on the bus that made him feel uncomfortable.

After Robert and his Grandad had been to the post office and had a look around the market and found themselves in front of the cafe. The door jangled unnecessarily as they walked in; they were the only people in the place apart from an enormous guy with long hair and a leather jacket on pondering his order by the till, the lady behind the counter looked up at him, pen and paper in hand waiting.

Robert and his Grandad stood behind him. Robert sidled forward a little,

'Are you a Viking?'

The man looked around at the word Viking and realise a small boy was addressing him, the man with him, presumably his Grandad looked a little stunned at this, his mouth was open and eyes swivelled around.

The small boy was looking up at him, head bent right back eyes beadily looking at him.

The man half-heartedly laughed, 'Well no, but perhaps I like to think so,' and winked.

'You look like a Viking.'

Robert felt his Grandad's hand on his shoulder pulling him back a bit, 'Robert, don't be rude, I'm sorry.'

The man smiled 'And what do Vikings look like?'

'Well some of them are big like you, others, just normal sized.'

'Robert!' snapped his Grandad.

'Hey don't worry about it, I've been called worse,' one side of his face lifted in a smile.

The man seemed to have decided his order during this conversation, told the lady what he wanted and moved to sit down.

'Robert?' asked his Grandad, nodding at the board on the wall behind the woman with more than a hint of tension in his voice.

'Can I have a cheese and ham toastie and a banana milk shake please.'

'And I'll just have a mug of tea please, love,' added Stan to the lady.

As his Grandad had placed the order, he turned and was mildly perturbed to find Robert had taken a seat next to the biker. It wasn't a big café, but it was empty apart from them and Stan would have chosen a spot that put some distance between their tables.

Robert was swinging his legs on the chair, his Grandad knew that this was a sign, he was bursting to ask something and wasn't sure if he should or was trying to pick his words carefully. He sat down in from of Robert, and fixed him with a look.

'So anywhere you want to go after this?'

The man next to them lent over, and in a stage whisper said, 'There's Viking treasure in the museum.'

Roberts head nearly swivelled off as he spun round, 'Viking treasure!'

'Yep, well not much, but some, some silver coins some farmers found a long time ago, a couple of rusty blades, a comb, a leather pouch all of which was in a jar.'

'Wow, Grandad?'

'Yes, we can,' replied his Grandad without letting him finish.

'What sort of blades are they?'

'Well there's a sword, though it's not in very good condition, and smaller one, kind of like a really big knife, or a really small sword I guess.'

'A Scramasax!' Robert gasped.

The man paused, mug of tea halfway to his mouth, looked at Robert and then at his Grandad, 'Yes a Scramasax, how do you know that?'

'I've been on the interwebs at Grandad's and when I'm at home Mum lets me go on the laptop and I've been looking up about the Vikings ever since they got me that cd of ocean waves which turns my bed into a Viking ship, but I think it was supposed to get rid of the monsters under the bed,' he paused, 'I wonder what happened to them? Maybe they can't swim?'

Robert looked up deep in thought; his Grandad just stared at him, lips pinched forward like a duck. The man nodded sagely, took a sip of tea and said, 'I'm pretty certain monsters under the bed can't swim, otherwise they would live near water and not under beds. Makes sense when you think about it.'

Robert looked off into the middle distance whilst he considered the internal logic of this argument and completely the missed the conspiratorial wink between the two men. Finally, he nodded, that was it. The monsters were dealt with. It was a simple matter of deciding after all.

'The pouch is that for a lady, or a man, or shaman?' he asked.

The man nodded again, clearly impressed, 'Well, we don't know, there's not really much decoration on it so it's difficult to tell. I guess it could have been a shaman's.'

The next 30 minutes were spent with Robert eagerly asking questions as to whether the man had been to Scand-in-a-via and had he seen the northern lights between mouthfuls of toastie and milkshake, all of which the man answered in good humour, but then his lunch time was done and he had to go back to work. He bid them farewell, shouted a thanks to the lady at the counter and went out the door.

When they got to the museum, the man they'd spoken to in the cafe was on the front desk, he nodded and smiled, 'First floor, second room on the left,' and pointed up the stairs before they'd even said anything. Robert shot up the stairs, his Grandad, nodded some thanks and smiled back.

Robert was in the room, nose and hands pressed against the glass cabinets, 'Hey Grandad, look at this, and this, Wow!' Robert didn't really notice that his Grandad wasn't taking much notice.

A few minutes later the man from the Cafe appeared, 'You ok, Sir?'

'Excuse me, that jug, there, what does the symbol mean? asked Robert.

The man from the cafe, peered over and replied, 'Nobody knows, we think it's just decoration. Your Grandad, is he ok?'

Robert turned around, his Grandad was sat in a chair in the corner, looking very pale, a distant look in his eyes and his head was kind of one side, he seemed to be staring at the floor.

'Grandad?' Robert dashed over and shook his arm, his Grandad slowly lifted his head and looked at him but didn't look at him with a weak smile.

'Does your Grandad have anything wrong with him?'

'He's... he's not to eat chocolate and sweets unless he goes funny, it's called Diabeatles.'

'Diabetes.'

'Yes, that's it, but he's never done this before.'

'No problem, kiddo;' and unclipped a radio from his belt, ' George, this is Dave, I'm in Dark Ages I've got a gentleman here who's taken a bit of turn, probably diabetic, can you bring some hot sweet tea and a chocolate biscuit.'

Robert had knelt down at his Grandad's feet and gripped his hand; his Grandad smiled back, 'I'm ok, just a bit out of puff, those stairs. I think we'll use the lift next time, eh?'

A few moments later a man appeared with a chocolate bar, 'Marion's bringing some tea,' he handed the chocolate to the other man, who unwrapped the end and gave it to Robert, who in turn waved it under his Grandad's nose, 'Come on Grandad you have to eat this.'

He looked at the chocolate bar, as if considering it carefully.

'Now!' shouted Robert with all the indignation a small boy can muster.

Stan took the bar and bit the end and chewed thoughtfully. And then another bite, his eyes seem to refocus and he was now aware that two museum staff looking at him with very concerned expressions. A lady in blue pinny appeared, all out of breath with a cup and saucer, which she pushed towards him and immediately seemed to take over.

'Here drink this my love, it's got 4 sugars in, you'll be right as rain after this, a nice cup of tea always good for the soul.'

Robert took the empty chocolate wrapper off Stan and he took the cup of tea off the lady. He sipped it gingerly and immediately seemed to perk up, a hint of an embarrassed smile on his face.

'Ah well, that was, erm, thank you for the chocolate and the tea, er, how much do I owe you?'

'Nonsense, it's on the house sir,' said Marion, flapping her arms slightly.

'Thank you, that's very kind,' said Stan as he drained the cup.

There was an awkward silence whilst everyone looked at Stan and he looked a little sheepish. The man they'd met in the cafe, seemed to realise it had got awkward, 'Right then,' and took the empty tea cup off Stan and said, 'Do you want us to call you a taxi?'

Stan nodded, 'Yes I think that would be a good idea,' and carefully stood up, 'thank you, you've been very kind.'

Once home Grandad made some more tea and went and sat in the living room, Robert followed him and put the T.V on, spending an age to decide what to watch he settled on an old Time Team program, he looked over at his Grandad who had his eyes closed and was making an almost but not quite snoring noise.

When his Mum arrived, the tale was told, Robert got a pat on the back. And when they got home, the tale was retold when his Dad came in. His Dad was very pleased with events, saying how brave he was.

Robert didn't feel particularly brave, things had just sort of happened, but nevertheless the day had ended with a good feeling as he closed his eyes and hoped to dream. As he slowly slipped into sleep he half remembered what he'd blurted out in the cafe, about the monsters under his bed, the cd and it turning his bed into a Viking ship, but the words were lost, blown away on the wind.

Robert did dream of them, but he was not with them, more watching from above, Ragnar knew, he could see him, looking up, smiling, looking straight at him. Robert tried to wave but had no arms, he tried to shout but his voice was again snatched away on the wind. Ragnar smiled, nodded as if he knew, then pointed towards the horizon before them.

More days passed, Robert spent his time on the laptop and drawing the symbol he'd seen on the jug and the pouch in the museum and sometimes helping Grandad in the garden.

Chapter 25

And then one night he just woke up, with a jolt, sat bolt up and found himself on the boat which had just slammed into a stone beach, the sound of stone and wood and sea all scrunching in his ears. The boat lurched at a crazy angle and Robert stumbled out and looked down as the men formed a semi-circle, scurrying across the beach.

Ragnar was on the beach, he half turned to look over his shoulder and saw the small boy waving from the boat, he waved back, the other men turned to look and a small cheer went up. Villi ambled back, held up his arms for Robert to jump down into.

'We almost thought you weren't coming back little fish' he rumbled.

'Yes, so did I for a while.'

The boat had sailed in the last known direction taken from Robert's head until it literally struck land. And then they walked in that direction. They had walked through wood and across moor, over hills and down valleys and they had not seen a soul.

A hand sign and the men stopped, not for the first time Robert marvelled at how utterly quiet such large, well-armed men could be in a wood. Villi leant over to Robert and whispered, 'The tree line is ahead, we must watch and see, stay hidden.'

Robert nodded and crept forward, cracking twigs and snagging and snapping at the undergrowth. He found a tree stump which he could kind of lie into with just his head poking over the top but still remain hidden by the large low bough which dangled a cluster of leaves in front of him, some of which had been nibbled on.

Stretching before them was a long, wide valley, low hills on either side and it was incredibly green and dotted with a myriad wild flowers, purples, blues, yellows and red. They stayed there for hours. Someone handed a water skin around which Robert took a swig from and too late realised it was mead, stifling a choking cough, he wiped the tears from his eyes. Then remembered he had some dried meat in a pocket somewhere, he retrieved that and started to chew on it. And chewed and chewed and chewed. There was no sustenance here, only chewing. Robert concluded that it was all the relentless chewing which conned the body into thinking you'd had a meal.

Out in the valley Robert could see a family of deer moving and eating and watching. Above them an eagle or some large bird of prey hung effortlessly on the wind, barely visible. Bees buzzed and skylarks sang; it all seemed fairly idyllic.

Villi tapped Robert on the shoulder, 'Come on, we're moving, walk in the shade of the trees, and don't dally.'

'Where are we going?' asked Robert.

'That way.' Robert followed the line of Villi's finger to a promontory not that far away, on which was a small stone tower, 'How can I have not seen that?' he muttered to himself, shaking his head in disbelief.

As they broke the tree line, the deer watched them thoughtfully; they were still a long way off so instead of running, the deer stared, bottom jaws moving rhythmically. The line of men kept in the shadow of the trees, occasionally having to duck under low branches. Legs swished in the long grass, and the smell of heather beckoned. Robert looked up at the building; it seemed to be just a square tower surrounded by a low wall, built by piling roughly the same size stone on top of each other, the surrounding forest cleared from its base. The only noise seemed to be bees and skylarks.

Thunor vaulted the wall, putting one hand on the top and skipping over. Nothing happened. The other's followed and still nothing happened. Ragnar broke the line and walked up to the tower, touching the stone, running his fingers across the rough surface and moss; he pressed an ear against it and momentarily closed his eyes.

'Some of you stay by the wall, but spread around it. No man unwatched,' said Thunor. The men jogged into a large circle surrounding the building, spaced such that each man could see at least two of his companions.

'There is no entrance, no windows' muttered Ragnar to himself, looking up, then walking around it again.

The only decoration was on the south side, looking away from the valley towards the nearby line of hills, it was a small stone head, crudely carved, almost childlike, and placed in the middle of the wall but high up, very near the top.

'Well?' asked Thunor.

'It's old, really old,' peering upwards, 'Other than that, I've no idea,' shrugged Ragnar.

'You're a big help.' He replied, still not taking his eyes off the tower.

'Is it a look out post?' asked Robert.

'Could be, but how do you get in?'

'Maybe a tunnel?' added Robert.

Ragnar and Thunor looked sideways at each other then at Robert.

Ragnar smiled, 'Sometimes you need a small boy's big imagination,' and the two men started looking in the long grass for signs of a tunnel or doorway.

Nothing.

One of the men had jumped down off the wall and then shouted, 'What about this?'

He was pointing at a large stone in the wall, where the rest of the wall was made of small bits, like a regular dry stone wall. Ragnar prodded it and ran his fingers around its edges. To the right of it one stone was an odd shape compared to the others, it had a chamfered surface, some care had been taken to make this stone. Ragnar put is hand on it, it moved, he pushed and it went in. There was a grinding noise and the large stone slipped into the ground revealing a tunnel that led into the mound towards the tower.

There was a waft of dry, stale air.

Robert beamed with pride, Villi smiled and punched him the shoulder in a blokey way and sent him flying into one of the others who caught him, grinned and ruffled his hair, 'Smart boy..'

'Who builds an entrance to a tower on the outside wall?' asked Villi.

'Someone who is either trying to be a bit too clever or doesn't care much about any foes; or doesn't have to, I guess. Who's coming?' and Ragnar crouched into the gloom.

Thunor nodded at the man who had pointed at the stone in the first place, 'You'll fit,' observed Thunor.

The man, though not very tall, was very wide and had to twist sideways to get in the hole, then onto all fours, there was a thud then some swearing which disappeared into an echo. Then it went quiet for several minutes.

Ragnar's face appeared over the wall at the top of the tower. A hand reached up from behind the wall, grabbed his throat and pulled him down, Ragnar's face grimaced in agony as it disappeared from view. Then he stood up again, laughing, waving the death grip hand. Robert thought this highly amusing, the rest of the men rumbled and chuckled but Thunor just shook his head, with maybe a hint of a smile about his eyes.

'What do you see?' He shouted.

Ragnar's eyes scanned the horizon, looked about the tower, checked it for markers or pointers or something, 'Nothing. Though there is a barn about a mile that way,' and pointed down the valley, 'Which can't be seen from down there....'

Ragnar disappeared, a minute later he reappeared out of the tunnel closely followed by his companion...

and both looked unperturbed by the experience, Ragnar grasped Robert by the shoulders and spun him around, staring intently at his forehead. Then shrugged his shoulders and set off walking in the direction of the building.

'Come on,' Thurnor waved his arm, and the rest of the group followed, not bothering to hide now, but eyes and ears still alert.

'What was in the tower?' asked Robert.

'Nothing, a staircase to the top and a viewing platform.'

'A lot of work to build some stairs when there's hills all around' mumbled Villi

Ragnar looked over his shoulder, 'I agree,' and pulled his thoughtful face.

They walked for maybe another thirty minutes, birds, bees, rabbits, and unseen things scurrying about them in the undergrowth for company. Then Ragnar stopped, checked Robert's head, then turned ninety degrees towards the hill and set off walking.

As the land rose, the plant life changed, from grasses to bracken and it was heavier on the legs, they had to push their way through and up. By the time they crested a small rise, Robert was quite out of breath and his legs ached. Before them, another stone building, this was long and low though and looked abandoned.

Robert looked back, at the edge of the forest.

'Why is the tree line so straight? It's like someone has cut them back into a straight line?' asked Robert.

Heads turned, nodded and then all turned back and looked at Ragnar.

Ragnar looked at a few of them, his twinkling eyes slashed from side to side, then he pouted a bit, looked up and said 'Dunno, clearly they've been cut, possibly the same reason we cut trees, for farm land and for wood and I assume they may have lived here.'

'And why,' asked Thunor, 'Is the watch tower down there and the farm house up here...hidden? Why isn't the watch tower on high ground so it can see further?'

Again Ragnar pouted, 'Dunno, you got me there, why is that?'

Thunor scowled.

'And that stone face was pointing away, looking away from the valley.'

There was silence, and some shuffling of feet.

'The face was looking south,' shrugged Villi.

'So let's go see what's on the south of this,' continued Thunor and flicked one of his hands.

The men seemed to know that this meant some of them go round one way and some the other.

Robert got the impression that this was just a ruse to stop people asking awkward questions, he looked at Ragnar, who realised that Robert knew and he winked.

It was beginning to dawn on Robert that Thunor and Ragnar had a deep understanding of each other and worked well as a team, guiding the rest of the men.

Behind the farm the land rose quite steeply. And there were lots of lumps and bumps in the ground, before more trees which covered the hill top.

Robert clambered up to where Ragnar was stood, slipping at one point, he had to scramble on all fours.

Ragnar was looking over the roof of the barn, and you could see the whole valley from this little lumpy outcrop, 'Nice view,' he muttered and stood with his hands on his hips and took a deep breath in. He turned grabbed Robert's face in his palms and gently spun him around.

Thunor looked about, 'Well any ideas? Anyone?'

Silence. Then one of the group said, 'Camp, fire, stew?'

Thunor looked at the speaker, then at Ragnar who shrugged in agreement.

'Ok, then, get to it, it looks like someone's had a fire in this barn, so let's make the most of having a roof.'

And with that the men wandered off in various directions, several to the nearby tree line.

'Villi, Robert, you two stand watch.' Robert caught the quick wink from Ragnar to Villi, which Robert knew was the adults 'secret' code for watch the kid and keep him out of trouble or such like. But Robert didn't mind, part of him was pleased with the responsibility, he noted that Villi was looking South and East, so Robert turned and stared hard North and West, he caught a flicker of a grin pass over Ragnar's face as he hobbled down, but then thought maybe it was pain from his hip.

Robert could hear axes chopping at wood, two of the men talking and laughing.

Slowly the sun set and strange shadows cast along the valley floor; the sky, the world grew tranquil. Birds stopped singing, except for one, Robert wasn't sure if it was a blackbird or a thrush but whatever it was it was singing its heart out; it was beautiful.

A bat appeared flying a figure of eight pattern over the barn, flitting and flickering in the twilight sky, which was now bright in purples, mauves and dark blues.

Darkness fell without commotion, seeming to slip in unnoticed. Firelight flickered out of the doorways and windows of the barn, inside men spoke quietly but occasionally laughter bubbled up and surged into the night air like waves on the sea. Robert thought about how much his legs ached, they'd been stood there for ages. Villi had never said a word, Robert looked around to see if he had fallen asleep stood up, but he watched the darkness intently. Robert started to fidget, put his weight on one leg then another. It was cold now.

Robert looked up and his mouth hung open at the number of stars in the sky, a pale dusty river of light, lazed across the black and everywhere he looked shone pinpricks of sparkling light, he never tired of being amazed by this. But soon even the most spectacular night sky he had ever seen was not enough to take his mind off the standing. Robert had stood until he couldn't stand any more, and then he stood some more. His thighs were shaking violently by the time other men loomed out of the dark. Robert realised at that point just how much he could see in the dark. It was all dark, just varying degrees of pitch, shapes and shadows, but they were quite clear, with distinct edges. The two new men stood in silence as Robert had and after what seemed like another hour but in reality, was just a few minutes, Villi grunted and walked towards the barn, leaving a friendly slap on the shoulder of the person who had replaced him.

Robert raised his hands to his eyes as they entered, he couldn't believe how warm it was, nor how bright.

'Stubborn in his bones this one, as well as strength' rumbled Villi, jabbing a thumb over his shoulder at the boy.

Robert grimaced a smile but was just too tired to feel the pride that was there somewhere.

Thunor nodded and smiled, 'Stubborn is good, we like stubborn.'

A space was made for them by the fire, Robert clambered to the floor, a rough wooden bowl of something hot with lumps in was pushed at him, he ate and drank and slopped it down his tunic and within minutes was asleep, leaning on Villi's arm. Villi placed a massive hand under Robert's head and turned him so he lay curled up on a rolled-up piece of cloth. The men talked and laughed quietly well into the night as Robert quietly snored.

Chapter 26

'Urngh' or something like that was the first sound from Robert. He was chilly and stiff and ached. Most of the men were still asleep. Ragnar looked to be asleep but his eyes were peeping out from under his lids. One of the men whispered huskily, 'Poke the fire boy and more wood eh?'

Robert leant over to a pile of small branches, placed them on the smouldering fire, then poked around with a third, sparks surged upwards and the heat with them. The man who had made the request nodded and smiled, then closed his eyes again. Robert sat cross-legged and stared into the flames.

He was aware that he was being watched, he looked around, Ragnar had not moved but there was now a conscious light in his eyes.

'What do you see boy, in the fire?'

Robert returned his stare to the flames, till his eyes burned.

'I see armies rise and fall, whole kingdoms reduced to ashes, towns and villages been and gone.'

Ragnar was physically rocked back by the words, 'Such is life boy' he said grimly, 'It's how you live, how you die and the stories you leave behind that count, everything else is for nought. Sooner or later, no matter how big the pile of stones, the wind, rain, sun and ice will wear it down to dust. Yet they can't wear down deeds and words.'

Robert pulled his face into a frown, and returned his attention to the fire, aware that some of the others had woken up, were listening and trying very hard to pretend they were still asleep. And suddenly uncomfortable with what he had said, as he'd no idea where the words came from, they'd just popped out.

Outside the world was flat, grey, and the sky with it, but it had a hint of orange, like ashes that still have the potential to ignite. Strange shadows and flat echoes glowered at them; the men were on edge not venturing far from the vicinity of their make-shift beds. Robert sat with Villi who was carving sharpened ends onto sticks. Thunor had sent two of the men to scout the valley, the rest of the men milled around, sharpening swords, axes and knives or sewing bits of clothes that had split.

Robert wasn't sure if it was cause or effect but slowly the laughter bubbled louder and the grey mist dissipated, revealing a crisp blue sky. Robert stood up stretched and stepped over to the edge where the land gently dropped away to the valley below in the distance the family of deer looked back, still chewing rhythmically and watching over them, high up circling an eagle or buzzard or something.

Two men broke the tree line and walked towards them, Robert shouted and pointed, watching them walk towards them, slowly they zig zagged around heather, tussock grass and small shrubs till they were back, bringing a new energy into what had been a lazy morning so far.

'Well?' asked Ragnar of the scouts.

'Nothing, just four standing stones, uprights, big as you.'

'How do we know this is where we are supposed to be, we won't know till the other side of the hill and we see what that the ember does on the boy's head?' said a voice from the back.

There was some murmuring of agreement.

Ragnar bit his lip, 'I'm going to think. My hands itch.' And with that he stalked off on his own and sat at the northern end of the bit of field the barn was in, crossed his legs, leaning his back against a small ash tree and closed his eyes.

Some of the men excitedly questioned the scouts about the stones, Ragnar opened one eye, he didn't have to speak he just glared at them with one eye and they stopped, some even staring at their shuffling feet, then they all moved away into the inside of the barn, leaving Ragnar and a couple of men keeping watch.

The day grew into a long pleasant afternoon; Robert watched the men make and mend and sharpen more, others returned with firewood and food foraged and hunted from the valley. More stew appeared from somewhere.

At some point Robert nodded off, his head slumping forward. He dreamed of his own home, his parents, his Grandad all stood in bright sunshine waving at him. He woke with a start.

Someone said 'Bad dream boy?'

Robert was a bit confused, and just nodded, unsure of where he was and looked round to the speaker. The man, he couldn't remember his name, smiled a toothy grin from his red, weather worn face.

Robert realised that he should have been terrified by him, all leather armour, straps and sharp edges and looking more than a little bedraggled, his long blonde hair and beard running down his front in plaits. But he wasn't and Robert smiled back, stood up and stretched.

'I need a wee.'

The Viking winked, 'Watch out for beasties...'

Around the back of the house, part way up the hill was a convenient bush. When he'd finished, he looked out over the valley rather than where his feet were going and he slipped off a tussock of grass, landing heavily on his behind. Standing up he looked over his shoulder to see if anybody had seen him slip, the sun was just sat above the hill line behind him, throwing long and bizarre shadows right towards him and down the hill towards the barn. Strange curves snaked back and forth, and a line of lumps which looked for all the world like the armoured spines on a dragon's back which had been covered in grass. These led up to a head, horse shaped but three or four times bigger; you could see the line of the ears, the nose, the mouth, where the eye would be. And there was an eye, it blinked open, a clod of earth and grass tumbled from the lid, then it snapped shut. A cry spluttered from Robert's lips, 'Ragnar, Villi!!'

All the men came running, and stood looking at the small boy on the hill, he looked at them wide eyed and pointed at lines and lumps in the grass, the colour drained from his face. The men looked at each other and then at Robert then at the hillside. Ragnar stepped forward, clambered up and stood next to the boy. He looked, pouted in that thoughtful way that he had, then his mouth dropped open. His hands flexed out in the 'Don't panic, don't move, stay still' symbolism used ever since upright apes saw something bigger than them with pointier teeth. This freaked the men, startled, staring wide eyed; foes were easy enough to fight when you could see them but foes that only the Shaman and a world walker could see where an entirely different thing.

There was a low rumble and the ground shook slightly, then a shuddering breath, like an old man waking from a deep sleep. The ridges under the grass flexed. The men leapt for their lives down the hill, weapons were drawn before they even landed. Ragnar gripped Robert by the elbow and they scampered backwards, never taking their eyes off the now flexing and moving grass which then raised up; grass, earth, rocks, stones, rubble and soil rained and clattered down about them, on them, over them.

There was a noise like a dog shaking itself, but it was a dog wearing armour plating. Dust, soil and bits of grass filled the air in a great cloud.

Faces and sharp edges appeared from behind the barn, a stone wall and some shrubbery; Ragnar and Robert were just kind of stood staring, stock still hoping that what they were looking at didn't notice them. Robert sneezed from all the dusty earth in the air, then yelped as Ragnar's iron grip squashed his elbow.

The dragon sat there looking a little dazed if the truth be told, a long tongue licked its lips and then it seemed to notice them for the first time and made a strange 'mew' noise. It hobbled to its feet, peering at them down its snout; back plates (that Robert had spotted under the grass) flexed and then with a lazy, slow, effortless stretch and beat of its wings, it launched into the air, kicking up more earth, dust and grass. Everyone ducked as the massive creature sailed into the air at head height, skimmed the roof of the barn and then began climbing in a long spiral over the valley towards forest.

The men relaxed a little, looked at each other and then dragon, which was climbing higher and higher.

Where it had lain was a large indentation in the earth, a slash of dark red soil amidst the greenery.

'Stairs' said someone who liked to state the obvious as Thunor and Ragnar and a couple of others had already edged forward and were peering down stone cut stairs that led down into dark.

'Shall we go?' asked Ragnar.

Thunor pursed his lips and looked up at the dragon that was now a small dot on the horizon and then at some of his men.

The blonde man from the barn said, 'What if it comes back?'

'And it's going to be dark soon.' said someone else.

There was a general murmur of agreement.

'What bearing does that have on anything Canute, it's going to be dark in the tunnel' snapped Ragnar.

'Yes but we'll know it's light up here.' There was a pause then Canute added for further clarification, 'if we went down when it was light.'

'And we'll only have to worry about things in the dark down there, instead of things in the dark down there and up here' added another voice.

'You know there are strange, terrible and ferocious things abroad in this land and it's us! We're Vikings; we're what everything else is afraid of.'

There was lots of nodding, and ayes, and goes without saying, but not much conviction. And nobody was looking anybody else in the eye, least of all Ragnar.

Ragnar glared at them all.

'We'll need to organise some torches,' mused Thunor.

'And rations' added someone else.

Followed by, 'and water.'

There was much more enthusiasm for the preparation.

Thunor nodded and then everyone was skipping down the hillside with an eager air.

Ragnar looked down the tunnel, then at Thunor sighed and stamped off.

No one slept much. Men watched the skies for the now missing dragon (one chap was suitably rebuked at shouting the alarm when a passing bat flew a bit low for his liking) and some men watched the stairs for would be terrors rising from the depths: And others watched the night generally, as this seemingly was the best time for horrors to come lurking.

Robert thought about this, 'Ragnar?'

'Mmm?'

'Why do ghosts and things come out at night?'

Ragnar raised an eyebrow; the men within earshot grew nearer. Those out of earshot grew nearer to see what the men who were nearer were listening to, wide eyed, and hands on swords.

'Well erm?' said Ragnar.

Robert reconfirmed the question, almost as if for himself, 'Why don't you see ghosts and things during the day?'

'Well some people do, I mean, it's at night because, well, it's your sight see, yes that's it, your vision is your main sense for perceiving the world, so at night when it's pretty much useless, then your other senses kick in and that heightens your ability to see through the veil. And at twilight, that's a crossing time, it's a boundary time, and so the boundary between worlds is thin. Those with strong sight, like myself, can see at all times'

Robert was still staring at the fire absentmindedly, most of the men were looking very nervous, wide eyes swivelling in pale faces.

Thunor cleared his throat and glared at Ragnar, who nodded as if jolted, and added, 'But you can rest assured, that there's nothing around us at the moment, you have nothing to worry about.'

'I wasn't,' replied Robert matter of factly and winked.

Ragnar grinned.

There was a sudden easing of tension in the rest of the room, but still some furtive glances to be made into the night. And a certain amount of heated but whispered discussion as to who was sleeping near the door and windows.

Chapter 27

Dawn broke. Broke is an exaggeration; more like it seeped into the night, edging its way from one horizon to another, bleaching the shadows from around the camp.

Ragnar sat at the stairs, cross-legged, eyes closed. Men crept about preparing for what might come next, but no one disturbed Ragnar. As the sun crested the hills on the other side of the valley, his eyes snapped open and he stood up.

'Ready then?'

There was some shuffling of feet and then one of the men said, 'That seemed a little easy, that dragon flying off last night, a little too easy.'

'We're Vikings things are supposed to run away from us. Or fly away,' replied Ragnar.

Some of the men turned to check the sky.

'What if it's a trap, or he's gone for friends, or there's another dragon?'

'Why would there be another dragon? Who ever heard of their being two dragons, they're famous for not getting on with anything else.'

'Aye well, but strange things have been happening a lot recently,' the man's eyes flicked to Robert and then back again, then added 'a lot' for extra emphasis.

'And have we not come away with the prize every time?'

Canute asked, 'How do we know we're supposed to go down there, I mean we've been following that glowing thing on the boys head, we won't know till we get to the other side if this is the place.'

There was a general murmur of agreement.

'By Odin's blood, it's just a tunnel!' yelled Ragnar with some ferocity. Everyone took a step back.

Ragnar turned to Robert, 'Climb up and go stand on the other side of the opening, then face this way.'

Robert clambered up, slipped, stumbled and eventually found himself looking out over a beautiful valley and a line of grumpy looking armed men; he put his fingers to his forehead but could feel nothing.

'Satisfied?' demanded Ragnar.

There was some mumbled agreement, Ragnar eyed the men, 'Whoever is coming, stand in a line here.'

Thunor nodded at three of the men to stay behind and guard the entrance, the rest lined up.

Robert lined up with the others, and nobody at all thought this was odd. Except perhaps for Robert, who could hear his Mum's voice off somewhere telling him to 'not' do whatever he was about to do for some very good and pointed reasons.

Ragnar reached into his bag, pulled out some dried leaves still attached to their twigs, and a small flask. He emptied a few drops of the liquid in the flask into his other hand, then sprinkled it on the leaves, smearing it over them. He then raised the leaves and his arms and eyes to the sky and muttered. He flicked the leaves and some splashes of whatever it was over the line of the men. And then returned the contents to this bag.

The men looked at each other up and down the line, 'Is that it?' one of them asked.

Ragnar looked up, raised an eyebrow and sighed. He then waved his arm almost like a ballerina thought Robert and then was surprised to see a wash of yellow sunlight fall from Ragnar's hand and ripple down the line of men.

'Better?' Ragnar asked sarcastically.

The men nodded and were now ready for action, although the three being left to guard the entrance did not look too thrilled, keeping a wary eye on the sky.

The tunnel was made of hard packed earth, here and there tree roots, entwined and knotted, could be seen in the flickering shadows cast by the torches. The men were tense and moved slowly, many struggling to get through due to their size, leather armour and chainmail scratched and gouged at the earth walls. Robert, in the middle of the line, noticed they were spaced apart, and then figured that it was so each man could draw his sword without hitting the man in front or behind. Then he thought about what it might that they would be drawing their swords against and felt butterflies in his tummy. Then he remembered he was with a bunch of Vikings armed to the teeth, their shaman and who knows what he brought. He suddenly realised he didn't know very much at all about Ragnar.

A line of hand movements ricocheted up the tunnel from one man to the next and all stopped instantly, the sound of breathing rasped in time with the guttering flames. Robert watched a small black beetle, its carapace glinting in the light scurry into a hole no bigger than his thumbnail. The tension faded a little and they carried on; they seemed to be walking in a wide spiral that was circling towards some central point.

The tunnel opened out into a large chasm, the dome of the hill above them, the hill was hollow, it had been mined out. Robert mouth opened to say wow, but Villi clamped a large hand over most of his face and shook his head, using his eyes to point to the centre of the chasm.

Behind Villi's hand Robert's mouth hung open; no noise would ever explain or illustrate what he could see. A small waterfall ran out of the far wall, which fed a stream, this trickled over moss covered rocks and stones, and around an enormous pile of gold. Some of the gold had been washed downstream slightly, mainly the coins Robert noted. In the gloom, small trees and saplings struggling to grow towards the beams of light that filtered through holes and cracks in the rock above, illuminating the scene below with pools of light. Shimmering dots of gold spun and flickered lazily in the beams of light.

On top of the pile of gold, as if having made a nest out of the metal, was another dragon; it snored gently, nostrils and wing membranes vibrating.

There were then quite a lot unbelieving looks and gestures and frenzied arm waving that all summed up to, 'That's another dragon! You said... etc'

Ragnar ignored them.

The dragon was about the size of a large van. It was all lumpy, like it had been thrown together with spare parts, clumps of plated scales, co-joined and malformed. It slowly creased and flexed as it breathed. You couldn't really make out its original colour, greens, browns, golds, reds maybe even a hint of yellow, had all smeared into one sludgy mess. The overall effect was added to by the profusion of moss and lichen which coated the beast and up high in between its shoulder blades a mass of ivy seemed to flourish, cascading a trail of the plant along the dragon's ribs.

There was a pervading aroma of sulphur and other accelerants. When it breathed there was a back rumble which sounded faintly like flames were about to go 'whoomph' which echoed gently around the inside of the hill and provided a low background menacing rumble.

Villi physically picked up Robert; his hand still clamped over the boy's mouth and hauled him over to a large boulder that looked like it had fallen out of the roof, crouching behind it; next to them, hiding behind another stone thick with ivy, Thunor and Ragnar. All around the cavern Robert could see faces peering over whatever hiding place had been chosen by the men. The dragon's snore rasped loudly and it rolled over onto it's back wriggling and writhing in ecstasy, like a cat lying in a sunbeam. The sound of gold coins tricking and tumbling down the pile as it struggled to hold the dragon's weight brought groans from some of the men.

One of the dragon's eyes snapped open, then the other, it craned its head, furrowed brow and looked around, all still upside down.

Every man tried to make themselves as small as possible; the dragon relaxed, lay its head down, once again seemingly snoozing, flicking one back leg as if swatting an imaginary fly: Then with a great crash and unnatural speed it spun around on to all four stumpy legs glaring into the dark recesses of the chamber. Gold coins and swords and torques sprayed and clattered and tinkled about, flashing and glinting in the darkness. The dragon squinted into the dark, then coughed and spat a small ball of flame into the shadows at regular intervals. The rocks nearest glowed a bright orange and then slopped off into a hissing liquid, one small tree was instantaneously converted to pure charcoal and then crumpled to the floor. What didn't burn, melted, shadows danced and flailed and then disappeared. The air was filled with the smell of hot rock and carbon, hissing, bubbling and spitting.

The dragon peered about, one eye slightly larger than the other, pupils dilating and fixating, then after what seemed an age, it settled down.

Having played with his Auntie's cat often enough, Robert recognised that this air of relaxation was in fact a ruse, the dragon was ready to strike at any moment.

From behind the various hiding places, lots of relieved faces turned to look at each other, shrugged shoulders and then one by one everyone looked at Ragnar; who was thinking.

Then he looked at Robert and beckoned him from his hiding place. Robert considered this; considered the plinking sounds of cooling rock, the smell of burnt carbon in the air and politely declined the invitation. Ragnar waved his arms some more, and nodded his head vigorously. Robert peered over the rim of his hiding place and hurriedly hid back. The dragon was peering with one good eye around the cavern, the other seemed to be a bit dim and unfocused.

With great emphasis Ragnar pointed a finger at Robert then at his own forehead then at the Dragon. Robert looked around the various hiding places, or the ones he could see from where he was and everywhere he saw pasty, sweaty faces staring at him. All he could hear was his pulse banging in his ears, his hands shook, his stomach was doing somersaults, and then seemingly without any thought processes taking places, indeed part of his mind was screaming what are you doing, his legs stumbled forward, almost as if he was a puppet on a string, his eyes were so wide he thought they might actually fall out of his head. The dragon, slow and ponderous turned, it wasn't used to the squishy things being up front and in his face, they usually hid till they were crisped... this was new.

Nostrils the size of Robert's head sniffed and wrinkled, then it squirmed forward on the pile of gold, better to see him with his odd eye. The gold crumpled and crumbled and cascaded under the dragon's weight. Some of it within tantalising reach of one of the men.

Robert could see him out of the corner of his eye, but didn't recognise him, couldn't remember seeing him before, which was odd as he wore a bright red jerkin under his bits of leather and chain-mail, he was just so obvious, where everyone else was in dull earthy, colours.

He leaned and strained to reach some trinket and Robert realised that the bright red was far too easily seen, quicker than a blink of an eye, the dragon's head snapped round and blew a ball of bright, white blue fire at the man. He disappeared in the flame, there wasn't even a scream, no dust, just wisps of glowing sparks carried away on the tendrils of heat. On the back wall was a vague black outline of the man's shadow in black carbon. Robert nearly wet himself, in fact it was only because he'd had nothing to drink in a while that he didn't. Instead he slumped to his knees, his head bowed forward. Before him the floor was illuminated, as if he was wearing a miner's lamp. He touched his fingers to the glowing spark on his forehead and felt a tremendous heat leaving his body. He threw himself backwards and as he fell, fingers of light, followed by arms, a head, a body and leg oozed from the mark, slipped effortlessly like a fish through water, stepped out of his forehead and stood up; Robert scrabbled back towards Ragnar, crab like, not taking his eyes off the Djinn.

The dragon sat back and watched mesmerised by the creature of flame. The Djinn flickered, weaved and bobbed gently on its tendril of fire it moved about on. It stared at the dragon, on the back of its head a second face formed and looked for Ragnar.

'You gave your oath. One coin. We hold you to that oath.'

Ragnar stooped out from his hiding place and nodded solemnly.

'How do we find this one coin Ragnar?' asked Thunor in a not very quiet whisper.

Ragnar pursed his lips then said, 'I've no idea. I never expected us to get this far.'

Thunor's eyes narrowed, and then he snorted back a quiet laugh. Slowly and very measuredly the rest of the Vikings congregated towards Thunor, never taking their eyes off the Djinn and the Dragon both of whom were just staring at each other like long lost relatives.

The Djinn then held out its arms and with the tip of its fingers held the sunstone, flames flickered and danced around its edges but it did not appear to char or burn. The dragon grunted and nodded almost imperceptibly; as this unfolded the Vikings retreated away towards to the wall where they had come in, just on the off chance that someone decided to take umbrage at their presence.

Suddenly the colour and texture of the Djinn changed, he went all bright white and extremely hot, then rocketed skywards. There was a tremendous roaring noise, made all the louder by being in a relatively small dome, a streak of fire like a falling star returning to the sky hurtled for a small hole in the roof and then was gone. Dust, earth, bits of burning plant, hot rock and cinders whirled around in a maelstrom of gold coins and hot metal. The group of men coughed and sputtered, patted out small fires that burst into life in their beards and bits of leather armour. As the chamber cleared of flying debris they realised that the dragon was glaring at them with uneven eyes. Everyone stopped what they were doing and stared. The dragon stared back. Then its brow furrowed as it had reached some sort of conclusion.

'I think...' said Ragnar out of the corner of his mouth, 'that we should run.' They didn't need telling twice.

The dragon started to take a deep breath in, a very slow and deliberate one. The group of battle hardened warriors ran for the tunnel, they ran like small boys being chased by a farmer for stealing apples, there was no finesse or strategy it was just get out of the way as quickly as possible.

Having got use to the dimness of the cave, the sunshine outside was blindingly bright. The first one out tripped on a tree root or rabbit hole or something and the rest tumbled over him like fools before the high chair. A great 'Woof!' noise followed by a boiling cloud of fire burst out of the hole and washed over them.

Chapter 28

There was some muffled shouting that sounded like it was coming from underground. Villi rolled over and off Robert who sat up gasping for air, then he started laughing, and Villi joined in.

A crumpled voice said, 'I'd just like to point out that I said there might be another dragon,' he was interrupted with a thwack noise to the back of the head and he shut up.

Thunor shouted rather gleefully, 'Hey Ragnar, your bum is on fire,' pointing at the flames that danced about Ragnar's rear.

Ragnar turned and patted out the smouldering that had been the rear of his breeches. Looking around most of the men were severely singed, bits of beards, hair, and eyebrows were gone, much of which had only just grown back after the incident on the ship. The laughter was interrupted by a thump that shook the earth and another cloud belching from the hole, this time just dust.

'That sounded suspiciously like the roof of the tunnel collapsing,' said Villi with resignation.

'What just happened?' asked Canute who was lying on the floor smoke ebbing from his leather armour, 'and what of Russ?'

A solemnity passed over the men, they looked unsure, as if trying to process what had happened.

'And what do we tell his wife?' continued Canute.

Villi rumbled, 'His wife left him for a fish merchant in Dansk. That's why he was here.'

Many of the men shook their head at the absurdity of this.

'So, he had no one?' asked Canute

'He had us,' replied Villi with some gusto.

This caused a murmur of agreement and nodding of heads.

Ragnar raised a wagging finger, 'He was a Viking, he died doing what we do, and love. And know, he sits in the Great Hall, with Odin, and his kin, and all the other warriors. Do not worry my friends, he is well.' He emphasised the word well.

The nodding of heads turned to wistful smiles.

'As long as he does not sit to near the fire in Valhalla eh,' said Canute.

The men laughed guiltily, and Canute got a friendly kick from Villi.

'So, what do we do now?'

Ragnar ignored the question; he was looking at Robert who was stood mouth open and looking troubled.

'What's the matter boy?'

Robert said, 'erm,' and shook his head. He grew really uncomfortable at finding everyone looking at him. He opened his mouth to speak but no words came out, instead tears welled up in his eyes.

Ragnar bent down, 'It is done boy, there is no more use being sad at his passing than being sad that the moon came up last night, there is nothing we can do about it. So be glad he was with us, be glad that he died well, and even now rides for the Hall. Do not spoil today for what happened yesterday eh? We will meet him again, but for now he's just sits in a different room of a great Hall.' Ragnar forced a smile.

Robert bowed his head and stared at the grass, he understood the wisdom of this, but his emotions were in turmoil. The reality of what had happened, what was happening surged inside him and tears leaked down his cheeks. He then felt embarrassed that he was crying.

Ragnar put a hand on Robert's shoulder and squeezed.

'To answer Canute's question as to what just happened, was that payment was made, our fellow traveller was granted access to a place he could not otherwise have been allowed in. And that is pretty much all I know about it,' said Ragnar, trying to change the subject and focus of everyone looking at Robert. But it didn't work.

There was silence. There was still the distant cry of a buzzard, the shrill, merry chirp of a skylark, the gentle blustering of a faint breeze through the long grass and long hair and rasping of a grasshopper nearby, but on the whole silent. The men stood in a line, all charcoal and burned, wisps of smoke slinked lazily upwards from various bits of them wondering what to do about their lucky charm who for all the world looked like a small boy crying.

White fluffy clouds fleeced across a bright blue sky. Robert closed his eyes and turned his face to the sun, letting the warm rays soak into him. Then a shadow closed over him, Robert opened his eyes to see Thunor towering over him and looking very serious.

Slowly he knelt down, not small feat in all his armour, and as he did so he spoke 'We kneel to no man, we do not even kneel to our Gods, we stand and stare at them, in the face. Ask them for strength and wisdom.'

He took Roberts tiny hands in own massive shovel like hands, 'But by the Gods, by Odin, Thor and Tyr, that was the bravest thing I've ever seen boy, truly we are blessed you are with us.'

Robert looked around, and spluttered a laugh through the tears. This was all real and not real at the same time and it suddenly became too much.

He looked around at his band of Vikings stood around him, all nodding and smiling in agreement, all black and burned. And he said, 'Erm.'

Thunor laughed, and pushed Robert over as he clambered to his feet, 'You and your erms, boy.'

Everyone laughed, Robert laughed as he sprawled into the long grass, and as he fell, something small and golden and round, fell from a crease in his jerkin and lay there gleaming in the sunlight.

There was a general noise a bit like an 'Oooh!' but perhaps also a gasp as well and everyone stood very still.

One of the men said, 'Erm..'

Ragnar produced a small, thin knife from the recesses of his clothes and crept forward then flipped the coin over with its tip.

On this side strange marking spiralled from the edge towards the centre, getting smaller as they went, it seemed to be writing but like no writing any of them had seen before. On the other side, some sort of creature, with whirls and dots, and possibly two tiny birds made from smaller dots. Ragnar reached out for it tentatively and gripped it between two fingers, lifted high above his head and peered at it with his beady eyes, watched the sun light flash and gleam of the shapes and edges.

Shaking he head, he muttered, 'Th.... this is the coin,' he looked at Robert and shook his head in disbelief.

Smiles broke out across faces, there was even a small cheer. Villi reached down and hauled Robert to his feet, 'Come little fish back to the sea!'

There was another cheer, and then they set off, scampering towards the tree line.

On the way back someone did raise the issue that someone else had said that you never get two dragons in the same place. But it was a short conversation and over quite abruptly. It was never mentioned again.

The walk back to the boat didn't seem to take anything like as long as it took to get there; their path was lit by a low summer sun, a dull orange orb in the sky that guided them through the woods. Slowly oak and ash gave way to rowan and elder then to heathland, which halted abruptly at low cliffs.

The waft of salt and the crash of waves on a shingle shore were evident well before they saw the flat sea to the horizon. Their ship was leaning to one side, rammed up the beach, a fire had been lit and three men stood watching, the one higher, stood on the front of the boat, waving vigorously when he saw them.

Chapter 29

The jovial mood evaporated quickly, it appeared that the boat had some kind of problem, Robert didn't understand what, but most of the men stood looking at her, nodding sagely.

The men who had guarded her did not want to leave her alone and venture to the nearby woods for materials, so now time would have to be spent mending her. And possibly another night on another blustery cold beach.

Robert sat near a fire that had been built, idly drawing in the sand with a stick.

'What's that?' asked Ragnar.

Robert looked down at the shape he'd drawn in the sand.

'I, err,'

Ragnar scowled and leaned forward.

'On a jar, somewhere, I'm not sure where but it was on a jar.'

'A jar!?' Ragnar slumped to his knees, rubbed the lines out of the sand and said, 'Draw it again boy.'

Robert drew the shape, the shape he'd seen on the jar and that he'd drawn now many times at home and at his Grandad's and now on a beach who knew where.

Again, Ragnar rubbed it out, 'Again, thrice is the charm' he spoke hoarsely, eyes fixed on the sand.

Robert drew the shape a third time, sat back and looked at Ragnar who stared wide-eyed and shaking at the sand.

After what seemed like an age, Ragnar said, 'A jar, the jar, the last jar, it exists. You must tell me where you saw it.'

Robert squirmed, 'I can't. You wouldn't understand. I don't understand. It's not somewhere you can get it. I can't get it.'

Ragnar leant forward and gripped Robert's shoulders, stared him right in the eyes, 'You promise me this boy?'

Robert squirmed some more, 'I promise, I've seen it but can't get to it. What is it?'

'This is the last jar, an item that was thought lost, perhaps never was, but you've seen it. It belonged to the Picts. When you saw it, what else was there?'

'A broken comb, sword, a seax, and a bag,'

'How were they broken, deliberately, they still break things as an offering to their gods,' he said almost as an aside.

'No,'

Then there was a long pause, Robert was acutely aware of the others watching, as the boy and the old man stared at each other, Ragnar relaxed, he knew the boy wanted to say something but was afraid, finally Robert spoke.

'Broken with age, I think, they are just very, very old, thousands of years old.'

Ragnar slumped back on his haunches, looked at the boy with a new sense of awe, opened his mouth to say something but didn't and so closed it again.

There was a long silence where the two just looked at each other.

After what seemed like an age, Robert spoke, just to break the silence,

'The bag, had a design on it as well, but it was faded, only part complete, it kind of looked like this,' Robert drew the symbol in the sand and waited.

Ragnar looked at it long and hard and then nodded.

'This takes us on new adventures boy,' and got and walked off towards where the Chief had been watching from.

The two men walked away from the camp, Thunor leaning to one side, listening intently to what Ragnar had to say.

The mending of the boat slowed, the noise of carpentry had gone to be replaced by the sound of gentle surf on polished stones, the men more intent on watching Ragnar and Thunor and the boy sat by the fire than fixing the boat.

Villi walked over and sat down next to the boy who was staring intently into the fire. Canute followed and handed Villi a strip of dried meat, who handed it to Robert, 'Come on little fish, there's no reason to look so glum, eat, you will feel better.'

Robert looked round, half smiled, took the meat and tried biting a bit off.

'It's good eh?' grinned Canute.

Robert struggled to find an appropriate answer so just went with an mmm noise instead.

Thunor marched back to the fire, made sure that all eyes were on him and said in a loud voice, 'We're not going home, we're, we're going to see the Picts.'

There was stunned silence amongst the men, they looked at each other, then Canute said, 'Did you just say we were going to see the Picts?'

'Yes.'

'Are you insane?'

There then followed much shouting and finger pointing and gesticulating which escalated into pushing and shoving.

Ragnar looked around and found a large branch on the beach and stormed forward, holding the branch aloft like a staff, the end glowing with a bright white light.

The sudden appearance of light caused the men to stop arguing and take a large step back, forming into a circle around him. Ragnar stood in the middle and slowly turned, looking at each man in turn, glaring at them.

'Be still, be quiet,' he barked, 'What's got into you recently, you spend as much time being Viking as you do bickering like old women! Enough! Stand back.'

The men were suitably cowed. Ragnar stood in the middle of them, still slowly turning, pointing the light at each in turn.

'The boy has seen The Jar of the Last Breath. I knew the Picts had it, but they always swore it was lost. It holds the secret of how to draw the last breath from someone, from you. As well as the inscription we already have from the Djinn coin, we will be all powerful, none will ever best us. Imagine the stories!? This is the boy's purpose to lead us to greater things. You'll remember this moment and take great gladness from it. You'll be able to say, I was there, that night with Thunor, Villi and the boy Robert, the World Walker. Remember it, for you are joined by it, as one under the stars: For it is the doom of men that they forget!'

'The last breath you say?' said Villi, hand stroking his beard.

Canute interrupted, 'I, I'd just quite like to go home, we've been away nearly all summer, my wife is going to kill me and we don't have much gold to show for it,' a lot of the other men agreed.

Ragnar's shoulders visibly drooped and he rested the end of the staff on the floor, the light slowly dimming.

Canute continued, 'We've been to other side of the world and back, stories is all well and good, but gold is possibly better.'

'There's more to life than gold, knowledge!' said Ragnar.

'Maybe for you Shaman, but I can't spend knowledge; it doesn't buy my wife a new coat when the traders come up from the south.'

There were more murmurs of agreement.

Ragnar nodded, seemed to give in, then his eyes unfocused and he spoke in a sing song rhyme.

'Aye, that's what I say. And when I have the jar I will say more; I will say, I am the sky, I am the ground, And I am the streams that run through it and the lochs that fill it. I am the heather, And the bones of the earth, And I would have your dying breath. So blow, blow into this bottle. Blow hard and blow deep. Blow from your centre and your core. Blow from the very pit of ye. For I will hold your dying breath. And none shall have it save me.'

Robert felt goosebumps, felt the hair stand up on the back of his neck.

There was a stunned silence which seemed to stretch out for a long time, then Thunor spoke, 'I hear you Canute, and Odin knows I'll be hearing my wife when I get home to. But think of next summer when we have all this, we'll need a bigger boat for all the gold we'll have.'

'Besides it's on the way, we have to pass it to get home,' added Ragnar.

None of the men spoke, just looked at each other, then kind of shrugged and dissipated into the night.

The evening into darkness was subdued, men spoke quietly to each other, no stories tonight, no roaring fire, just a small glowing pit.

Paul Hodson

Chapter 30

Robert felt like he'd barely slept, the night had been cold and draughty. At first light people started milling around checking the repairs on the boat. Satisfied that she was once again sea-worthy, she was pushed back into the water with brute force, sweat and some swearing. Breakfast would be dry bread and dried something that Robert couldn't identify and a cup of sour water.

The sea was rough, dark waves hurled themselves from one horizon to another, white spray splashed across the boat, the men laughed, laughed loud with glee.

'Now this is a sea worthy of a story,' bellowed Villi as he stumbled past, floor of the boat rising up to meet his feet then dropping away again. Robert just nodded and smiled, not convinced. He'd found himself his usual spot, sat on top of a barrel, in a corner tucked out of the way. He realised he had no idea what was in the barrel. It didn't matter right now though, it was something to hold on to as boat lifted and dropped away, lifted and dropped away...

Ragnar had appeared next to him, 'That symbol that you drew, and the jar, well that's something that's been spoken of for generations, for many generations, since when the square shields came to the great river. They built a wall across Briton, to keep the Picts out,' he paused as a particularly large wave hurled itself across the boat, then continued, 'They could not be defeated, and the jar was why. It's been lost of generations, spoken of as we speak of Odin's Spear, or the necklace of Freyja. Or so I was led to believe.'

'But why do you want it, you don't....I don't know, need them is not right, but you just go around collecting these treasures?'

'For the glory, men will sit around campfires and tell our story long since our bones and swords are dust. And men will know of us from our deeds. And when we die, we will be in the company of our Fathers, in the Great Hall and we will stand there with pride. It is for each generation to make the best of it. That's just the way it is. And for the knowledge!' He winked.

'But you don't see your wives, or your children, you're never home?'

'Heh, well they usually come with us!' said Ragnar, casually, and then moved to walk away.

'Come with you?' Robert was aghast; he could not consider his Mum going anywhere near a boat like this.

'Yes, many of the woman are very handy in a fight,' he seemed to wander off into his own imagination for a moment, his face broke into a smile, then a splash of sea spray brought him back to reality, 'They're quick see, and vicious, oh yes,' he winked.

'Why aren't they with us now?'

'Well, we left in spring see, been gone quite a while we have.'

Robert scowled, 'Spring?'

Ragnar looked at him, trying to fathom the question that he was asking, 'Yes spring, a time for growth, new lambs, birthing's and what not. You know woman's magic. We're better out of the way.'

Robert considered this with a nod.

'You look unsure to my answer boy?'

'Well where I come everything is shared, we don't have women's work, though my Mum does do most of the cooking. And cleaning,' Robert thought about this for a moment.

Now it was Ragnar's turn to look confounded, 'Woman are good at somethings and men are good at other things, that's a bit sweeping and we all muck in when we're about. It's not like one thing is better is than the other, it's all essential to the survival of the tribe.'

Robert nodded, in a ponderous manner, mulling over what had just been said.

Ragnar stooped down, 'It's like a sword, it has to be strong, but needs to be flexible, it has to keep its cutting edge and not go dull quickly, and it has two edges – but it's all part of the same sword. Yes? Any of those attributes are missing, the sword is useless. So it is with us. I talk to the Gods, Thunor is blessed in battle, Smvor with the forge. Villi's daughter makes mead that would knock a horse out, but by the Gods it's good stuff. Why would you have people doing stuff they are not good at, it weakens us all. That's why we normally bring the woman with us, they're quick and they scare the hell out of anyone who crosses us.. hehehe.'

Ragnar shook his head as he spoke, sea spray glistening on his silver hair.

Robert smiled. Ragnar tousled his hair and hobbled off up the centre of the boat towards where Thunor was sat.

Robert thought about the fact that people didn't sit around campfires anymore, nor did they know the names of their kin from 3 generations ago, let alone their deeds. It made him very sad.

Chapter 31

The sun was a dull orb; in the mist you could clearly see the roundness of its shape, grey yellow and lacklustre. Many of the men refused to move, muttering things about Old One Eye being abroad, Odin himself stalking the lands. Only Ragnar stood, proud, knowing, he had foreseen this the night before, when with eyes half closed he had had the sight. He looked over the side of the ship to the near horizon, arms folded, chin thrust forward, eyes daring the world. The only noise was the slow slide of Villi sharpening his axe, the rest of the men, including Thunor eyed the shoreline warily.

They had spent the night anchored in the middle of a wide, slow moving river, talking quietly amongst themselves, twice the number on watch as normal. This was the land of the Picts, the painted warriors, wild men of the north, who could swim through the dark unheard and slit your throat before you even knew they'd been. But none had come. Instead a dull morning had slowly pushed the night back, light bleeding through the fog, until at last the sun bleary eyed, pushed its way into the sky.

Thunor looked around at his men, then spoke in a loud voice to Ragnar, such that all could hear, 'You seem unperturbed by the omens Ragnar?'

'Why should I be perturbed, our Fates are woven. Beside the Grim Lord himself accompanies us, these are not his lands, they have their own Gods here, yet it is Odin's baleful glare which watches over us.'

This was said in a kind of sing song lilt, and some of the men appeared to relax a little, the whole conversation had just taken place to that effect. Robert nodded gently to himself, realising the magic in this.

Ragnar then added, 'We should move, slowly, we are not far from the place.'

Villi looked at Thunor who nodded and the men clambered down to their seats, oars where unhitched and then in perfect unison they began rowing; the noise of oars slashing water, now replacing the sharpening of axe.

After what seemed like ages, Ragnar pointed to the shore on their left, Robert could make out a large standing stone on the bank; it was thin and could only be described as gnarly, below it almost on the water line, a cave burrowed into the earth.

The boat was moored next to the bank, brightly painted shields slung over the side. Villi jumped down, then Thunor, Ragnar and followed by Robert who kind of fell, threw himself at Villi and hoped he caught him.

Robert was glad to be off the water and on dry land, it seemed considerably warmer on the bank than in the middle of the river.

After a short walk pushing through some particularly dense ferns, they were at a cave entrance. Clear water ran out across bright sand and then tumbled into the dark water of the river. They stepped into this stream, Robert was shocked into a sharp intake of breath at how cold it was, even though the water barely covered his feet.

Slowly they edged up the dark tunnel, leaving the glare of daylight behind, Robert's feet stung with the cold. The tunnel had a curious tangy smell, sharp and musty at the same time.

'Perhaps a torch would have been useful?' muttered Thunor.

Ragnar waved his hand for him to be quiet.

The tunnel bent slightly and up ahead there appeared to be a gentle light. And then the tunnel opened into a chamber.

It was a perfect circle made of sand coloured stone. In the middle, water bubbled out of a crack in the rock floor and became the stream, which they had just walked up. Robert immediately forgot his cold wet feet. In a semi-circle against the back wall, each in its own niche was a severed head, seven in total.

Their skin was taut, pulled tight over the face, black hair hung limp and bedraggled, all their eyes were rolled back just the whites showing, mouths hung open. They all had blue swirls tattooed on their faces, and what looked like horses or dragons. The one in the middle had a simple gold band around its head, its hair tied back in a knot. In features they all looked to be near identical, as if they had belonged to the same person, or perhaps brothers.

'Where's the light coming from?' asked Villi, which was unusual, Villi just normally accepted what was before him without question but there was a background ambient light but no obvious source.

'Shhhh!' replied Ragnar

Then the was a 'slop' noise and as one all the eyes on all the seven heads rolled forwards, the whites replaced by pale blue piercing stares, the heads bobbed as jaws moved. And then a snap as their mouths slammed shut, heads bobbing forward on the suddenly closing jaw. Robert physically jumped back.

'Speak!?' they all chimed.

The noise echoed around the chamber.

Robert stepped behind Villi, who put a protective arm across him, the other hand already had his axe ready.

'Speak your question,' they bellowed in unison.

Ragnar said 'Err,' which was unusual for him.

The heads spoke again, 'Speak, speak your question, you may ask one of us, one question and we will speak the truth.'

The jaws stopped, the heads lolled forward slightly but their eyes remained focused on the source of water in the middle of the chamber.

Ragnar paced sideways a little, watching intently, but the eyes did not follow him.

He then walked backwards to the chamber entrance, waving his hands that the others should do the same.

Back on the river bank, Robert blinking in the bright light could see the rest of the men on the boat craning over the side to see what was going on, he shrugged his shoulders at them in what he hoped was a helpful and communicative way.

Ragnar scratched his head, and his beard, then held his chin with one hand and peered down the river, eyes not really focused on anything.

From out of the tunnel came the unmistakable sound of people trying not to laugh, or at least not to laugh loudly.

Ragnar glared into the dark hole, then crept forward,

the others followed. As they got nearer they heard a voice say, 'Did you see the look on his face, Speak!... Ppffffttt, I thought he was going to wet himself!'

There was lots of sniggering. Then Ragnar jumped rather nimbly into the chamber, the laughing stopped instantly and there was that horrible slopping noise of eyeballs rolling back in heads.

Ragnar peered at them.

Chapter 32

One eye belonging to the head on the left, slowly rolled forward, looked around, saw that Robert was looking at it then rolled back so that only the whites were showing and tried to pretend that nothing had just happened.

Ragnar stalked backwards and forwards, bristling with indignation.

'Do you know who I am, I am Ragnar, Shaman, and this is a World Walker (pointing at Robert with a vibrating finger) and I would have you do my bidding before I bring great doom upon your house!'

One of the heads said, ''Nooo nooo no noo ni nam, ni nam nagnaa, naman.'

The room was full of hysterical laughter, the heads rocking and bobbing backwards and forward, fourteen eyes crying.

Then it stopped, very suddenly and the one in the middle with gold band, said, 'No, seriously, what do you want?'

Ragnar paused, thinking and then just said, 'The jar.'

A perplexed look passed backwards and forwards amongst the heads, they even managed to move a little sideways so they could see each other and then the middle head said, 'Jar?'

'Yes you know, THE jar?'

'No, I've no idea what you are talking about.'

Ragnar lowered his voice to a kind of stage whisper, 'The jar of the last breath!'

'Oh,' said all the heads together.

Then the middle one, 'Never heard of it. Now if you don't mind we've got important business to discuss. Off you pop.'

'What can seven heads stuck in this room have to discuss?'

'That's for us to know and you to bugger off.'

'Don't make me get angry!'

'Nont nake ne net nangry, pfft, what you going to do, sprinkle us with some Elf dust?'

'No, but I could take you outside and throw you in the river, one at a time.'

The head's jaws snapped shut with a crack of teeth, 'Bring it on stumpy, I'll take some fingers with me, besides don't you think that's been done before.'

One of the other heads joined in, 'Yeah, last one that tried that bled to death.'

'You can't bleed to death from a lost finger,' sneered Ragnar.

'No, but when he was bent down trying to pick his fingers up, he fell over, smacked his head on the floor. Then bled to death.'

'Yeahhh!' said one of the others in a menacing tone.

Ragnar pulled a face still not believing.

'Stabbing him repeatedly in the face helped as well,' one leered trying to be menacing.

'How did you manage to stab him?'

'I jumped him, pulled his dagger out with me teeth, then jumped him some more. Don't make me do the same to you.'

'Yeahhhh...!' said all the heads at once. 'When you've been stuck in here as long as we have you got time to sharpen your skills see.'

'Oh,' was about all Ragnar could say. Robert had never seen him lost for words before.

There was a pause whilst Ragnar pondered, lips

pinched together. The heads all swivelling and nodding, looking at each other, as if in the hope they could egg each other's bravado on.

'Look we may have got off on the wrong foot,' Ragnar said.

'Oh that's easy for you to say, you come in here ranting and raving, then mock us for being temporarily separate from the rest of us and us not having any feets!'

'Where are your bodies?' Robert interrupted, peering from around Villi.

'Why?' was the very suspicious reply from the head with the gold band.

'Erm, no reason, just curious.'

'Hmm. So you're the World Walker are you?'

'Erm'.

'Heard a lot about you,'

'How?'

'You know, here and there,' the head sniffed.

'So what did happen to your bodies?' asked Robert.

The head with the gold band fixed him with a stare, 'You're standing on them, they was thrown down the well.'

'Oh, sorry,' said Robert.

'S'ok, was a long time ago, besides which, probably best thing that ever happened to us. It was an amazingly freeing experience. Then some blooming bad tempered Shaman melted the rock over them and cast a spell on us, causing us to be trapped here for eternity.'

All the heads sighed and looked wistfully into the middle distance and then glared at Ragnar.

The one with the gold headband said, 'So Mr Shaman, what did you want again?' with more than a hint of sarcasm.

A few of the others joined in with mutterings of 'Yeah, shaman'.

'The boy has seen the jar,' Ragnar announced.

'We know. We're an Oracle, it's kind of what we do.'

Ragnar continued only a little bit deflated, 'And I'd like to know where the jar is now?'

'Would you?'

'Yes.'

'And is that your question?

'Yes.'

'And which one of us are you asking?'

Ragnar looked up and down the line of heads, then said, 'You're all one, your kindred in flesh and in spirit, it doesn't matter which one of you I ask, you're each one and the same!'

The heads nodded, looking at each other, up and down the line, clearly impressed.

'Nice answer, very good. But no. We don't make the rules. You know how this goes. This is a magical item of great power, why should we just hand it over to you when all the others who have come looking for it failed.'

'What happens if we fail?'

'I think you'll find it's when boy? And the last one, well let's just say he was very tasty,' the head that had spoken grinned maniacally and winked. Then one of the others snapped his teeth together for effect and made 'mmmmm' noises.

'You have one question. And if we get it wrong then you will forfeit something. The boy.'

'The boy?'

'Yes.'

Robert felt the floor fall away, his stomach somersaulted.

'No!' Bellowed Ragnar, 'That is not happening.'

The boy felt like he'd stumbled but despite his sensations, he hadn't moved.

Ragnar scowled at the heads, glared at them under his brow ridges, 'You will not even begin to suggest such a bargain. I have not travelled the length and breadth of the world, sailed every ocean of this world, to banter words with you fools.'

The atmosphere changed, it had been menacing then jovial and now the pendulum had swung back to downright frightening; all the light seemed to suck out of the chamber, the whole world focused down onto one head in the middle, the gold band glinted in the dark.

The voice was low and deep with fury, 'Do not come into our House Ragnar son of whoever, and tell us what the rules are. We were here long before you were even a twinkle in your Father's eye. And we will be here long since you wain. We are as old the hills, as old as the bones of the earth.'

Ragnar bowed, 'I apologise, I forget myself in my old age and my excitement.'

Robert actually took a step back, he'd never seen Ragnar so conciliatory, then he realised he was holding his breath, and let out a gasp.

The head in the centre turned and looked at the boy, the light bled back into the chamber.

'Step forward boy.' The voice commanded.

Robert hesitated.

'Come one we won't bite,' and snapped its teeth together with a grin.

Robert pushed his face forward and took a step.

The head broke into a smile, 'Fire in this one eh?'

'You have no idea,' muttered Ragnar.

'Ah yes the Djinn, an old trick. A good one,' replied the head with a grin.

It continued, 'You have the coin?'

Ragnar thought, then said, 'What of it?'

'I'll trade you the coin for the location of the jar.'

Ragnar looked over his shoulder at Thunor who was scowling in a 'don't you dare' kind of way.

'We went through a lot for that coin' said Ragnar.

The head simply nodded, then said, 'Anything of value has to be struggled for.'

Ragnar felt around in the hem of his cloak, and pulled out the coin, flashed it in his fingers.

He examined the coin closely as if teasing, 'What's this to you?'

'We are a well, and people throw coins down wells, it's a tradition that always pleased us.'

Ragnar nodded slowly, inside he was checking all the angles and trying to find the trick.

The head swivelled a bit and looked at Robert, 'You boy, take the coin off the old man and place it where the water comes out of the ground. And as you let it go make a wish, but make it a good one, for our magic is strong.'

Ragnar lifted the coin out of Robert's reach and turned to look at the heads, 'The location of the jar is not the wish,' he emphasised.

'No, give the coin to the boy and we will tell you the location of the jar Ragnar son of Ragnar, the wish is extra, we're feeling generous today, besides, it's the person who drops the coin that gets the wish, we're making a business transaction with you Ragnar.'

Ragnar's eyes narrowed and slowly he handed the coin to Robert who gripped it lest it fly away.

Robert could feel Thunor vibrating, bursting to say something but he held his tongue. The water was still freezing cold, Robert let out an almost joyful gasp as the sensations ran up his leg. For the first time he saw all the colours in chamber; the silver sheen to the water, the reds, browns, yellow and orange smudges in the rock, which now he realised were some kind of drawings, symbols and men with spears throwing them at lumbering beasts under a great sun. He could feel everyone's eyes on him as he closed his and made a wish, his lips almost moved as he thought the words. The world held its breath, the only noise the sound of the water gurgling and splashing as it made its way from earth to sea.

Robert opened his eyes and placed the small gold coin in the head of the water fountain that burbled from the rock, a coin so beautiful and shiny he didn't think he would ever see the like again. He looked around the room at everyone whose eyes were fixed on the coin, he looked down and let go, his fingers now nearly numb he clenched his fist. The golden disk bobbed and span slowly on the silver water, then slowly sank down the shimmering column, before disappearing into the black crack in the floor from where the fountain came.

'Tis done,' said the head, with a nearly smile on its face, then it turned to Ragnar, 'The jar, is south of here.'

'South?' Ragnar was clearly surprised by this.
'Yes south, sail for Ellan Vannin.'

Ragnar looked at the others; Thunor spoke, 'My cousin lives there, we will get a warm welcome.'

The head continued, 'Then sail east for the coast of Briton and until you come to a large bay, with 5 rivers emptying into it.'

'I know this place also, there is a roman castle to the south of the bay on the largest river and a large building to the new god. We stole their gold once, when I was out 'fishing' with my Father.' He added with a chuckle.

'Then you may also know on the coast not far from this castle, there are two churches to the new white god, one on the cliff tops, one in a hollow beneath.'

Ragnar nodded, 'Aye, I know this place, there's a stone there, called the Druid's stone and some mounds where their ancestors lay.'

'In the cliffs, between those two buildings lies a secret cave, inside is the jar.'

'I have been there as a boy!' gasped Thunor, ''They made for poor foe and poor pickings. It was there all along?'

'Yes' whispered the head, 'things go full circle Thunor. Where there were poor pickings lies one of the greatest of treasures. Ironic eh?' And then added, 'your Father is well Thunor, he drinks in the Great Hall.'

Thunor bowed slightly at this and the head nodded with a wink.

Ragnar spoke quietly, 'Why there, why? The stories say that it belonged to the Picts?'

'It did, and we let that story lie, but then a would be King came, with his band of warriors and his mage, Myrddin Emrys. In battle none could stand against them, Myrddin knew all the tricks all the secrets; he could turn his King into a bear, a mad, ferocious bear, with swords instead of claws and an armoured hide. They slaughtered all who stood against them, Saxon, Pict, Briton; purged the whole west coast from the southern seas to the northern ocean. They stole the jar and took it back south with them.'

'How did it end up there though?' asked Thunor.

'Greed, lust, men fall asleep; even magicians can be fooled by a pretty face. It was stolen by the followers of the white god, after they had put the King and his followers into a sleep for eternity. And they buried it. They took it to a place of ancient magic, soured the land with salt and blood of their new god; grew two of their houses to contain the magic. And hoped that the world forgot; some did, most did, even more will. Only a snippet, a refrain, a story told to frighten children will remain. They will not cease till the old ways are gone.'

The three men looked at each other, 'So, we go there then?' asked Villi.

'Aye.'

Ragnar bowed to the heads, the other men nodded, Robert kind of did something in the middle and they left the dark chamber for a bright and breezy mid-afternoon sun. Robert could feel the silence of fourteen eyes staring at him as they left.

'Don't worry,' said Ragnar, as they blinked their way through the ferns back towards the boat, 'We wanted what was on the coin, not the coin itself, and what was on the coin, is now in here (tapping his head). So you'd better keep me sweet,' He giggled and cackled to himself, Thunor just nodded and grunted.

Chapter 33

Ships in every direction, all the same, all with dragon prows of different designs scudded over the waves north, south, east and west. Robert was amazed, some of them came so close to each other, heading for the island with splash and spray, the thrumming of ropes and the whip-crack of sail against the wind. Jokes and banter were bellowed to those boats near enough, abuse hurled with smiles and laughter. Robert stood near the prow, wind pulling at him, salt in his face and still the underlying sweet smell of the wood of the boat. Despite the apparent speed of the boat the island seemed to only inch closer. And in every boat that came along side someone knew someone on it.

Eventually the town came into view, wooden piers full of people, sacks and barrels, people shouting at each other. And the smell; it was a different smell to the town in the south, Robert guessed the lack of heat, but it stilled made him gag and wrinkle his nose. The oars came out, the sail was pulled down and stored and slowly they came to a halt and the boat was roped to the side. Robert tried hard to disguise his disgust, even came close to being sick as he jumped onto the quay. A nearby seagull screamed at him from a wooden post then flapped lazily over the town into a sky full of other screaming birds and smoke from hundreds of chimneys.

It was a maelstrom of activity, hammering, banging, sawing, shouting, Thunor, Ragnar, Villi, Robert and a couple of the others walked up the hill towards a large hall, it was slow going, everyone had something to say to them, everyone seemed like long lost friends. Near the top of the hills some very serious looking men in chain-mail that looked like it was made from fish scales stopped them, 'Thunor, long time, how goes it?'

'Well, my friend,' they gripped each other and briefly embraced, 'Is he in?'

'Aye, go up,' the Guard turned to a dirty, scruffy looking child, crouched nearby, 'Boy!' the guard yelled, 'Run ahead and tell Sigurd that his cousin is here!'

The boy sprinted away up towards the hall.

Sigurd was similar to Thunor, yet different, you could tell they were kin, but where Thunor was dark and brooding, Sigurd was all fire and bright red hair, red beard and bright blue eyes.

'Thunor, you son of a dog!?' he bellowed, arms wide as he lumbered out of the dark doorway, 'Why did you not send word, I would have had a feast worthy of my kin!'

'We are just passing cousin.'

The two men hugged and slapped each other on the back, Sigurd then said, 'Well you are most welcome, all are welcome in Sigurd's Hall, come we will burn much wood tonight, and drink much mead,'

As they got to the doorway, Sigurd paused put his hand on Thunor's shoulder and said, 'I heard about your Father, he had a good send off, his story will be told for many generations to come.'

'Thank you cousin, I err, ' Thunor just kind of shrugged and seemed a bit lost for words. Sigurd nodded, and then started shouting orders at people in the musty hall.

Soon the party were sat at a long table, the rest of the crew had joined them, drinking honey and eating a hot meat in front of a fire. All was well with the world as the men talked and laughed and boasted.

'So why you here cousin?'

'We've had poor pickings from the Picts.'

'Aye we've heard they've left, it's said they just got on their boats and sailed off, left, the whole of their lands are empty. Not that there's much there but blooming trolls and rain mind. But nobody knows where they went!?'

'Well, we head south, then around and back up the east coast, see what we can take from the Cymry and Saxons before heading home.'

'Aye, it's a good trade to be in at the moment, this new god of theirs is bringing much gold to his houses, and most of his followers have no sword arm, never practice and are always on their knees whining. I heard you'd been south, far to the south.'

Robert's ears pricked up at this, although it had been said in the flow of conversation and seemed to be just mentioned in passing, but there was a probing nature to it, Sigurd watched the party very carefully, but all faces remained impassive, except for Ragnar who winked at Robert when no one was looking.

Ragnar sat up, 'We went to see an old friend of mine, he'd found some books for me. Might be the last time I saw him, given his age, eh?' he added absentmindedly.

'Books! Bah, stories for children and old men!' barked Sigurd.

'Indeed,' was the only reply he got from Ragnar whose eyebrows wriggled like angry caterpillars, then he followed this by a loud slurp from his cup and proceed to fish something out of it and then inspect the end of his finger.

Sigurd was not sated at this and a ''Hmph' noise and a shrug was his response, Robert could see him looking, trying to find something to add but the conversation had stumbled to a halt. Sigurd forced the issue by standing up with unnecessary boisterousness, 'Your man there Villi, he's got some arms on him, how about a little wager, for an arm wrestle, eh? A gold piece says I can take you?'

Villi looked at Thunor who nodded and great cheer went up. The two men sat down at a small table and were immediately surrounded by the whole room, all shouting and pointing and spilling their drinks. Banter and betting followed. Robert hadn't moved, nor had Ragnar who looked at him and rolled his eyes. It had been a curious exchange that had come to feel uncomfortable, but to Robert's relief everyone was now shouting at the two men arm wrestling in the middle of the room.

From within the throng of people Robert could hear grunting and sharp exhales of breath, then the unmistakable roar of Villi, and a thud, followed by Sigurd roaring laughing. There were cheers from the crew and groans from the household. As the party separated back to various tables, Robert caught sight of a glinting gold coin being tossed from Sigurd to Villi who then nodded at each other.

Then night seemed to drag on, people told stories (with much audience participation), recited poetry and raised toasts, Robert had not really spoken nor had he been spoken to, he was full and warm and sleepy and being ignored. At some point he'd managed to fall asleep at the table despite the drunkenness around him. And the next thing he knew he was scratching at straw that was poking him. He found himself in a cot of sorts, stuffed with what he thought of as horse food and covered in a scratchy blanket that smelt funny. He nestled down, not really wanting to get up but then realised he could hear something scratching about in the straw beneath him. He sat bolt upright and clambered out, rooting through the straw he couldn't find anything so very nearly got back in, then decided a better option would be to sit at the table until someone he recognised appeared. Already some of Sigurd's hall were milling about poking fires and stirring pots.

Sometime later Ragnar slumped down next to him and slid a bowl of what might have been porridge across the table. Robert tried it. He couldn't decide whether it was awful or didn't really taste of anything, but it was warm and he was feeling cold.

'Still with us, eh boy?'

'Erm, yes.'

'Good,' Ragnar winked, 'thought you might have wondered off in the night?'

Robert shook his head, trying to swallow a mouthful of porridge.

'It's good stuff eh, sticks to the ribs.'

Robert laughed, 'that's what my Grandad says about things, mainly custard.'

'What's custard?'

'Erm it's kind of a sweet sauce, but it's bright yellow, I think it's made with bananas.

'What's a ban... never mind. Do you think I'll ever meet your Grandad?'

Robert stopped and thought hard and then just shrugged, it seemed an unfathomable question.

Ragnar nodded, then licked the bowl out.

Robert decided against licking the bowl and had left quite a thick coating of porridge in the bowl which he'd smeared around so the casual observer would think there wasn't much left, but a closer examination would reveal quite a bit... Robert didn't want to appear rude.

The rest of the men slowly roused themselves, most poured buckets of cold water over their heads and then shook themselves like a dog. Robert decided he didn't like that idea, it was bad enough getting a wash in warm water, let alone stuff from the nearest pond.

Later in the morning they ambled down through the town to the quay side, it was as busy as when they first arrived and smelled just as bad. Sigurd had arranged for some supplies to be brought down to the boat and Ragnar had shown one of Sigurd's wives a potion that when put under bandages help heal black toes and fingers after winter sailing.

And slowly the rest of men came back to the boat, some were happier than others, some richer and some poorer.

Sigurd and Thunor hugged each other and slapped backs, 'Come back again cousin, it was good to see you, kin is always welcome in Sigurd's Hall.'

'Aye, sorry to have surprised you, next time we'll send word, but it was a good night, your mead kicks like a horse!'

Sigurd roared laughing, but it was an infectious laugh, 'So, where are you going now?'

Ragnar looked out to sea, 'We'll head for the coast and follow it round and back up the other side, get home in time to help with the harvest. And see what gold we can't lighten on our way.'

Sigurd chuckled, and slapped Thunor on the back pushing him towards the quayside, 'The gods will be with you, give those whining, weak armed Christians a good thrashing, teach them some manliness, eh?'

As Robert hauled himself over the side, pushed by Villi and pulled by Ragnar he spoke in a quiet voice, 'Why does he want to know where we are going so much?'

Ragnar smirked, 'Well boy, we're a competitive bunch and he doesn't want to think we've got one over on him. The fact that he knows we've been so far south will have pricked his ears. He's half a mind we're on the trail of some treasure. Which we are, but we wouldn't tell him that. Otherwise we'd be mysteriously delayed whilst one of his own boats slips out,' Ragnar tapped the side of his nose conspiratorially. 'You've got to get up early to get one past us eh?'

Thunor and the rest of his men clambered aboard, ropes were cast off, and the air was filled once more with good natured abuse and name calling. Robert felt the now familiar motion in his tummy, the rise and fall of the ocean, and that smell, wood resin and lord knows what.

Chapter 34

The bay was wide and flat, to the north, mountains
tumbled down to the sea, to the south, low scrubland
with low, dark hills beyond. The boat followed a deep
channel that meandered through the mud and sand
until they came to a suitable place, most of the men
jumped a shore into thick wet sand that made a
splash noise as they landed. The other three stayed
behind. Everyone was in full battle gear, sword,
spears and axes gleaming and shields bright. Robert's
heart thumped in his chest to see such a sight. The
first group scattered to the line of coarse grass that
marked the water line. Villi carried Robert over his
shoulder and then dumped him unceremoniously on
his butt, scanning the tree line and horizon for
danger. There was nothing, only the noise of the wind
in tussocks of grass, the buzz and rustle of insects and
the distant cry of estuary birds.

Once satisfied that there was no immediate threat,
Thunor spoke to them, 'So either we meet some
peasant fishermen and they run off, or we meet some
Saxons who will be camped at that fort up the river
but could be wandering, keep your senses sharp,
we're heading for those cliffs,' and he pointed across
the inlet to a rocky outcrop that tumbled down to the
sea, it was about 40 foot high in places, and ran the
coastline ragged for maybe a mile.

At the far end small square building could be just seen with perhaps a tower.

One of the men turned, 'they're not really cliffs, as cliffs go, is this the right place?'

'Aye it is, there's two Christian houses here, and I remember seeing a doorway that went nowhere.'

Some of the men nodded at this, Robert just frowned but thought better of asking.

The men walked in full armour and weapons without so much as a single complaint. Robert had found it hard going, although there were no hills, it seemed to be a never ending landscape of rabbit holes and lumps of grass over which he stumbled constantly.

'Always get up, that's the secret little fish,' said Villi who handed him a leather pouch in with some water, 'Take only a sip, we don't know where the fresh water comes from here, seems to be salt marshes in every direction.' Even whilst Robert took his sip, Villi's eyes cast around for danger.

Robert nodded and wiped his mouth with the back of his sleeve, handing the pouch bag back, Villi fastened it on his belt.

Soon they could see smoke rising from somewhere beyond the headland, they hadn't seen another soul yet, only birds and bird song to keep them company.

Much of it the sad baleful wailing of estuary birds, this was seen as a bad omen amongst the men. Robert could see them muttering to each other, always out of earshot but he could feel an atmosphere developing.

They skirted along the edge of an ancient wood; to their left was a wide flat beach, bright with large stones, which gradually got smaller until the wet sand gleamed all the way to a grey sea. On the horizon, distant hills scattered under white clouds.

When they found a track through the grass on the edge of a wood, Thunor raised a fist and the line of men squatted down onto one knee, one hand on swords and axes. He flashed his fingers and two of the group peeled off, one right, one left and scurried forward, keeping as low as possible before throwing themselves down behind some cover. They lay there for what seemed like an age, perhaps longer, Robert was bored and fidgety and was getting eaten by midges, the smell of the sea mixing with damp wood and leaf mould. There was no conversation, just birds, bees and other insects flitting about. The square building could be made out quite clearly from here, it must have been visible from anywhere in the bay. Robert could smell some kind of wild flower but didn't know what it was, lavender maybe?

Robert seemed to spend the whole time there scratching, itching and rubbing to the point of wanting to run across the beach and into the sea just to make the irritations stop.

Finally the signal to move, ever so quietly the men moved, senses keen for any movement, Thunor drew his sword, Robert gulped hard as the rest of men followed this unspoken command.

The church was quite visible now, but the path they walked on dipped behind some burial mounds which we covered in tiny white and purple flowers. Thunor had stopped and was muttering something, then he waved his hands about and stopped, he walked over to a single standing stone, it was about 4 foot high and looked like it had been recently beaten, bright gouges in the stone and about it a fire had been set with signs of digging about its base.

Most of the men made warding signs with their hands at the sight, Ragnar turned to Robert, resting his hand on the stone, 'What have they done? Is this how they drive the old gods out, the Elves, the wild wood; with fire and axe?'

He looked like he was about to cry, Robert felt himself go red, and simply nodded.

Ragnar turned away, wiped his face and walked towards the others.

Below the church a cluster of dishevelled mud round houses appeared which clung to the edge of the beach, on the sand some crude nets, and a couple of round boats. Robert had never seen boats like this; they looked like tea cups without the handle. And the place stank of rotting fish and sewage and dead seaweed.

There seemed to be nobody home; fires still had some flames in them, and some baking pots with might have been food, were still warm, but there were no people. Each hut was checked by two men, all returned shaking their heads.

Thunor half closed his eyes, and muttered to himself, 'Have they just run off waiting till we've gone, or have they gone for help?'

'We'll find out soon enough,' replied Ragnar, 'Come on, this way.'

They followed a well-trodden path into a cluster of trees and found themselves looking at a small stone building, with a sturdy wooden door, it was nestled in a hollow below and between the chapel on the cliff tops and the village; surrounded by wild flowers and at the back some boxes with bees bumbling in and out looked out over the sea to a long coastline curving north. To one side of the clearing was a stone cross, delicately carved with scenes and figures, Robert walked over to it and marvelled, tracing his fingers along the stonework, the rest of the men gave it a wide berth.

Ragnar appeared at his shoulder, 'Do you know the stories they tell?'

'Some of them I think,'

'Where you come from are our Gods still worshipped?'

'Some still, not many though. Though they still have a strong influence, the days of the week are named after them and a lot of our stories are based on your stories, Tuesday for Tyrs Day, Wednesday is Woden's Day, Thursday...,'

This seemed to please Ragnar immensely.

'But a lot have no God.'

'No Gods?!' Ragnar seemed genuinely shocked by this, 'Truly how can that be?'

Robert shrugged, 'I don't know,' shook his head and walked off, Ragnar stood and watched the small boy walk through the wildflowers, then seemed to wake as if from a dream and followed him.

Villi and three others went to the building, Villi tested the door, it was locked so he kicked it, there was a loud crash and splintering noise as the wood burst and the other two men rushed in... then silence. Still no other people. Robert didn't get chance to look inside the building.

'Well they said it was between the two, which I make is this way,' muttered Ragnar and hobbled off. Robert followed him. Hidden behind some holly trees, was a stone archway, a doorway, but there was no wall for it to be in, it was free standing, two uprights and a lintel. Thunor was already stood in front of it, one hand on his chin as if in thought, 'I remember it being bigger, and less holly,' he said.

Ragnar walked slowly up to it and dug into his pouch, then tossed some dust into the air.

The air around the doorway shimmered and pinpoints of light twinkled in the air. Then nothing happened for a long time, except for Ragnar glaring at the portal.

'Someone find me a stick,' he said.

Considering they were surrounded by trees this proved harder than you might think; you can never find a stick when you need one. Several were examined then tossed away, till one of the men found one that was not too long, not heavy, just right in fact. He handed it gingerly to Ragnar who snatched it and then tossed at the doorway. It did not come out the other side. There were several, strange unmanly like noises, and most of the men took a very slow and almost imperceptible step back.

Thunor walked around, everyone could seem him, slowly he bent down, found a small stone and threw it towards Ragnar, it never made it, the stone just winked out of existence.

'Strange magic is this,' whispered Ragnar.

Robert could feel the tension rising in the men, as if something was about to burst.

Ragnar looked up and sighed, 'Well come on, spit it out one of you, you've been muttering since we left this ship, say what needs to be said.'

There was a pause then one of the men said, 'The thing is, we've been thinking,'

Ragnar raised an eyebrow at this, opened his mouth to reply but then just nodded for him to continue.

'There's not a man who doesn't respect your decisions, but the thing is, we don't want to live for ever, we want to go to Valhalla and be with our forefathers, swapping stores, eating and drinking and fighting, I mean that's as good as it gets.'

One of the other men added, '...and the Valkyries, don't forget the Valkyries,'

There was a general muttering of agreement, especially on this last point.

Ragnar put his hands on his hips and pushed his lips forward, he looked over at Thunor, who half nodded and shrugged in agreement.

There was a long silent pause. The tensions was shattered by the sound of a man running towards them in full battle gear, they all turned as one, weapons ready, but he was one of them. The sweat poured off him, he was completely out of breath, bent over double panting, vaguely pointing behind him and gasped 'Horses'.

Chapter 35

'Shield wall!' bellowed Thunor.

The men had lined up in an instant, shields locked together, swords and axes at the ready. Thunor was in the middle, Villi on the far left hand side. Ragnar grabbed Robert by the shoulder and stood behind the line, then he pulled a small evil looking sword and a large knife from the recesses of his cloak and stood waiting. Robert suddenly found that his arms and legs were shaking, he clamped his sweaty hands under his armpits, folding his arms tight across his chest. Ragnar squeezed his shoulder slightly but did not look at him, instead his eyes squeezed together and scanned ahead. Robert thought about drawing his own sword, but fear got the better of him and he stood rooted to the spot.

Men on horses appeared at the entrance to the church, there was about a dozen of them, in long mail coats and strange looking helmets. One of them had gold edging to his armour, clearly their leader. And there was a priest with a long staff which ended in a crucifix.

One of the Vikings let out a growling roar and all the men banged their weapons on the shields three times. Robert felt his bladder spasm, then something unexpected happened. The leader of the Saxons slowly slid off his horse, took a few steps forward, carefully took his sword from its scabbard and laid it on the ground. Then the Priest got off his horse and stood next to him.

There was a pause, then Thunor extricated himself from the shield wall and took a step forward, 'Ragnar?' he said.

'Wait here boy,' said Ragnar as he walked around the shield wall, as he passed Villi he said in a not very quiet stage whisper, 'This could be a trap, keep your wits'.

Robert edged forward into the gap that Thunor had left and pushed his head between the men, scraping his ears on their armour.

Thunor laid his sword and shield on the ground, carefully such that everything was in easy reach if need be.

The Saxon spoke first, 'I am Aeldric and this is Godwulf,' the Priest nodded slightly.

Ragnor had managed to conceal his weapons back about his person as he hobbled up to Thunor's side, he pointed at the Priest wagging is finger, 'You, lay down your staff Priest.'

Godwulf looked at Aeldric who paused then spoke with a really strong, strange accent. The Priest appeared either not to understand or not wish to comply. Aeldric repeated this time more forcefully, and the Priest, with obvious protest laid the staff down.

'And you are?'

'Thunor son of Ealric, son of Eolric and Ragnar son of Ragnar, son of Odin!' growled the chief with a flick of his head.

There was an uneasy silence that Aeldric seemed eager to fill, 'And what is it you want, there is no treasure here, as I am sure you will have seen,' peering over the Vikings to the shattered church door.

Thunor ignored the question, 'How you come you know our language?' his eyes narrowed as he spoke.

'I was in the north as a child, with my uncle, his Earl had men as guards who spoke your tongue.'

'And your priest, how come he speaks as us?'

'You ask a lot of questions for someone who has desecrated the house of god and is backed into a corner,' hissed the Priest, though he mangled the words a bit.

'There is no house of gods, these are just a ruse to rob the poor and stupid,' interrupted Ragnar, 'and if you think we're backed into a corner, come and get us...'

Aeldric raised his hands and waved them vaguely in what he hoped was a calming motion.

Thunor growled, 'If you were so sure of the odds you would not be talking, I suspect your Uncle told you a tale or two about how we men of the north fight our battles.'

The Saxon looked a bit fidgety and uncomfortable with how the conversation was going.

Thunor scowled, 'And I think you are delaying for some reason,' his eyes flickered around the trees that covered the low cliffs about them, 'Perhaps you wait for reinforcements from the fort up the river?'

The Saxon's eyes widened at this and he struggled to bring his face back under control.

'I know more of these lands than you might think, I know where you live, where you sleep, where the best places are for an ambush; tell you what we will do, we'll go back to our boat and we'll wait for you there, eh, or maybe we'll head up the coast a little, come back in at night time and take your heads whilst you sleep, like the Picts.'

The Saxon's head bobbed back and then cast a quick glance over his shoulder, Thunor used this moment to bend down pick up his sword and shield, and turn his back on the Saxons in a I don't care about you at all way, he winked at Robert. Aeldric looked furious. But not as furious as the Priest.

'Come on lads back to the boat.'

The shield wall dissolved, the men turned and walked towards the headland via the muddy beach. Robert spotted a few of them pulling tongues or going cross eyed at Aeldric and the Priest, not to mention a couple of other gestures Robert wasn't so sure about but didn't like to ask.

'Nice touch that, turning your back on him,' shouted Ragnar as they scuttled across the sand, That really upset him, haha.'

Thunor had a face like thunder, 'Keep your eyes peeled for the buggers, that had all the markings of a trap. Watch for archers.' was all he replied.

'We could have had them,' said one of the men.

'Aye, but I like to know who I'm fighting and on ground of my choosing, not a bloody tree lined ridge behind us and he was stalling for some reason.'

By the time they'd reached the headland and the boat was in view, the tide was coming in, the men was pushing through ankle deep water and the half moon bay opened before them; white stones, dead seaweed and muddy sand.

'Now what?' asked Robert.

'Now we push the boat out a couple of lengths and have a think.'

The priest used the end of his robe to wipe the dust of his staff, 'They have desecrated the house of god and you do nothing,' he hissed, 'The bishop will hear about this.'

Aeldric was still watching the band of Vikings plod over the wet sand, 'Well the bishop can come down here and give them a stern talking to if he wants,' he looked at the Priest who remained silent.

'No, I thought not. And whilst you're at it, you could ask him about the merits of building two churches next to each other, to protect a secret location? You may as well put a huge banner up for the whole horizon to see, 'Treasure here'... because that's what these boys do, hunt for treasure.'

Godwulf was furious, shaking with rage but remained silent.

Aeldric picked up his weapon, and mounted his horse, pointed at one of the men, 'Go find the archers, tell them to come find us at the edge of the bay but keep out of sight, we'll keep a watchful distance for now.'

Godwulf turned, and snapped 'And what about me?'

Aeldric looked at the tall, skinny, belligerent man, 'Well, you can join us priest or you can head back to the fort, the choice is yours,' and turned not waiting for an answer.

'But I must have some men to escort me back to the castle.'

'Your god will be with you, isn't that enough? It's what you're always telling us. Besides I've got a war band armed to the teeth just over there, I am not sparing any men to walk you back to the castle.'

Aeldric smiled as he heard Godwulf rap his staff on the ground in anger but he kept the glee to himself and his horse as they slowly sauntered towards the woods on the ridge.

Chapter 36

The boat lifted and lolled again on the gentle roll of the tide. Robert sat on his barrel out of the way, the men half-heartedly pretended to do various tasks about the boat but in reality where either muttering to each other or watching Ragnar and Thunor at the prow, sitting by the dragon head talking intently, the pair of them kept casting glances towards the distant trees. Ragnar reached into a pouch and threw some small stones onto the floor, he paused, then scooped them up and the conversation continued.

Back at the fort, it was cold and damp, as it always was; flaming torches coughed and spluttered in the draughts around a long wooden table in the private rooms for the Bishop, about it sat two hunched figures, Godwulf and the Bishop, they gnawed noisily on animal bones. Barely visible in the gloom away from the table a servant stood waiting, not listening to the conversation.

'Do you think they know about the cup?' asked the Bishop.

Godwulf licked his fingers noisily before replying, 'I don't know, I don't know. That dolt Aeldric thinks they were just looking for treasure in the churches. But when we arrived, I'm sure they'd been looking at the doorway.'

'Perhaps they'd found it by chance?'

'Perhaps. But the pagans had their own stories about the cup.'

The Bishop snorted, 'Simpletons, we cannot let them get hold of the cup that touched our Saint Patrick's lips.'

'No, there is much protection there, we have killed the old magic, with salt and prayers and fire, but.... It could be coincidence.'

'I don't like coincidences, Godwulf.'

'Yes your Grace.'

Godwulf, nodded in agreement, but his eyes were focused on a candle in the middle of the table and he seemed lost in thought. He opened his mouth to speak, his head moved slightly to one side then he seemed to think better of it.

'Well, spit it out man' boomed the bishop and forced the issue with raised eyebrows and thrust of his head.

Godwulf's lips pinched together, then he said, rather too quickly for his own liking – 'Are we sure that this is The Cup, they have stories about a cup that's very similar to St Patrick's?'

He was cut off by a scowl from the Bishop, 'They are ignorant' he stressed each syllable for extra emphasis, 'My grandfather saw the miracles the cup performed, only a relic touched by a Saint, can have such power,' he paused, 'Or are you telling me you believe in heathen magic?'

Godwulf choked a little, ''No, no, no, no... that would be foolish.'

'Yes. And heresy' replied the Bishop gruffly without looking up from the roast chicken he was dismantling.

Godwulf nodded forcefully and gestured agreement with greasy fingers.

'Go down to the beach and watch how this unfolds and keep an eye on Aeldric, tell him I want them dealt with.' The Bishop looked up from his food and glared at him.

Godwulf thought about opening his mouth to speak again, pointing out that that was where the Vikings were, and there could be fighting and bloodshed and lots of, probably one sided violence, but instead dipped his fingers in a small bowl of water, wiped them on plain cloth, stood, bowed and strode from the table into the dark.

He rode out on a horse taken from the stables, skirted the old roman fort, that lay derelict, left to its ghosts and headed for the fishing village. As the crow flies it should not have taken that long, but he had to ford a river, skirt an inlet and then take the high ground around a marsh along the estuary so it was a couple of hours before he saw the two Saxon soldiers watching the road.

'Where is Aeldric?' he demanded.

The Soldiers paused, then one of them spoke lazily, 'In the wood, south of the chapels.'

Godwulf sniffed at the lack of respect and headed off in the general direction.

Once out of earshot, the other guard asked his companion, 'Do you think you should have told him to stay out of sight of the shore?'

'Probably,' came the reply. They both broke into a grin.

As Godwulf crested the mound by the chapel a gentle breeze from the sea buffeted him and sounded in his ears. Down the long grass bank towards the pale beach he rode his horse, upright and with purpose but in no rush. He squinted in the bright light and watched the wooden dragon slowly bob on the waves just off the shore of the long curved beach. The locals called this Half Moon Bay, a pagan nonsense.

There was the whistle of an arrow hurtling through the air that startled him from his reverie and the horse pulled up as the arrow thumped into the ground only a few feet from him. He looked to the tree line on his left where it had come from and he could see Aeldric stood motioning him to come to him with a wagging finger on the edge of the wood. He would tell the Bishop about this, how dare that impudent man.

'What do you think those idiots are up to?' rumbled Villi, resting his chin on folded arms on the bow.

'Dunno' was the illuminating reply from Ragnar, 'but I reckon old fella there is in for tongue lashing for giving their hiding place away.'

'But we knew they were there,'

'Aye, but they don't know that.'

The Priest rode up to the tree line was about to speak but before he could say anything Aeldric launched a tirade of abuse at him that even made some of his men blush, it was all about tactics, and strategy and subterfuge and spending less time on his knees and more time with a sword in his hand.

The Vikings couldn't understand a word of, as it was all in some strange language, but you could get the general idea given the tone, and frantic yelling that carried over the noise of the odd seagull.

Aeldric didn't wait for a response he stepped out of

the tree line, put his hands on his hips and glared at the boat.

'That Aeldric bloke is really annoyed with yon priest,' muttered Villi.

'Yep,' replied Ragnar.

Godwulf hissed through gritted teeth, 'The Bishop wants them stopped.'

'Aye, and as I told you before, the Bishop is more than welcome to come down and have a word with them,' he turned to face Godwulf, 'Or better still, you go down there, swim out to their boat, and see how many of them you can smite with your stick before they chop you up as sea bait. And not wishing to make this personal but my gold is on the boys in the boat.'

The Priest turned, twitched the reins and walked slowly down to the shore line.

As Godwulf started to move over the wet sand where the tide had moved out, Ragnar began muttering a strange slow chant, it became more and more frenetic until he loudly whispered something and seemed to flick the words with the fingers of his hand towards the beach.

A small wave pushed across the bit of sea to the beach like a mini tidal wave as if carrying the word.

The horse reared up and squealed, dumping Godwulf with an almighty splat in the wet mud.

The Vikings were impressed with their shaman, and then roared laughing as the horse shot away up the beach kicking wet mud all over its dismounted rider.

Alderic just stood, hands on hips and watched the Priest try and extricate himself from the mud, he could feel the tension rise to almost breaking point in his men hidden in the undergrowth; they really didn't like magic.

Finally on his feet, Godwulf roared abuse and called down God and his Angels and Christ himself to smash their boat. The men on the boat, again had no idea what he was saying but got the general idea.

'He's a fiery one that one ain't he, what's he saying?' asked Thunor.

'Got no idea, be all killing and an eternity in pain and stuff, that's what they normally shout about.'

'Odd for a religion that bangs on about love and mercy and forgiveness,'

'At least with Thor you know where you stand, upset him and bang, a wallop from Mjollnir.'

There was a general murmuring of agreement on the sound principle that foreign religions were crazy.

Robert coughed politely, 'I can tell you what he said. If you want?'

'You can?' asked Ragnar, eyebrows ruffling up his forehead.

'Yes, I can understand him.'

'Ragnar looked perplexed, 'How's that then?'

There was a long pause, Robert shrugged, 'Dunno really, just can.'

The Vikings accepted this like they accepted most things, with good humour and the view that it would all work out alright in the end.

'So what did he say?'

'God, his Angels and Jesus himself is going to sink the boat.'

'Oh..' Ragnar was completely unfazed by this, but some of the other crew looked a bit uncomfortable, it didn't do to go around upsetting other people's gods.

'What's an Angel?' asked one of the men, pronouncing the word like it didn't quite fit in his mouth.

Ragnar looked at Robert, who pulled a face, that

said…. Ermmmm… 'A sort of messenger I think.'

'So they come to tell you before they sink the boat?'

'No, I think they join in with the sinking as well.'

'Oh.'

'Why don't we shoot this messenger then their gods will think that the boats been sunk and he's just gone off with more messages?'

There was a look of that's a really stupid question, wait a minute there might be some merit in that, passed amongst the men.

Villi rumbled, 'You can't shoot messengers, who said that?'

'Not anybody I know' added Thunor who seemed to have grown bored with the conversation.

'What do you want?' he shouted at the Priest.

'What do you want?'

'Gold!'

'You would smash and desecrate the house of god for petty baubles?'

Thunor looked around at the crew, and shrugged his shoulders, like it was a dumb question to ask.

There was a pause.

Then Thunor replied, 'Yes. Why, do you have anything else?'

'No,' came the reply.

Thunor turned to the crew, 'Right lads, time to decide, do you want this bottle or not?'

The man shuffled and looked uncomfortable, they didn't like being asked their opinion by the chief, it was his job to make the decisions.

Thunor pressed them, 'Ok hands up who just wants to go home.'

Slowly all the hands went up.

Thunor looked at Ragnar who forced a smile and dropped his shoulders.

'Right then let's be having you then, let's sort this boat about.'

There was a flurry of activity and then a sail appeared with a gentle woofing noise and slowly the boat began to spin so it faced out of the bay.

'Where are you going?' shouted Godwulf who had been watching all this unfold from the shore.

Ragnar responded, 'Home, you have no gold for us to take!'

By this time Aeldric had walked down from the tree line and was stood little behind the Priest, arms folded and a little unbelieving that they were just going.

'Where's home?' asked the Priest.

'The North. All of It!' came the gleeful riposte. And with that, they were moving out to an ocean swell, the hiss of water, the thrum of ropes and the sting of salt their companions for the many days it would take to get home.

'What just happened?' asked Aeldric.

'I've got no idea. But the Bishop will be pleased.'

Godwulf turned and stepped from wet sand onto the line of small stones and seaweed, 'Would you be so good as to have one of your men bring my horse back?'

There was a flicker of a smirk around Aeldric's face, then he simply replied, 'Certainly Godwulf,' and he turned up the beach towards the tree line shouting orders.

Chapter 37

Coming out of the bay into the greater ocean, the sea was wild and mountainous; waves lashed at the boat pushed on by a howling wind. The men bellowed laughing, shouting good natured abuse at each other, their default method of companionship. Robert gave up sitting on the barrel and instead wedged himself up its side, trying to keep out of the way and the spray. As they rounded the headland, the world settled into fall and rise. Slowly Robert's eyes fluttered closed and he fell asleep.

In his dreams, he was neither one place nor the other, he saw his parents standing on the boat and Thunor on the bus when he was with his Grandad, he couldn't tell if he was dreaming or awake. Everywhere he looked, it's like both worlds where overlaid and merged at the same time. And then he fell into the deepest of sleeps, a dreamless sleep, where he truly was neither one place nor the other.

'Come on sleepy head, get up.'

Someone was shaking him.

'Urgh, where am I?' Robert muttered.

His Mum took a step back, her brow furrowed in a question, 'What do you mean, where are you? You're in bed! And now it's time to get up.'

'Why?' Robert pulled the duvet up.

'Because I say so,' snapped his Mum, 'Your Grandad's coming for Sunday dinner today, and I've got things to do.'

Robert wasn't sure why that meant he had to get up, but he knew better than to be on the end of his Mum's sharp tongue and scowl; it was going to be a long day.

'Wash yourself and clean your teeth before you get dressed,' she said as she scurried from the bedroom.

Robert lay there, all the images and thoughts, tastes, smells and textures whirled about his head, he could see Ragnar and Villi and Thunor and the others clear as can be if he closed his eyes, their smell and sound lingered with him. He shook his head, and swung his legs out of the bed. Maybe he should say something to his Dad. Or his Grandad. But then they'd tell his Mum and she'd tell him to act his age not his shoe size or grow up or something. He didn't see what all the fuss was about growing up, it looked boring from what he could see, they never seemed to have any fun.

Downstairs was cold and noisy. His Mum was banging around in the kitchen.

'Where's Dad?'

'He's gone to the supermarket. You could have gone and helped if you'd been up.'

Robert bit his bottom lip at the implied criticism, 'I'll help him bring the bags in,' he said. But he thought, 'He probably went to get away from you'. And then was shocked at what he'd just thought. He turned and headed for the living room to look out the window. Sitting staring out the window was infinitely better than sitting in the kitchen.

Across the road Mrs Winterbottom was gardening and Mr Winterbottom was washing their car. He watched them, old, slow, weary and wondered what stories they had to tell their children; or even if they had children. Everyone in the Viking village knew everyone else; they lived like one large family. He'd lived here all his life and he knew nothing about the people who lived across the road except for their name, and that was only because he'd heard his Mum and Dad mention it and it made him laugh.

He saw their car swing into the top of the road, there was a passenger. Dad had obviously stopped to get his Dad on the way. Robert grinned as he opened the door, gave them both a hug.

'Hello sleepy head,' said his Dad, ruffling Robert's hair.

'You're up?' said his Grandad with feigned surprise and a grin.

Robert rolled his eyes and stamped to the back of the car, reaching into collect the bags. Some of which were very heavy.

'Your mum been feeding you spinach?' asked Stan as Robert strained at carrying a particularly heavy carrier bag.

Robert had no idea what he was talking about, 'Why would she give me spinach?' he replied through gritted teeth.

It was Stan's turn to shake his head.

Robert almost made it to the kitchen before the bag split and vegetables tumbled all over the kitchen floor.

His mum tutted, 'Robert, be more careful!'

'The bag split, how is that my fault?'

'Well, if you want to eat food that's been kicked around the kitchen floor be my guest.'

He turned to look at his Dad who had come in behind and opened his mouth to say something, the anger building in him.

His Dad squeezed his shoulder, 'Go keep Grandad entertained.'

'It's a few potatoes Louise, hardly the end of the world,' he heard his Dad say as Robert walked up the hall, followed by his Mum huffing.

Robert stamped into the living room and plonked himself down on the sofa with some force.

'What's up kiddo?' without looking up from the TV magazine.

Robert shook his head, almost vibrating with anger, then just said 'Mum.'

Stan nodded wisely, and then said, 'There's a documentary on tonight about 1066.'

Robert replied quickly, 'That's well after my bedtime Grandad.'

Stan looked up for a moment, then roared laughing, tears rolling down his face. This cause Robert to start giggling and Brian came into see what the noise was about. Through fits of giggles Robert recounted what happened, Stan was still wiping tears from his face.

'Very funny, and I thought I was the funny one!'

'What time is it on, Grandad?'

'Eight o'clock.'

Robert's frowned returned, 'Mum'll never let me stay up and watch that.'

'We'll see. You want a brew Dad?' Said Brian to Stan.

'Aye, be rude not to if you're putting the kettle on?'

'You want some apple juice Robert?'

'Yes please.'

Brian left the room, Stan still flicking through the magazine, Robert staring out the window; after a while, Robert's train of thought began to run in circles and he began to form a question.

'Grandad?'

'Hmm?'

'When you were my age, did you know everyone?'

'What do you mean everyone?'

'Well, all your neighbours and people in the town?'

Stan put the magazine down and looked off into the middle distance, 'Yes, yes I did. But there were less people back then, but we had bigger families, which sounds odd. But we didn't move around so much. My parents lived two streets away, and my uncle and aunty lived next door. And then when I was a bit older than you, I used to knock about with my cousins. Who lived no more than three streets away.'

'Why don't we do that now?'

'Work I guess, there's not the same local work now. I was a steelworker and all my family on my Dad's side worked steel. And my mam was a cook.'

He smiled and Robert thought he saw tears well up in his Grandad's eyes, but Stan turned away, before continuing, 'but the steel works aren't even there anymore, it's a housing estate. So, people had to find other work.'

They both became aware that Brian was stood by the living room door.

Stan leant over as if to whisper loudly, 'Your Dad could never have worked there anyway, he doesn't have the muscles for it,' and winked.

Brian smiled as he put the drinks down on the coffee table.

'But he was always much cleverer than me. And people's pay for brains over folks that can work with their hands, just the way of the world.'

Stan looked up at Brain, 'And he's done alright has the

lad, I'm very proud of him, and perhaps I don't tell him as often as I should, he's provided for his family better than I ever could have.'

Robert was acutely aware something profound was going on, both men on the verge of tears.

'Shut up, you daft auld sod,' muttered his Dad.

Stan pulled a tissue from his trouser pocket and wiped his face.

'Why do you ask?' said Stan from under the tissue.

'Well, the Vikings, they knew everyone where they lived, like one big family and you did. And your parents and Grandparents all the way back to them. But my Dad he moved, and he didn't do what you did, and everything's different.' Robert stared at the floor.

Brian sat down next to him, put his arm around his son, 'That is very insightful. And an interesting point of conversation. And it makes me very proud of you that you're asking such things.' He hugged Robert till he was nearly squashed.

'I guess technology changed things and that there's a lot more people.'

Robert frowned.

Stan looked down at the small boy.

'And just because you don't get the answers you want, doesn't mean you stop asking the questions. You must always question things Robert, even if you have to change the people you're asking or the questions you're asking, until you get the answer,' Stan tapped him on the leg as he spoke, to emphasis the point.

'I instilled that into your Dad, and that's why he's clever than me, because he asked more questions. That's why he can spend his days at a work he enjoys rather than a work he has to do just to earn money.'

Robert was aware that the conversation had the possibility to tip over into one of those lectures about doing well at school but his Mum shouted that dinner was ready and saved the day.

After initial compliments about the food, everyone was quiet, focused on eating. Robert was nearly finished when he piped up, 'Mr and Mrs Winterbottom from across the road, what did they do for jobs?'

Brian looked and said, 'Wasn't he a teacher?'

'No,' replied Louise, 'Their daughter was a teacher, he was gardener, he spent the last few years before he retired, up at the hospital looking after the memorial garden. Mrs Winterbottom used to take sewing in, she made some lovely curtains for Barbara next door to her. But I think her eyesight isn't what it was.'

'That's right, she married that bloke that played cricket, she taught up at the high school.'

After a couple of more mouthfuls of food Brian said, 'Why?'

Robert shrugged, 'No reason, was just wondering, they were in the garden as you came home and I just thought that I didn't know anything about them.'

Stan said, 'I knew Frank Winterbottom's Dad, he was a foreman at the Steel works when I started, tough old bugger he was. He was fair, but he didn't stand for any messing and woe betide anybody who got on the wrong side of him.'

'What does that mean?'

'What?'

'Woe betide?'

'Well woe is trouble or unpleasant things. And betide, don't know actually, I think it means like being surrounded by, when the tide comes in. So, it's you'll be up to your neck in woe.' And he made a kind of duck noise out of the sound of his mouth and drew a line across his neck.

He always did that when he was talking about someone getting it or dying. It still made Robert smile.

Brian, put his knife and fork down, 'Betide just means to happen, so woe will happen to you,' he looked sheepishly at Stan.

Stan smiled, 'See, I told you he was smarter than me.'

The dinner plates were cleared, Stan shuffled into the living room with a mug of tea whilst Robert, Brian and Louise tidied up and loaded the dishwasher. Robert was particularly pro-active working on the theory that this might stand him in good stead when it came to the negotiations around watching the documentary on 1066 later.

By the time Robert got into the living room, Stan was asleep in a chair, and his Dad was slumped down, not far from sleep. There was an old war movie on the TV, but the volume was low. Robert pulled the laptop from under his Dad's arm and flicked it open.

Afternoon slipped into early evening, Stan woke himself up snoring, which caused everyone else to giggle. He yawned and stretched sleepily.

'Cup of tea?' asked Louise

'That would be lovely, thank you. Probably best to make a move after this?'

Brian nodded, 'Sure, whenever you want Dad.'

After the tea, Stan left with hugs for Robert and Louise, and a 'See you in the morning.'

By the time Brian had got back, Robert had left the TV papers folded open on tonight's page and he'd found a pen, which he'd artfully left pointing at the documentary.

It didn't work, Brian seemed oblivious to the hint, instead he found some papers he had to read for a meeting at work the next day.

Seven o'clock came, and like clockwork, Louise said, 'Robert time for bed.'

Robert almost burst and stared at his Dad, eyes bulging, trying to mentally shout at him.

'Why are you looking at your Dad like that?'

Brian looked up, 'Hmm? What?'

Robert swivelled his eyes to the TV.

Brian's brow furrowed, then he said, 'Oh, I said Robert could watch a documentary about 1066 later.'

'What time is it on?'

'Eight.'

'That's a bit late?'

'He's on summer holiday, he's got no school tomorrow.'

'I've still got to get him up.'

'Will you get up tomorrow?'

Robert nodded vigorously.

'It's a documentary?' said Brian, as if this implied something special.

Louise raised her eyebrows and sighed, 'Well you can get washed and clean your teeth and put your PJ's on now, then straight to bed afterwards.'

Robert leapt up and thundered up the stairs. He was back down by the time it was seven minutes' past and he realised he'd still got nearly an hour to wait. Which was going to be a long time because there had clearly been some kind of exchange of words between his Mum and Dad, he could tell by the way they were studiously ignoring each other.

He sighed and slumped into the sofa. And waited. The TV volume was still really low from earlier. And he waited. Eight o'clock came; Robert hunted around for the TV remote and turned the sound up.

It was worth the wait.

At nine o'clock the credits rolled, Robert stood up, turned the volume down, left it on the arm of the sofa next to his Dad and walked out of the room , throwing a 'G'night' over his shoulder.

Louise looked across at Brian and then her eyes followed Robert up the stairs. He was also looking to the stairs, he then flicked his eyes to his wife and said, 'Which bit of that makes you surprised?' stood up and followed Robert up the stairs.

Chapter 38

The boat hurled itself from wave top to wave top, all spray and salt and they never looked back and they never looked to their side, onwards and forwards, always the way there were going.

A pod of dolphins raced them for a while, easily skipping ahead. Ragnar said this was a good omen and the men were pleased with this; despite the disappearance of the boy. Ragnar has said it was a sign that the boy would return.

Robert was woken from his deep sleep by a full bladder. He considered getting up and going to the bathroom but then thought, if he ignored it, he might make it till morning. He was really comfy and he might not get back to sleep if he got up now. But it was too much, his bladder won. He slipped out from under the covers, still with his eyes closed. Robert considered this too, smiled to himself, thinking that it was not that long ago there was no way he'd have walked about in the dark with his eyes closed. As he put his feet down from the warm bed to the floor he found that his feet didn't touch a carpet, instead they crunched into dead leaves, he was cold and could see the dancing of red firelight flickering against his eyelids.

There was the sound of several large, burly men, hurling themselves into the darkness as quickly as possible from a resting position, as a small boy suddenly materialised by the fire, or seemed to step out of the air. Only Ragnar had not moved, he looked at the boy, eyes twinkling in the flames which he absent-mindedly poked with a twig, 'Where you been boy?'

Robert yawned and wrapped his arms around himself, looking down at himself; he was always amazed to find himself, not in his pyjamas but in clothes, smock top, rough-hewn pants and strange leather shoes. He went and sat next to Ragnar by the fire; 'Asleep' he replied.

This seemed to satisfy Ragnar who turned back to the fire, gazed into the flames and nodded his head gently. In the dark around them, Vikings sheepishly looked at each other, one or two flexed their shoulders or heads in an embarrassed, I was just practicing, kind of display and each slowly returned to their previous snoozing positions without making any further eye contact, or mention of what had just happened.

Robert remembered he needed a wee. Stood up and looked about, Ragnar pointed into the dark with a stick – 'White tree yonder,' he muttered and returned his attention to the fire.

Out of the circle of light and heat, Robert stumbled about with his hands outstretched on the presumption that he was going to trip over a branch or root. At first he was unable to find his way, but then he just kind of followed his nose, to the point where he couldn't stand the smell any longer and did what he needed to do. By the time he'd finished, he could make out some of the brighter stars glinting through the leaf canopy.

Back at the fire Robert slumped against Ragnar, wrinkled his nose at the aroma from the old man and fell into a light sleep, peppered with dancing shadows and whispered words.

Villi nodded at Ragnar and looked at the sleeping boy, 'What does it mean?'

Ragnar stared deep into the flames, 'The gods have chosen him to accompany us on our travels. Know that we are blessed and they watch over us, Villi. The gods are with us,' he emphasised that last part and looked up into Villi's eyes.

Villi smiled, almost triumphantly and sat back on his haunches content with this knowledge.

Daybreak arrived, feebly and wet. Men coughed themselves awake in the damp air, hacking the night from their lungs. It wasn't raining but the moisture in the air swirled about their heads and eddied slowly around the trees, trapped under the leafy canopy.

'Where are we?' asked Robert rubbing his bleary eyes.

'A couple days north of where we were,' replied Ragnar.

'I've been asleep for days?'

'I don't know, you went...'

Robert looked at the swirls in the mist, 'It's all got a bit weird, I'm not sure what's happening Ragnar.'

'Well everything has worked out so far, so I don't see why it won't in the end,' replied Ragnar and smiled, putting a hand on Robert's shoulder.

'Where we going?'

'To see a Kelda.'

'What's a Kelda?'

'A well or spring,' and then added because he knew what was coming next,

'Because it's looked after by a God.'

Robert's head rocked back at this news.

Villi interrupted with a furrowed brow, 'It's not going

to be like that one with the all those heads in is it?'

Thunor walked by, 'I hope it's worth the effort,' he grumbled and kept going, nagging people into their allotted tasks.

Ragnar smiled as he watched Thunor walk away, his head lolled to one side as he considered a response to the others, 'No, well yes, but there's only one of them, and they weren't gods really, they were... Erm, different. This one is, this one is very, very old.'

'You have a lot of gods,' said Robert looking confused.

'And Goddesses,' added Villi helpfully.

'And Goddesses,' nodded Ragnar, scowling slightly. 'And there are Gods and Goddesses of place, of the land. Each land has their own. The Gods of this land hold a special place and we would do well to pay them a visit and say hello, pay our respects to them before we leave for home, be glad of their presence.' he smiled down at Robert, who seem satisfied with this response.

Robert realised that they were not far from the river, where the boat was tied up in the middle; he could just make out the shadow of the dragon's head looming through the mist. The locals really must have been terrified by this sight, if there were any locals to see it, for in this strange world, there rarely appeared to be other people. He wondered if that was because there were so few people, or were they frightened off by Thunor and his men?

They left the shadow of the boat and walked along the riverbank, skirting around the forest. By midday they'd crested a rise up onto a moor, the river trailing off north towards some distant hill. Below them in a dip surrounded by three hillocks was a huge boulder. The dip was maybe half a mile wide, almost circular and it looked for all the world like the boulder had been dropped from the sky and making a huge dent in the earth. The men were silent, not edgy or wary, a respectful sort of silence. Ragnor looked over his shoulder, 'Villi, find me some wood, a suitable limb,'

Villi nodded once, turned and headed back towards the forest. There was some grunting noises and then the sound of wood being dragged through undergrowth and then being hefted. He walked out of the tree line carrying a large branch on his shoulder. He walked past where they were stood, down the slope to the point where the land began to flatten and then stood the piece of tree upright on the floor. With one hand he took his axe and seemed to randomly chip large bits off until a rough looking face appeared. Then he cut an upside down capital T on the right hand side, then he sharpened what was apparently the base and smacked it into the soft earth with the back of his axe, forming a kind of crude totem pole.

Everyone walked down to the pole where Villi waited. Ragnar touched the wood, closed his eyes and said 'Thor's place, protect her.'

The process was repeated from the west, except this time, one hand was carved on the left side of the pole, the right side left blank. And Ragnar said 'Tyr's place, protect her.'

In the north, the face only had one eye and Ragnar said, 'Odin's place, protect her.'

Finally the men moved around what was now some kind of circle around the boulder to the east where Villi was placing the last pole. Robert couldn't see what was on it, because he was behind, but Ragnar walked up and said, 'Freyr's place, protect her.'

He reached up and patted Villi on the shoulder, Villi wiped the sweat from his face with this back of his other hand then hooked his axe back on his belt.

Robert was confused, the posts had clearly been placed south, west, north and east around the boulder, and some distance from it, and it was clearly meant as some kind of protection, but Ragnar kept saying 'her' as if the boulder was a woman.

Ragnar walked towards the boulder, slowly, everyone else strung out in a thin line against the imaginary boundary formed by the posts. Villi rested a huge hand on Robert's shoulder. There was silence. Apart from grasshoppers, and bees, and skylarks and shushing of the wind ruffling the grass and the hiss of the trees swaying gently beyond the rise; Robert felt like he'd never heard anything like this before; for a silent place, everything was so loud. Ragnar knelt down on one knee, stretched out and placed his right hand on the face of the massive rock.

Words filtered back, Robert couldn't quite make them out, Breed or Bride or some combination of both, other strange words that Robert did not know, a different language, it flowed like thick honey and had a poetic, lilting rhythm.

Ragnar stood, hobbling slightly then got going as the stiffness eased from his joints and walked back, 'This way,' he said and strode off.

Thunor scowled at Ragnar, who was oblivious and merrily striking out for the horizon, the other Vikings looked at each a few shrugged their shoulders, looked at Thunor, who had a face like thunder, and with a twitch of his head stalked after the shaman, muttering to himself. The rest of the men gave Thunor a wide berth.

It soon became apparent that the place was also located in the top of a Y shaped area where two small rivers had joined before heading on to the estuary, which filled most of the southern horizon – beyond mountains hustled up towards the sky.

Robert looked at the mountains, they looked familiar, he was sure he'd seen them before.

The men waded over the river, Robert rode on Villi's shoulders, as the giant sloshed through the water and dark shapes could be seen flashing away from the commotion into reed beds below them.

By late afternoon they were well up onto the moors, all the men were cheerful, bantering and throwing jokes at each other. Even the Chief seemed in a good mood, having been silent and sullen most of the day.

They came to another river; this one was narrow, but quite deep and had cut a groove into the moorland. Rocks and small boulders had tumbled and jumbled into the slash and the water skipped and skittered over and around the obstacles. They found a relatively narrow point and began leaping across the gap, goading each other into falling, but always reaching out a hand and grabbing people to safety as they leapt the gap.

Villi swung Robert, grabbed him by an arm and the back of his pants and hurled him at the other side, the men cheered, Robert laughed, he landed rolled and put his hand in a big pile of sheep poo. Everyone else thought this was hilarious. Villa thundered into the ground next to him as he was wiping his hand on hillock of grass, 'Don't worry little fish, it will make you grow and you'll become big fish,' and chuckled at his own joke.

Robert shook his head, sniffed his hand, wiped it some more and then scrambled after the rest of them.

They followed the river they'd just jumped, vaguely north as it meandered across moorland towards the distant hills. Behind them the sun was getting low, the sky was vibrant and full of new colours.

Ragnar and Thunor huddled together and were talking, the rest of the men wandered along behind them, strung out in a line, seemingly without a care in the world.

The two men stopped walking and turned. The rest of the men stopped walking and looked at them, waiting for one of them to say something.

'It'll be dark soon, we can either camp here, or down there at the edge of the wood?' asked Ragnar.

'What's in the wood?' asked one of them.

'Trees. Bears, wolves, rabbits, squirrels, and crawly things,' replied Ragnar.

One of the others, Krik, a tall thin man with pale yellow brown hair that hung in braids down his chest said, 'What happens if we stay up here?'

'Well, if you want a fire you'll be seen for miles.'

'By what?'

'Whatever is out there,' said Ragnar slowly waving a straight arm at the view, leaving the men to conjure worse beasts from their imagination than would ever come skipping over the horizon.

'What do you suggest?' asked Krik, the other's letting him do the talking, whilst they studied the horizon, the woods and Ragnar's face.

Ragnar, waited, pinched his face and then said, 'The woods; we can deal with bears and wolves, and besides we'll have fire which will keep them away. I've no idea what's out there,' and pointed at the horizon again.

There was a moment's pause, some of the men looked at the horizon, then there was a kind of unanimous agreement that the woods would be the best options followed by lots of muttering and furtive glances about them.

Robert thought that Ragnar might be counting to ten under his breath, but he couldn't be sure.

They started to ascend from the moor towards the tree line, until the point where they found a huge oak quite some distance into the forest. Ragnar patted the trunk and smiled, slumping down into its roots. He rummaged around a bit found sound some dried moss, pulling it apart, and beginning the ritual of teasing fire from dead plants.

All the men had jobs, they scurried off to get firewood, others went to fill a metal pot with water from a stream. Some of the others just disappeared into the forest. Sometime later these came back with five rabbits. They were dead. Robert watched with revulsion as the rabbits were butchered, skinned and skewered on sticks over the fire. The cooked meat was then chopped up and dropped into the pot, one of the men stirred it with a stick, then people scooped up bowls of the stuff.

Robert helped himself with a small wooden bowl Villi had given him, then looked at it pondering the contents. There were a range of unidentifiable leaves floating on the top and lumps that might have been potato. But Robert was pretty certain they weren't potatoes. He gave it a sip, it tasted earthy and bitter and strong and wasn't actually that bad. The food always looked worse than it tasted.

The wood encroached, and the darkness behind it, and the world was reduced to a circle of flickering fire light, which men brought to life with stories of their forefathers. Robert, having a full belly, felt the heat from the fire warming and comforting him and desperately tried to fight the need to just close his eyes. But slowly they flickered shut and his breathing deepened. His ears were still just about awake, and took in sonorous tones of the men weaving their tales.

He found himself up in the trees, looking down on a pool of firelight. He gasped in shock for as he looked down seeing himself, asleep, leaning against Villi's arm.

Beyond the circle of light, keeping watch, five of the men stood in a rough circle, beyond them, only night and the blackness of the surrounding woods. Robert felt like he was in a lift as he shot up even higher, now above the trees, the sky was dusted with coloured stars to every horizon, it was like something out of a movie; spectacular did not convey his sense of awe at what he could see. Beyond the wood, a clear area that seemed flat and different to the rest of the land, it felt bounded, and a light mist gathered on this place. Robert could see shadows moving about in the mist, strange looking men. They did not leave the mist, instead they circled a large golden eagle that glinted and gleamed in the starlight. Some kind of statue, wings and talons outstretched.

He woke up with a yelp. The men stopped talking and watched him intently. Ragnar leaned over, smiled and said 'Speak, what did you see?' nodding encouragingly.

'I saw the stars, and a field, flat, full of mist, and I could see the shapes of men in the mist, but they would not leave a golden eagle in the middle.'

Ragnar smiled, 'We are not far. Don't worry they will not leave the eagle, they will not venture from its glow.'

'What are they?' asked the Chief.

'Squareshields, ghosts of Romans, their emblem was an eagle made of gold, the most precious thing in the world to them. The Picts came for them when they warred and killed them all in the night; stole their souls and their eagle, now they mourn their loss, a disgrace to their ancestors. They can neither leave nor move on till they reclaim their eagle.'

Some of the men immediately put hands on sword hilts and began looking about.

'Tsk, don't worry so much, the Picts have not been this far south in a generation,' said Ragnar shaking his head as the men stared intently into the darkness.

Robert slept soundly, as only a small boy can. Ragnar snored and rasped as only an old man can. The rest of the men barely slept, alarmed by every sound in the night time wood, lest they be ghosts, or worse, Picts on the hunt.

Chapter 39

By dawn Ragnar was ready to move off, the rest of the men were weary and lacklustre through lack of sleep. Not helped by Ragnar insisting they get a move on and eat on the hoof. The men moved slowly, and carefully until the forest began to thin and they found themselves before the raised, flat expanse of earth that Robert had seen the night before.

'This is it?' asked Villi.

Robert nodded his head.

'Wait here,' said Ragnar who then strode out towards the centre of the field.

He walked slowly in a circle, as if smelling or tasting the air for several minutes, then walked back to the waiting band of Vikings, 'They'll not bother us, the only fight they have is with the Picts.'

This seemed to placate the group, but Robert eyed him suspiciously, Ragnar caught his eye and twitched one eye in the tiniest of winks. By lunchtime they had crested a small ridge, below them a wooded ravine and water could be heard running over a jumble of stones.

Ragnar squatted down and watched the trees below, his eyes squinting in the bright sunshine. The rest of the men looked at each other and looked about and then as they realised not much was happening, sat down on the grass and waited. Robert had pulled a long piece of grass out of the ground with a head on it that looked a bit like wheat and he was slowly taking it apart and letting the seed heads blow away on the gentle breeze. One of them landed on Ragnar's side and though it would have been impossible for him to feel it, he suddenly rose to his feet, taking in a sharp intake of breath, which surprised the others.

'Thunor', he said, 'Myself and the boy will go to the Kelda, which is over there,' and he pointed down towards the thick woodland below them, 'Over there, towards that tallest tree is an old earthwork fort, complete with ramparts and a ditch, I will meet you there before sun down. I am minded to say that you should perhaps make it more defensible than it is.'

Thunor, nodded, then added, 'Why was the fort abandoned?'

'It matters not.'

'Is there bad magic there, spirits, some curse or....'

He was interrupted by Ragnar who turned swiftly, narrowed, 'Would I send you there if there was!'

'No, but....'

'There are no buts, we will need those walls and ditch before the night is out.'

They held each other's stare for a fraction longer than was necessary, Robert realised again that this was theatre, put on by them, to answer any questions the men might have, to mould opinion and cast it in one direction.

'Robert come,' and Ragnar set off down the hill side. Robert scampered after him, half turned and waved at the others, who nodded at him with smiles and half waves.

Once they were out of earshot Robert asked, ''Why do you and Thunor do that, pretend to argue but then nobody asks any further questions thing?'

Ragnar chuckled and smiled and ruffled Robert's hair, 'Well it's just that, it stops further questions. It's a tricky thing, getting a group decision and they are all free men, with free minds, and once they set their mind to it, it's a fool's own job to try and change it. Thunor rules because he is strongest with a sword, and the gods smile favourably on us, but every man has a say, and if they all, or most, decide on a course of action, then that is that, so we say these things and try to persuade them without them knowing, because it would take too long to explain what I know and how.'

Robert frowned, 'How do you know the things you know?

He nearly walked into the back of Ragnar who had stopped and was looking up thoughtfully, 'Because I watch and listen, and taste and see, and don't spend as much time yammering away with empty words. I am a Shaman, it's what I do.'

Robert looked down, 'Yes... I think I understand.'

Ragnar turned, put one hand on Robert's shoulder and bent down to look him in the face, 'You will boy, you will. But for now, let us be still in our minds and breathe and walk slowly and with reverence for we approach that which is truly sacred.'

Robert nodded again, his face all serious.

Ragnar continued, 'I need you to understand this Robert, we will be on sacred ground.'

Chapter 40

Robert looked about him; it was perfect oak woodland, with a stream running through it. And then they followed the stream deeper into the wood.

Ahead of them a mound in the earth, almost as wide as a house, seemed to thrust itself out of the ground. In the front a large hole, the sides and tops propped up with lintels of pale stone. Ragnar looked over his shoulder and nodded for Robert to follow, but place his finger on his lips and whispered, 'Be quiet'.

Inside was dark and it quickly grew completely pitch black. Robert felt his way along the tunnel, keeping his head low and following the shuffling noises ahead. Which he hoped was still Ragnar.

Inside was sodden, Robert was aching and cold and wet as he kept finding himself ankle deep in freezing water, slipping slightly on the stones, sloshing the water high up his trouser legs. The darkness seemed to pale and up ahead he could see light and all his woes were forgotten. The tunnel opened out into a cavern. Robert let out a long sigh, not realising he'd been holding his breath.

At the back of the cavern a figure slumped against the base of large flat rock, which was covered in carvings the like of which Robert had never seen; whirls and spirals and men and winged men and huge fat naked ladies. Before the figure, a simple hole in the ground through up which crystal clear water bubbled. All of it was surrounded in a huge crescent of flickering candles.

Ragnar inched forward, the figure stirred.

'We are the sons of Odin and we bring the wolf and the raven,' said Ragnar.

The figure moved, sat forward and laughed once, 'That old fraud! We have spoke words many times, the wanderer has been and gone and shall come again; being all mysterious with his hood up in the dark. Do you see any Ravens?

Ragnar had to shake his head.

'Do you hear any wolves?'

Again Ragnar slowly shook his head.

Robert's mouth hung open, the figure was dishevelled, and filthy, and you could not tell where beard and hair began, it just all tumbled down over his body. Robert wasn't even sure if the figure had any clothes on. On his head was what looked like the top of the skull of a deer, with antlers rising up and splitting into the dark, they bobbed and moved as he spoke.

The figure pinned them with a stare from huge, round, owl like eyes, and without looking down, used the exceptionally long fingernail of his first finger to scratch in the mud before him, then he smiled and wiped the markings out of the mud with the side of his hand, the rest of his fingers seemingly gnarled and twisted with arthritis. And then he just stared at them.

Robert felt hot and prickly, beads of sweat blobbed out onto his forehead and face, even Ragnar didn't look his usual confident self, then he licked his lips and spoke, 'We brought offerings to the Kelda,'

'Words and wood scavenged from the forest, – hardly gifts fit for a Queen. And yet in your travels you have gathered many secrets and your tribe is wealthy.'

'What use does she have for trinkets, the stuff of the earth, she is already richer than imagination, all dwells within her?'

The hunched figure broke into a smile, then laughed, 'Haha, you have a cunning way with words, just like your Alfather. He walks this way and that, and all he has are his words.'

'What would she have?'

There figure's face seemed to go slack and his eyes either unfocused or focused on a place far away. The only sound was that of the water gurgling in its hole.

The figure stayed motionless for what seemed like an eternity, then his eye snapped back up to them and he pointed at Ragnar which his excessively long index finger nail.

'You will be found worthy, with sword arm and words of steel, you will hear the lamentations of her enemies in defeat. She will gift you their plunder for your service.'

Ragnar nodded deeply, almost a bow, but not quite, and his eyes remained fixed on the figure.

'First a test' the figure continued, 'The shades in the Eagle's Field will come this very night, to the old fort, where your kin gather even now. And I will watch from tree, root and bough, from owl, fox and vole and I will judge you worthy.'

Ragnar nodded again.

'And I would have your word, your bond, your oath, before all your Gods, before the Gods of this land, before me, and before Her. Before the Gods of your Father and your ancestors, I will have your oath.'

Ragnar reached into the folds of his cloak and pulled out his evil looking blade. Robert felt like all the blood and light drained out of the scene, all he could see was Ragnar's blade.

He held it before him and dragged his other hand down the cutting edge, blood welled up and ran onto the floor, making splatter patterns and splatter noises. Robert thought his eyes were going to pop out of his head, he'd never seen so much blood.

As the blood ran, Ragnar spoke – 'I give my word, before all the holy gods and their houses, as this blood is my witness.'

He held the blade loose in his right hand and squeezed his left hand together, blood still oozing out between his knuckles and fell.

'Good Ragnar, good,' then he drew some more symbols in the patch of red earth before him; Robert felt nothing, he was numb.

'Now wash your hand in the water.' The figure murmured.

Ragnar knelt down and slowly pushed his hand into the pool. It was a strange thing, that Robert thought about later, water has certain qualities, it looks and sounds, but this water, it was if it was enhanced it was more water like than any water he'd seen before; it tinkled and shone and danced and was silver and white and flashed and then dark swirls of blood detached themselves from Ragnar's hand and Robert watched them spiral and swirl away, mingling and disappearing. Robert could see whole worlds and lives rise and fall in those patterns.

Paul Hodson

'Life for life' whispered the figure. 'Know this Ragnar, know that she looks over you, she walks with you, and that if you break your oath then you will be lost for all time, your people, your places, all gone. Not even dust. All of the gods will venge their wrath upon you.'

Ragnar stood up, winced a little.

The figure looked at Robert, as if suddenly remembering he was there, looked through him, 'An odd fish this one, well out of his waters. I bid him take some water.'

Ragnar turned and looked down at him, Robert looked up, eyes wide and feeling utterly uncomfortable, Ragnar pulled his water bag off his belt, unfastened the top and gave it to Robert, 'Fill it boy,' he said softly.

Robert took the bag, and knelt down, pushing the leather bag into the water which gurgled and glugged playfully.

Robert's senses were completely overwhelmed all he could perceive was the noise of the water and the shimmer of its surface.

Then the figure said, 'Truth goes both ways, remember this. Now go. The sun sets and you must race the twilight, find your men, and have them prove their spirit and sword arms are worth having.'

Robert lifted the bloated bag from the water and handed it to Ragnar, noticing that the gash on Ragnar's hand was now no more than a red line, he looked up open mouthed.

Ragnar took the bag, looked to the figure before them, his mouth open to speak, but the figure was slumped into a deep sleep, his head bowed, and the antlers wobbled slightly as he gently snored.

Ragnar, bowed his head slightly, a look of contentment on his face, he looked at Robert, grinned and turned, back tracking down the stream to the world.

Outside was bright and Robert couldn't figure out if he was too warm or too cold such was his mind beguiled by what he'd just experienced, covering his eyes against the glaring sky.

'Come Robert, we must get to the others quickly.'

Robert looked over his shoulder, the sun was on the horizon, and then turned and ran after Ragnar, shouting, 'the cut on your hand?'

But Ragnar did not answer.

They made no attempt to be silent or stealthy and were heard and then seen well before they were close. Ragnar hobbled along at an alarming rate for a man with a really bad limp.

It was already well into twilight as he crested the earth walls, and from the top he bellowed, 'The shades come, arm yourselves, best them like any other foe and know that the Gods are with us!'

He grabbed Robert's hand and waved his arm in the air like he'd just won the battle.

A great cheer went up, swords and axes were unsheathed and great excitement ran through the men as they scattered to the earth walls.

Chapter 41

'Boy, in the middle, do not move, do not stray, do not have someone have to come rescue you, do you understand?'

'Yes, but your hand!'

'It was a healing spring boy, a holy place,'

Robert nodded and Ragnar pushed him down the slope towards the centre of the flat earth that stretched for 50 yards to a low wall that circled them.

Ragnar hobbled away waving his short sword in the air, almost ranting, 'Know this, this is a test, which we will not fail, our fates are written, we fight for the Kelda, and we stand against this night, she will stand with us!'

Robert went through a gambit of emotions that started at terror, then went to, well everything has worked out ok so far, to, is this even real, and back to terror. And he realised that if something did get past the Vikings, he was on his own.
Alone.
Unarmed.
In the middle.
Unarmed? He had his sword, well knife really; and what was he going to do with it, was he prepared to start waving it around, to use it? This is ridiculous he

thought to himself.

He looked around and spotted a hefty stick, it would probably worry someone's shins and that was about it but it made Robert feel marginally braver. Hitting things with a stick felt different somehow.

Then a cry went up from the men on one section of the wall, 'Here they come. For Odin!!'

The Vikings banged their swords and axes on their shields and made a terrifying roar.

A bank of fog was forming under the trees, it moved slow and was illuminated from within, in it the shadows of Roman soldiers swirled into shape. They moved in a line, the centre of which a triangle of maybe 50 odd men, a line of ten, then nine, eight, and so one till the one man at the point of the triangle, clearly their fiercest warrior.

Thunor shouted at Ragnar, 'I thought you said their fight was with the Picts!'

'That was yesterday!' he replied.

Thunor scowled and then walked away from where the enemy was to the other side of the fort. Robert found this very curious.

Ragnar stalked backwards and forwards, yelling encouragement, calling on the gods and ancestors to come stand with them: Pointing at the men not on the wall under attack to stay vigilant lest they be flanked.

The line of shades stopped and then as one they threw spears which arched through the air silently, spears made of condensed fog, someone shouted 'Shield!' and as one the men raised their shields, everyone heard the thump of the spears into wood, felt the shield slam back into their arms with the impact but then the spears just seems to evaporated leaving no trace of their ever having been there.

There was a look of stunned amazement on the faces of the Vikings as they looked around themselves for the spears.

Ragnar yelled at them 'Watch the enemy!! Not your shields!'

The line moved forward to within almost a sword's length. The Romans hefted their oblong scutum into position on their arms, wickedly sharp gladii pointing outwards at the Viking line. Then they lunged ferociously up the embankment. There was screaming and shouting and the general clash of arms... but the Vikings held the higher ground.

The Romans lunged again, one of the Vikings braced his back foot against a stone which moved, tumbling him backwards off the wall, landing heavily with an 'Ooophh' noise. The line of Vikings almost broke. Almost.

Ragnar yelled something incomprehensible, and pointed his sword through the gap that had been made, which then glowed a fluorescent blue and a bolt of blue light hurled from its tip into a Roman soldier, he glowed a strange neon shade and then his form exploded into glowing mist which faded as it swirled up into the trees.

It was as if that was some kind of signal, all hell let loose.

Villi swung his axe over hand and it caught on the top of a Roman shield, he used his massive strength and reach to pull the shield forward whilst the man next to Villi punched through the gap made with the tip of his sword. The same thing happened, the roman exploded spectacularly into particles of moisture, which swirled about aimlessly for a few seconds and then streamed back towards the bank of mist.

The point-man in the wedge of romans punctured the Viking line and all sense of structure collapsed as the Viking warriors fought the ghosts.

From behind him, Robert heard an almighty roar and the Vikings who had been watching from the other walls charged forward, Thunor in the middle of them, he crashed his huge body into three soldiers bowling them out of his way, swinging his sword in great arcs, he ploughed through the legionnaires.

Robert could see why he was Chief, none matched him in battle: Wherever his sword cleaved, Romans were dispatched.

A flash of blue caught Robert's eye and another soldier was obliterated in a blue light cast from Ragnar.

As the line had punched through, the Vikings had folded around them catching the remaining roman soldiers fast within the pincer movement and then there was only a few left, Thunor quickly returned them to the mist. The men looked about, looked at each other all remained and a great cheer went up, despite the sweat and the panting, they were jubilant.

Thunor bellowed a great battle cry, like a wild animal. Robert was visibly shaking, unsure what to make of any of it, despite all the men around him, laughing, congratulating each other and recounting their particular part in the battle.

The overwhelming comment, was 'Did you see the look on their faces?'

Robert stepped away slight from the group to try and gather himself. He took a deep breath and looked out into the night. And with all the predictability of narrative causality, saw the mist creeping once more in the tree line. And in that mist, shadows and shades and oblong shields.

'Errmm......Ragnor, Thunor!!'

But the men were too jubilant in victory. With greater urgency Robert tried again. Still nothing. Hefting his stick he swung it hard against Thunor's legs, who spun round angrily.

Robert recoiled, and pointed quickly, 'Look, look, they are coming back!'

'Ragnar, what is happening?!'

'To the walls, defend, and fight,' shouted Ragnar.

'Why are they back?' shouted Thunor.

'Boy to the middle,' and he pushed Robert again towards the centre of the flat ground. 'I do not know Thunor, it just is,' he snapped.

Thunor growled and stamped away.

And then it started again. And again.

By the third wave the Vikings were exhausted, Ragnar looked frail and completely spent.

They were now being forced off the wall by the Romans relatively easily, dropping down the six foot into the space in the middle, no sense of order, just a desperate fight to survive.

Robert ducked this way and that, trying to stay out of harm's way. The men were struggling. Robert ran round dodging the fighting that that was now all around him, with a sudden urge to try and help he ran up behind some of the Romans and hit them as hard as possible in the back of the legs, he quickly learnt that the back of the knees was the sweet spot. As they fell backwards, their guard dropped and they were finished off with a thrust from a Viking sword or axe, their bodies exploding into component particles of water vapour, which swirled away in the starlight.

And then a paleness in the sky that none had really noticed, bloomed into pre-dawn, and the wisps of men who had been, grew fainter. The first rays of the light flashed through the forest, punching holes in the forms of the remaining ghosts and then they were gone, returned to the light as dawn broke across the landscape. They had been fighting all night.

The Vikings looked around, at each other bewildered and exhaustion etched in their faces.

'Is that it, are we done?' asked one of the men.

Ragnar, looked around exhausted and spent, 'I believe so.'

Villi swept Robert off the floor and held him high above his head shaking him at the men who cheered back, swords and axes waving in the air.

Thunor came over, took him off Villi, gripped Robert by his arms and stared hard at him, 'Well done, boy, I wish some of these men hit as hard with sword and axe as you do with a stick!'

Another cheer echoed through the forest.

Ragnar looked around, glee written large across his visage, 'Time for home boys,'

The men didn't need telling twice, with a quick look around and then they scampered towards the tree line, new found energy pumping their legs hard for the coast. Robert could just about keep up with Ragnar, and Villi thundered along behind them, occasionally one hand swooping down to pick the boy up when he stumbled, throwing him forward onto his feet. He quickly learned to land running or end up face down in sheep or rabbit poo.

The boat was turned, and they headed for the estuary, once Thunor was happy they were out of harm's way from anyone on the shore, the men settled down and soon most of them were snoring. Five were left on watch, and one small boy. Adrenaline was still soaring through Robert and he found a notch near the mast that he could perch on.

Thunor was drifting off, then he opened one eye for a last check, looked at the small boy who stared furiously at the shoreline, eyes alert lest danger sneak up on them and smiled and rolled over.

About thirty seconds later the stick dropped from Robert's hands with a clatter, the warmth of the day's sun on his back lulling him into sleep. One of the other watchmen, gently lifted him down, spread out a corner of a cloak from one of the others and laid him down.

Chapter 42

Ragnar did not sleep, he sat cross-legged, back ramrod straight, arms gently relaxed on his knees and slipped into a place between awake and sleep. He was in the cave, but it was bigger, indeed cavernous. Out of the darkness the footsteps of something massive crunched and boomed, but it was a slow gait, had all the time in the world - literally. A figure loomed into view, it was the figure from the cave but different. Here he was vast, a hundred feet high, deer hooves and legs morphed into a man's muscled torso, arms and head. Great bifurcating horns rose from his head and disappeared into the dark. Amidst these horns stars swirled and lightning nestled. He saw two ravens perched up there. The figure looked down at Ragnar, who did bow this time, in utter awe. When he looked up the figure was looking into the middle distance, with blind eyes of fire, then his head tilted down and he looked at and through Ragnar.

'I see you Ragnar.' The words were everywhere and nowhere and seemed to arrive directly in his head; he felt their power reverberating in the bones of his skull.

'Yes Lord' said Ragnar weakly.

'You are mine now, you are bound to me, and I to Her. You have done well; you are strong and wise. And that is all that can be asked. You have the spring water, that is your prize, use it wisely, the tiniest drop will yield health. When the time comes, I will come to you again and you will fight and you will win. My words give power to your sword arm.'

The figure turned his head, Ragnar followed his gaze, swirling in the darkness he saw another figure in the distance, but the figure wore the night like a cloak and a wide brimmed hat, the Milky Way swirling around the hat in a band. One eye gleamed from under the brim of the hat, and the two ravens flew from the antlers towards him.

'Go home now Ragnar, go to the gods of your lands and your father's lands. I have told them of your deeds. Your place is assured.'

'You do me great honour Lord.'

The figure almost smiled and then took a step back into the dark, slowly faded from view, the last thing to be seen where the horns of power and flaming eyes. Ragnar let out a startled breath and looked up at the sky from his place on the boat. He could see the same pattern of stars and maybe the outline of the horns. Two shooting stars flared and then disappeared.

Chapter 43

'Come on sleepy head, time to get up, Grandad is taking you out today.'

'Uh,' was Robert's response, somewhat stunned to find himself back in his own bed. He looked round trying to get his bearings, everything had been so, well weird lately.

'And put those old trainers on with your tracksuit bottoms,' his mum continued from the bathroom.

Robert sat up in bed, 'Where are we going?' he shouted.

'It's a surprise...'

'Come on Grandad!' shouted Robert.

His Grandad was quite some way further back down the hill.

'Your old Grandad ain't as fit as he was, or this hill is bigger than it used to be: One or t'other,' he puffed, 'and to think I used to cycle up this.'

Robert was almost jumping up and down on the spot, but Stan needed a breather, he doubted they were a third of the way up the hill yet, it had already been a long walk from the bus stop.

Robert couldn't contain himself any longer, he ran ahead, along a dry stone wall, then a gate, he looked back, waved and shouted that he was going in; Stan waved back and shouted to wait but he wasn't very loud and Robert already skipped through the gate. About a hundred yards from the gate across a mown field, was a cluster of stones, man size, in a circle. They looked ancient and gnarled and seemed to thrum with unknown purpose.

Robert was mesmerised by them, unsure if he should touch them. There was silence, but that noisy silence which contains the sound of daisies being brushed over by a light breeze, a skylark high and invisible and two crows that were sat on the wall, launched themselves into the wind, turning their wings seemingly hanging in the air.

Stan finally makes it to the field, Robert ran over and grabbed his hand dragging him to the circle.

'I'm just going to sit down here, out of the wind, and in the sun Robert.'

'Ok Grandad, I'm going to walk around the stones,'

'Ok, but stay close and don't talk to anyone ok?'

'Ok' said Robert as he skipped from view. Stan slumped down, the stone against his back was indeed warm and the sun was warm on his face. He wasn't sure he was going to be able to get up, but right now he didn't care, he was just glad not to be walking up that hill.

Robert wanted to touch every nook and cranny in the stones, he ran his finger over them all, trying to see any carvings or markings on them, but he couldn't find any, they just looked weather beaten. He felt like he could literally breathe them in. In the distance clouds started to build on the hill tops; one lone cloud scudded over and obscured the sun, the temperature dropped a little and Robert realised he should probably check on his Grandad.

He walked around, a little panic in his throat when he couldn't see him, then the panic mounted when he saw his Grandad's legs poking out, he looked to be asleep, a little sweaty sheen on his face.

'Grandad?'

'Grandad!?'

Robert shook his Grandad's arm, but there was no response, he looked like he was just asleep. Robert looked round but there was nobody else there. He stood still, trying not to let the panic take over, then thought, 'What do I do?' Then the next thought was what would Ragnar do? Ragnar would think.

He rummaged in his Grandad's coat pocket for his mobile, he tried his Mum and his Dad but couldn't get through, there was no signal. He tried 999.

Someone answered almost immediately, 'Hello, emergency service operator, which service do you require?'

Robert didn't know, 'My Grandad's ill,'

'Do you require an ambulance?'

'Yes, I er think so,' he squealed.

There was a pause, which seemed to take forever, Robert could feel himself starting to panic, could feel the tension rising up and twisting at his throat, but then he saw the two crows circling above come down and land on the stone nearest to them, and remembered where he'd been recently and what he'd seen. And more importantly what he'd done. The crows watched with interest.

'Hello, this is the ambulance service, where are you calling from?'

'We're at Castlewall Hill at the stone circle. My Grandad, I can't wake him up.'

'Your Grandad?'

Robert could what sounded like the clicking of fingers on the other end of the phone.

'What's your name son?'

'My name is Robert.'

'And how old are you Robert.'

'I'm seven. And one quarter. Nearly eight.'

'And do you know if there is anything wrong with your Grandad.'

'Yes he's got something to do with beetles, and he can't eat sweets and chocolate, unless he goes funny, then he can.'

'Ok then, you're being very brave Robert. How does you Grandad look, is he pale, sweaty?'

'Yes.'

'And is his breathing shallow or deep?'

'Erm...., shallow, slow.'

There was a pause at the other end.

Robert took the handset away from his head and looked at it, he could hear bells, or tinkling chimes; then he realised that a lady was walking towards him;

she had a pretty smile and no shoes, and had tiny bells around her ankles which jangled when she walked. She wore a purple top and a flowing purple skirt and had the most amazing gold necklace Robert had ever seen and big red hair.

'Is everything ok?' she asked, Robert was a bit dumbstruck, he could only stare at her smile, and flashing bright, bright blue eyes all enveloped in a wild mass of pale red hair.

She knelt down next to them and put her hand on his Grandad's forehead.

'It's my Grandad he's not well,'

'Yes,' she said, soothingly.

She looked at the phone, a tinny, tiny voice was shouting hello. Robert put it back to his ear, 'Sorry there's a lady here.'

Then Robert spoke to the lady, 'I've phoned an ambulance.'

'Then you've done the right thing,' she replied calmly.

The voice said, 'Are you ok Robert?'

'Yes, this lady seems very nice.'

'Ok, help is on its way, you just hang in there son, I'll stay on the phone ok?'

His Grandad moaned, the lady pressed her hand against his forehead and just said, ''Sshhhhhh,' very gently. He looked for all the world like he was asleep. She smiled at Robert, Robert thought he was going to melt.

'Robert?' asked the man on the phone.

'Yes?'

'Don't be alarmed or anything ok, but there's a helicopter coming for you, it was nearby and it's nearer than the ambulance, they've been practicing in the mountains.'

'Did you say helicopter?'

'Yes.'

There was silence.

'I've never been in a helicopter.'

'It will be fine.'

There was a long pause then Robert said, 'Can I go in the helicopter with my Grandad.'

'Pretty certain you will have to keep him company

son, you've been very brave this far, you need to make sure he gets to hospital ok. Is that ok?'

Robert sat up, 'Yes, yes.'

His Grandad moaned again, and the lady pressed her hand to his forehead again, she had an incredibly calm air about her, and his Grandad looked to have a bit of colour returning to his face.

Robert cocked his head to one side, he could just about hear the 'chop chop chop' noise of a helicopter, his stomach somersaulted and knotted. And then he saw it, looking for all the world like large insect slowly bobbing towards them.

He looked at the lady, she smiled at him, looked him in the eyes and he felt a little calmer. And then there was just noise and dust and wind, the spinning blades seemed to whip the breath from him, he tried to cover his eyes and face from the beating and all the bits that now whirled about him. Two men in red overalls and helmets jumped down, one of them shouted something at Robert and ruffled his hair with a gloved hand but Robert couldn't hear him.

He was grabbed by the hand and led towards the open door, then picked up and passed to a seat, where another pair of hands strapped him into a seat by a man who grinned and then gave him a thumbs up. He watched as now two men huddled about his Grandad and manoeuvred him onto a stretcher, there was a pause then the stretcher lifted and was hurried into the side next to where Robert sat.

The noise was overwhelming; it drowned out all his other senses. And then it intensified to something Robert would not have thought possible. There was a sensation of falling but upwards and being pushed down to the ground all at the same time. The only clear memory was of gripping the seat and looking down at the stone circle, it seemed completely tranquil, the lady looked up, smiled and waved, seemingly unaffected by the wind from the helicopter, her golden necklace gleaming so brightly in the sunshine. He would never forget her.

For a moment the helicopter lurched from one side to another, all the strange sensations were compounded by seeing the land through the window at a crazy angle, and then he was falling, sickening, he let out an involuntary shout, one of the men put his hand right in the centre of Robert's chest, smiled and gave a wink, the falling was over and they were hurtling forwards.

As the helicopter crested the ridge and banked around, the low sun flashed off something metal back in the strong circle, it was incredibly bright and blinded Robert for a moment, when he looked back, the lady with the necklace had gone, the circle was empty again.

Inside the helicopter was cacophonous, the men in helmets shouted at Robert if he was ok, he nodded and gave them a thumbs-up. His Grandad had opened his eyes briefly and the man shouted to Robert that that was a good sign. Robert looked out of the window, he could see the whole town to the mountains in the distance, he felt like he could see forever, but the whole experience was warped by the overwhelming noise.

And then they were coming into land, the doors banged open, people in flapping white coats helped Robert down and the trolley that his Grandad was on. The man from the helicopter ruffled Robert's head as he left and then shook his hand, Robert beamed at him, he couldn't remember anyone shaking his hand before. Then a nurse gripped his shoulder and they scurried across the car park, passed some automatic doors and Robert found himself sat in a long, quite corridor, with a can of coke the lady on the desk had bought him. The whole thing seemed like a really intense dream; he thought to himself that he'd be used to intense dreams by now.

He swung his legs off the chair and swirled the coke in the can to get some of the fizz out, the only noise was the faint rumble of air conditioning, the hissing of his can and in the distance a regular beep.

The door banged open and his mum ran up the corridor, picked him up and squashed him in a hug, 'You ok baby boy?' she asked.

He squirmed to be put down, 'Yes I'm fine mum, ask how Grandad is.'

His Mum walked over to the desk and spoke to the lady and then came back, her hand on her brow.

'He's going to be ok. He needs to remember that he's an old man.'

She slumped down in the chair next to him and put her arm around him and let out a long low breath. And then phoned Dad.

'Yes, yes he's fine, he's...he's fine, he's asleep. I'm just waiting for the Doctor, no you may as well go home, there's nothing, no, ok, see you soon.'

A tall, stern looking man arrived and he and Robert's Mum went into the cubicle where Grandad was, they were there for several minutes.

When she came out, she looked a bit happier and calmer - 'Come on kiddo' (she never calls me that, thought Robert) - 'your Grandad is fine and asleep'. They're going to keep him in overnight. We'll go home and get some tea and come back in the morning.

'You've been in a helicopter?' his Dad had his arms wide and wrapped them around Robert and scooped him up, 'I have never been in a helicopter, what was that like, that must have been so awesome?'

'It was, but was so noisy,'

Robert garbled through tea with epic stories of phoning the ambulance, the lady with the necklace and then the helicopter ride, which may as well have been a dragon the way Robert told it.

At some point later he fell asleep on the sofa, a deep, dreamless sleep, though he had a vague notion of being carried upstairs in his Dad's arms and being placed into a warm bed.

Chapter 44

The next morning he was still in his own bed. He pushed himself up a bit, half sat up, half not and pulled the duvet up to his nose and thought back. And it all seemed to break over him, everything that had happened, that might have happened and he struggled to really get hold of anything that was real. Were the Vikings? The dragons (he'd seen dragons!?), was the helicopter ride? Everything seemed to whirl around in his head, all the smells, sights, tastes, noise, it was like he wasn't in control of his own thoughts and they pummelled at him, spinning and spiralling around faster and faster. This opened the floodgates to the emotions and suddenly there were tears. His mum found him like that, tears streaming down his face.

'Little man,' and she hugged him for a long time. And then his Dad came into see where everyone was and sat on the other side of the bed.

'I think we've forgot, just what an adventure you've had and how brave you've been this few weeks, you seem to take everything in your stride.'

Robert sniffed back the tears, and nodded once, thinking, almost saying something about the adventures they knew nothing about.

'How about we go see Grandad, then go into town, we can go anywhere you want?

Robert nodded, wiped the tears from his face with his sleeve, 'Can we go to the museum?'

'Sure...'

His Grandad sat up in a ward full of other people and beamed at them when they appeared, Robert ran down and climbed up on the bed and hugged him, then sat on the edge swinging his legs.

'How you feeling?' asked his Dad.

'Ok, much better, got a decent night's sleep last night, despite this lot snoring,' his Grandad gestured with his head at the rest of the ward.

Robert looked round, there were faces that looked like nice old men, like his Grandad and faces that looked mean and nasty; he didn't like the idea of his Grandad having to sleep here with everyone else.

'Dad you need to be more careful, this is twice now, and both times with Robert....'

'I know, I know,' his Grandad squeezed Robert's shoulder, 'it's a good job this little fella is sensible. But I know, I need to be, I guess I didn't want to accept it. Anyway, I've never been in a helicopter before, and I don't remember being in this one.'

'This is serious,' said Brian.

'I know, Getting old, is not nice.'

Brian nodded, 'I know Dad, believe me.'

Stan nodded, and then smiled and then changed the subject.

The tension lifted a little, there was talk of food and drink and how horrible it was in the hospital. Robert's mum dumped the carrier bag supplies they'd got on the way. Which Robert checked over. They continued the conversation around what the doctor had said and what the nurses were like and then Robert had kind of switched off and let the words just waft over him.

Suddenly it was time to leave, everyone hugged Stan. Robert had never seen his Dad hug his Grandad before; this was new.

'So where to?' asked his Mum in the lift, as if she didn't know.

As they walked in the museum, the big guy Robert and Stan had met previously was standing by the entrance talking to the security smiled. Robert smiled and half waved at him, the man nodded and then said, 'How's your Grandad?'

Robert turned to his Mum and Dad, 'This is the man who helped Grandad last time.'

'Last time?' queried the man, as he offered his hand to Robert's Dad, 'Hi, I'm Dave, it was nothing, we just got him a cup of tea.'

'Thank you, thank you very much for that.'

Dave shook Robert's Mum's hand, 'Last time, makes it sound like a habit?'

'Well only two so far, being diabetic is taking him some getting used to, but he did it again yesterday, up at the stone circle, got a free helicopter ride, after Robert phoned for an ambulance.'

Dave broke into a wide smile, 'Dude that was you? Very cool, I heard about that, one my mates is on the crew, he told me last night, they'd got diverted, when he said who it was, I told him about you two in here, hah. Wondered if it was you. Well done fella, well done.'

He bent down and shook Robert's hand. That was twice someone had shook his hand in less than 24 hours.

Robert twisted about a bit on his feet, suddenly feeling shy but couldn't help grinning.

'So after being so brave, our treat, where do you want to go, and he said here,' said his Mum.

'Let me guess,' said Dave, 'The Viking section.'

Robert grinned some more and nodded.

'Come on then,' and Dave walked off up the wide stone staircase. They called off at a storeroom into which Dave disappeared and then came out with a handful of cotton gloves, which he handed out. Robert eyes lit up and he looked at his Mum and Dad, his Dad just shrugged.

Once at the section Dave showed them in, looked around, there was nobody else there, and then pulled an elasticated barrier over which said section closed on it.

He then walked over to a cabinet, jangled some keys and unlocked the cabinet.

'Put your gloves on' he said, as he pulled his on and then he reached in and took out the coins and placed them on a table at the side, very carefully.

'What's so special about these coins, is that they are from all over the world, or the known world back then.'

He held each one up in turn, and let Robert and his Mum and Dad examine them, one from somewhere in what was now Russia, one from Dublin, one from the Middle east, some from northern Europe, and one they didn't know where it was from, none like it has ever been found.'

Robert grinned, that was the coin, from the Kemry, suddenly his mind started racing, he was unable to keep pace within his own thoughts.

Dave put the coins back and slowly brought out the two swords and the comb.

'I'm not going to get the pouch down, it's very delicate now, the leather is so fragile as it's so old,' Robert nodded not really listening, Dave continued, clearly thinking about the merits of letting a small boy handle a complete and whole jar from the Viking period, 'And the jar is very, erm fragile also.'

Robert nodded again, and stepped forward, 'That symbol on the front is magic, that is the most precious thing you've got, that is the jar of the last breath, say the right words and it will hold you last breath so that no other can take it. It used to be in a well surrounded by seven heads, but then a king who became a bear and his wizard stole it, and then they lost it and some Christians buried it.'

He realised that the three adults were stood staring at him, and that perhaps he shouldn't have said that, but the words had just kind of fallen out.

'Is it?' Dave said finally to break the awkward silence, he looked at the strange little boy and then back at the jar, with the strange symbol scratched in the front, 'Is it,' he said again. And slowly nodded, got up and locked the cabinet.

Robert realised he'd gone bright red, and felt completely foolish. His Dad saved the day by saying, 'What have you been reading kiddo?' with extra emphasis on the word have.

Dave said, 'At least he's reading, and wants to come here. Gives me hope. Kids today...' he paused and looked a little jaded, 'well you know all that. Don't worry, you've clearly got a good'un here,' and grinned.

'Yeah he's alright, we'll probably keep him,' said his Dad and then ruffled Robert's hair with a smile. 'Anyway shall we go get some lunch?'

'Can I get a milkshake?'

'Sure. And thank you Dave, we really appreciate this.'

Dave and his Dad shook hands, then Dave shook hands with Robert's Mum, and then with Robert, 'Come back any time, maybe you can tell me some more about that jar eh?'

Robert went red again, and half nodded.

Lunch was had, with a milkshake and then they traipsed around the shops and then they headed home. When they got in his Mum went straight into the kitchen and started rattling pots and pans about. His Dad slumped onto the sofa and picked up the TV remote. Robert stood in the hall and looked at the kitchen door, looked into the living room then dragged himself up the stairs. He put his CD on and clambered onto his bed. He was still there when his Mum shouted that tea was ready. This came as something of a disappointment to Robert, but he went down, ate then sat next to his Dad watching something on the TV and suddenly it was bedtime.

Chapter 45

A strange smell wafted under Robert's nose which wrinkled in response, not quite malodorous, it had a sweetness too it. And then he realised he could hear the sound of chewing, slow chewing. Robert opened an eye, it was dark but he could just make out other large dark eyes staring at him. He let out a gasp, then realised that they were passive, almost kindly eyes. As his eyes got used to the darkness, he could make out the large shapes of cows, watching him. He untangled himself from the bale of hay he seemed to be half buried in and padded out of the shed into the pre-dawn light and headed for the great hall.

He found Ragnar lying by the fire, eyes half open. He broke into a grin when Robert appeared out of the shadows.

'Ah boy, glad you're back.'

Robert sat down next to him, and nodded, 'What's happening?'

At the back of the village, slightly set apart and almost in the forest was a solitary hut. Around it lumps of wood with crude faces hacked into them, rusted metal shapes and bits of twigs bound into elaborate shapes were strewn about the building: Which looked to Robert to be surrounded by every weed imaginable and a few he would never have imagined. As they walked through Robert dragged his fingers through the different leaves and stalks, a variety of aromas wafted about him and tickled his nose prompting him to stifle a sneeze. Ragnar placed a hand on Robert's shoulder and guided him around the back of the house, into what would have been the back garden, had there been a fence; or a garden, instead the forest beyond was the boundary. A pale rock outcrop protruded from the grass and moss, it was almost as big as the hut, which it was only a few paces from. It curved like a huge tooth and was covered in carvings of holes surrounded by concentric circles all connected by channels; sitting on either side where two figures in black cloaks with hoods pulled up over their heads, so they looked like black blobs. Robert judged from their size that they weren't much older than him. Sitting in the middle before the great stone was a woman poking something with a stick. She was hunched over slightly, wearing layers of rags and some red leather ankle boots.

'What do you want Ragnar?' she asked without even looking up.

'Nice to see you too, I thought I would bring the boy,' sweeping his arm as if she might not have seen him.

'Why?'

'He walks between worlds,' replied Ragnar, as if it was obvious.

She replied with a 'Hmph' and looked around at the boy. She had a small round stern face, framed with white blonde hair and set perfectly in the middle where eyes the colour of thunderclouds which nailed him to the spot.

Her face broke into a smile, Robert thought for a second the sun had burst through the clouds so bright was her countenance; he stepped towards her involuntarily, like some forgotten, secret part of his brain had taken over his legs. He then realised he had no idea what had prompted him to walk and stopped.

The woman broke into a laugh and tossed her head back 'Good boy,' she said, seemingly impressed with something and flashed another smile, this was more real, just as powerful, but different.

'I saw you,' she said, 'at the circle, you rode the shiny dragon, all noise and roar, she came for you, Freyja, The Lady, was there with you.'

Robert said, 'Erm,'

Ragnar looked down at him, 'Freyja?'

The old lady nodded and grinned, 'I saw her...'

Ragnar took a step away, not taking his eyes off Robert.

'Erm indeed,' said Ragnar.

There was a long silence, Robert felt very hot and uncomfortable and desperately thought of something to say,

'What are you doing?' he asked.

She thought for a moment, and then said, 'I'm poking these holes with a stick.'

'I can see that, why?'

'Nosey little one isn't he.'

Ragnar opened his mouth to speak but Robert beat him to it, 'The only way you learn stuff is by asking questions.'

This seemed to delight the woman who almost squealed, 'Well, it's a secret, I can't tell you, maybe you'll get to see sometime. Soon.'

'Oh um, ok?'

'Come on boy,' said Ragnar, 'time to leave Mother to her tasks.'

Robert turned, 'Bye' he said over his shoulder.

'Goodbye Robert' she said in a low voice.

Robert felt goosebumps run up his spine and he quashed a shiver.

He noticed Ragnar held her gaze for a little longer than was necessary, then they left the garden, again he felt left out, like there was some secret adult world of communication that deliberately went over his head. He sighed a little. Then said, 'Who was that then?'

'We call her Mother, she does Woman's magic.'

'So like a female version of you then?'

Ragnar's head bobbed, 'Yes, yes, that's right.'

'Why did we not stop long?'

'She's busy, she has things to prepare. I'm just showing you around, so people are more comfortable.'

There was a pause, then Robert said, 'Why would people not be comfortable about me, I'm the one away from home?'

'A good question boy; I don't know what's it's like where you come from, but er, well here people accept the unseen just as much as the seen, and you are sort of neither one nor the other, you're different. And different sometimes unsettles people. Especially people with no imagination,' he paused, then added,

'And I don't mean Mother by that,' very quickly, and checked over his shoulder.

Robert scowled, then changed the subject, 'So what's woman's magic?'

'Well it's things to do with hearth and home, and healing and childbirth and growing things. And looking after dying things, people, guiding people in and out of this world and easing suffering.'

'So what's man magic then?'

'Well that's all hard and metal, and minds and cunning, though women are far more cunning, they just don't brag about it like we do,' he laughed at his own joke as they trudged off through the mud.

'Which is best?'

Ragnar stopped and looked down into Robert's face, 'Neither's best, they're different, they are different edges of the same sword. They're not even separate.'

Robert screwed his face up in thought and was about to ask another question when a voice cried out for Ragnar.

They looked up and one of the villagers was motioning furiously for them to come; Ragnar suddenly sped up into a hobbling trot, Robert struggled to keep up.

'What is it?'

'It's Smvor, he's collapsed,' said the woman anxiously.

They ran to the smithy, outside a giant of man was lying on the floor, his face shiny with sweat.

'Get him some mead!' shouted Robert.

'Mead?'

'Yes mead. Hurry!' Robert stated this with such vigour and certainty that no one questioned taking instructions from a small boy. But given the adventures they'd share so far, why would they?

Ragnar turned towards the crowd, 'Well go on! Get some mead! The good stuff, we use for special occasions, not the regular swill.

Robert looked up, and stared at the sky for a moment. A moment long enough for everyone to be very aware that the boy was just stood staring at the sky. Some of the villagers looked up to see what he was looking at. Others didn't in case they saw something that disturbed their sleep for the next week.

'No wait!' shouted Robert, 'I don't care whether you think it's the good stuff or not, but what you bring has to be the sweetest, it's got to be the sweetest.'

The sound of feet scampering off in the distance was the only sound now. The smith was still motionless on the floor.

Villi's daughter pushed through the crowd, a plain brown jug held tight, and the contents slopping against the side.

'The sweetest we've got', she gasped, out of breath.

'Give him some, Ragnar lift his head, come on, quickly.'

Ragnar's top lip and moustache twitched vigorously from side to side, and one eyebrow raised, but he let the command in Robert's voice ride. Kneeling down he lifted the smith's head slightly and then pushed his knees so the head rested on him. Thunor, opened the smith's mouth slightly by gripping the lower jaw and Villi's daughter poured in a dribble of mead.

The mead stayed in the smith's mouth.

Thunor had pushed his way through the crowd, 'Now what?' he asked.

'He needs to swallow it.'

'Oh,' and Thunor began gently rubbing the throat of the smith whilst Ragnar gently moved the head up and down. The mead stubbornly refused to go down.

'Come on you big...,' Thunor then used a word that Robert had only heard once. When his Dad had hit his thumb with a hammer and his Mum had been really angry. You'd think it was her who had hit her thumb the way she'd carried on.

The smith spluttered, gurgled and coughed; most of the mead had been coughed out, but some had done its job. They tried again, and then again. Thrice is the charm as they say, the smith's eyes flickered open. Then shut. He groaned.

'Make him drink some, some big mouthfuls. Three I reckon,' said Robert.

Ragnar nodded and they helped the smith up so that he was now propped up on his own elbows. Villi's daughter let him take three big gulps.

'I feel awful,' he rumbled, ''What happened.'

'It's called a hypo glow kemic' said Robert very seriously.

Everyone looked at him blankly.

'And no I don't really understand what it is either.'

The smith made an attempt to stand up.

'Nope, I don't think so big fella,' said the Chief, 'You

can stay there for a bit while longer, don't want you falling on anyone.'

'He needs food now, I bet he's had nothing to eat today.'

The smith nodded in agreement.

'All I know is that it's some kind of in-balance, and you need to eat often, and when he collapses give him something sweet.'

'So what you're saying,' smiled the smith, 'Is I need more food and all the mead I can drink.'

This caused a ripple of laughter around the crowd of relieved faces.

'Yeah he's feeling better,' someone quipped from the crowd. A few people came over and slapped the smith on the shoulder and back.

Robert found his arm being gently gripped by Ragnar and manoeuvred away from the others.

'How do you know all this Robert?'

'My Grandad, has the same thing, and we got rescued by a helicopter!' said Robert excitedly.

Ragnar looked puzzled, then asked, 'What's a heli copter?'

Robert sighed and struggled to find a suitable description that wouldn't cause more trouble than it was worth, 'It's a type of Greek chariot.' He said slowly.

'Greek?' Ragnar pulled a face that seemed to imply he was impressed just by the fact it was Greek. 'Robert, again you have saved us. Thunor maybe the Chief of the tribe, the head, the strength but the Smith is the heart. His forge is....it has its own magic, the magic of steel, iron, of the plough and sword. Without him we are lost.'

'What about you?'

'Me? I'm, I'm just a guide, maybe even the brains, cause Odin knows, heheh,' Ragnar stopped talking and shuffled slightly, Thunor had fixed him with a beady stare.

'Brains eh?' said Thunor, smiled and walked away.

Ragnar followed him with his eyes and laughed, he opened his mouth to say something, and then changed his mind.

Chapter 46

That night they processed around the village Robert held high on shoulders. This was old magic; this was carrying burning torches around the perimeter and making sure that the darkness knew where the boundaries were.

Then they returned to the Great Hall, all the torches were lit, the fire in the middle roared and crackled like the laughter bringing new life to all the carvings in the wooden posts and ceiling.

And the mead flowed like the stories and song.

And Robert was at the centre of it all. He had a warm fuzzy glowing feeling but that could have been the mead. He'd ate his fill and was the toast of the tribe. One of the men had even made a song up about him, it was a bit rude in places and made Robert blush, especially when Villi's daughter made a point of coming over and filling his jug with some mead with a very enigmatic smile. Villi stood up and bellowed for the boy Robert to come forward. Robert was hoisted by his arms and passed over the heads from man to man down the table and then plonked on his feet at the top of the table in front of Smvor.

'Robert,' said Smvor, 'you have made it known that I can eat and drink my fill of mead whenever I want.' There was a roar of laughter and bits of bread where thrown from all directions. Smvor quietened the crowd down with a waving of his arms. 'Who are we, to argue, this boy who defeats Loki Spawn! This spirit walker,' he paused, and everyone cheered wildly, banging on the tables.

'What must their men and woman folk be like if their children are thus eh?' There was now silence in the hall and nodding of heads. 'Thunor asked me to make you something, and here it is, my finest work if I say so myself.'

From inside his tunic top he pulled a golden band, he took Robert's arm and pushed the band up such that it was around his bicep. Robert stared at it open mouthed, a gleaming, golden red dragon chased his tail around the band, amongst curves, spirals and knots.

'It's beautiful,' gasped Robert, 'The most beautiful thing I have ever seen. I will treasure it forever.'

The hall erupted in cheering, and Robert was again hosted by his arms and tossed down the table with laughter and shouting. At the other end of the table they threw Robert high into the air, Robert squealed with laughter. And again, and again. And thrice is the charm. And he never came down on the third one. He just disappeared into the darkness. A sudden silence crushed the villagers, only Ragnar remained stood, back straight, eyes daring the world and then he roared laughing.

Robert sat bolt upright in his bed, feeling like he'd just got out of the world's fastest lift. He looked over the side of his bed and where the carpet should have been was a village as if he was looking down from a hot air balloon, and as he looked around, mouth open he could see the sea and snow covered mountains and the dark forest. He could see the villagers who'd come out, looking up at the sky unseeing. And he could see Ragnar fix him with a beady stare.

Robert waved, Ragnar broke into a goofy grin and waved back. The rest of the villagers tried really hard to see what Ragnar was waving at and hoped it was Robert.

Thunor didn't even get to ask, he kind of mouthed some words hoping they'd come out as a question.

'He's gone home. For now. He'll be back,' and slapped Thunor on the back, 'Come on, that mead isn't going to drink itself,' and hobbled back inside to find more.

Slowly the villagers filled back into the hall, and the night closed in around them. Kept at bay by the songs and laughter of the tribe, the firelight and sheer joy and vitality of life.

Robert looked around his bedroom, then down at the village again, which was now rug and carpet. He got out of bed and gingerly put his feet down, it was solid. He walked around. And then got back in bed, pulling up the duvet, something cold and hard pinched against his arm: A golden band. A dragon chasing its tail.